THREE WEEKS TILL MARDI GRAS!

Sabrina abruptly staggered and clutched the microphone stand. Her expression was dazed, shell-shocked. Her sultry lips slackened into a drug-dulled smile.

She stumbled again, crashing into a second microphone, sending it toppling.

"Ladies and gentlemen," she said into the mike, then stopped suddenly.

Her eyes clouded.

Both knees buckled.

"Oh, Mother Mary, *help* me!" she pleaded in a lost-little-girl voice.

Seconds later, an obscene gout of blood erupted in a scarlet rope down her chin.

And somebody screamed.

TERROR LIVES!

THE SHADOW MAN   (1946, $3.95)
by Stephen Gresham
The Shadow Man could hide anywhere—under the bed, in the
closet, behind the mirror . . . even in the sophisticated circuitry
of little Joey's computer. And the Shadow Man could make Joey
do things that no little boy should ever do!

SIGHT UNSEEN   (2038, $3.95)
by Andrew Neiderman
David was always right. Always. But now that he was growing up,
his gift was turning into a power. The power to know things—
terrible things—that he didn't want to know. Like who would live
. . . and who would die!

MIDNIGHT BOY   (2065, $3.95)
by Stephen Gresham
Something horrible is stalking the town's children. For one of its
most trusted citizens possesses the twisted need and cunning of a
psychopathic killer. Now Town Creek's only hope lies in the hor-
rific, blood-soaked visions of the MIDNIGHT BOY!

TEACHER'S PET   (1927, $3.95)
by Andrew Neiderman
All the children loved their teacher Mr. Lucy. It was astonishing
to see how they all seemed to begin to resemble Mr. Lucy. And act
like Mr. Lucy. And kill like Mr. Lucy!

DEW CLAWS   (1808, $3.50)
by Stephen Gresham
Jonathan's terrifying memories of watching his three brothers
and their uncle sucked into the fetid mud at Night Horse Swamp
were just beginning to fade. But the dank odor of decay all
around him reminded Jonathan that the nightmare wasn't over
yet. The horror had taken everything Jonathan loved. And now it
had come back for him!

SPELLCASTER

J. EDWARD AMES

ZEBRA BOOKS
KENSINGTON PUBLISHING CORP.

ZEBRA BOOKS

are published by

Kensington Publishing Corp.
475 Park Avenue South
New York, NY 10016

First printing: August, 1989

Printed in the United States of America

Chapter 1

"Chick that good-looking is almost spooky," swore C. J. Guidry, the bartender. "Just *look* at that little unit!"

Obligingly, the off-duty Bunko detective at the end of the bar revolved sideways on his stool so he could watch the singer better.

Sabrina Nash unclipped her mike from the stand, and the combo behind her burst into "Iko Iko." Her Aztec-gold silk dress shimmered like day-glo foil in the spotlights. She chose a herky-jerky dance to accompany the lyrics. Her body was lissome, the copper hair mildly spiked. Innocent, wing-shaped emerald eyes were offset by full, sultry lips.

Thus preoccupied, most patrons at the Ragin' Cajun failed to notice when a seldom-used side door was slowly nudged open.

Had they been aware, some would have recognized the nattily dressed old mime who often worked for pass-the-hat money in the French Quarter. His face was still painted moonstone white from tonight's silent stint among the tourists. Now it was a lurid mask of reflection as he eased through the multicolored glow of the vintage Wurlitzer beside the door. He quickly located an unoccupied table and sat down, studiously avoiding eye contact with the waitress.

Guidry leaned across the gleaming mahogany bar to slide the cop a schooner. Folds of soft fat formed a tier of throw pillows under his T-shirt.

He winked at the cop and inclined his head toward the new arrival.

"Don't look now, but it's the Emperor himself. That old fart's talented, f'sure, but you ask me, he's got a few spark plugs missing. Been in every night this week, right? And ordered a Jagermeister. Then he just sits there staring off into the corners. Never touches the drink."

"He's here because of her," offered the usually quiet man beside the cop, nodding toward Sabrina.

But the Emperor paid little attention, either to the men admiring Sabrina from the bar or to the beautiful woman whose vibrant contralto was now spicing up an old doo-wop number.

Instead, he glanced furtively around at the walls, as if he mistrusted the eyes staring at him from the posters and portraits of local musical greats. His gaze fixed for a moment on the Fat Tuesday countdown calendar hanging between the dartboards: It still bore yesterday's date. A moment later he became absorbed in the long feathers of cigarette smoke, watching them trail lazily upward until the ceiling fans scattered them like fog in a sudden breeze.

"Check it out," insisted the bartender.

The Bunko detective, Alan Breaux, looked over his shoulder and watched the old mime for a few moments, merely to oblige his friend. Then he noticed something else and faced Guidry again, sporting a lopsided grin.

"You check it out," said Breaux. He jerked one thumb back over his shoulder.

In the middle of the dance floor, an over-enthusiastic tourist staggered like a punch-drunk boxer, trying to keep up with the music. He wore gaudy print clam-diggers, and his T-shirt proclaimed YOU NEVER FORGET YOUR FIRST PIG.

"Place is a frickin' zoo," C. J. admitted with weary candor.

A waitress bellowed and he hustled off to fill an order. Sabrina broke into a sultry blues tune.

The cop played a piano riff on his thighs. "Something, isn't she?" he remarked conversationally to the man beside him.

Steve Jernigan nodded, never taking his eyes off the singer.

"That she is," he agreed.

Jernigan spoke politely. He was clearly more interested right then in music than conversation.

Longstanding habit, not curiosity, impelled Breaux to study his taciturn neighbor more closely. Early thirties, he guessed. Medium build, clean-cut, good condition. The eyes were intelligent, but also sheltered a smoldering intensity, a silent absorption. Despite his obvious admiration for Sabrina, even she could not supply what this man was after.

"Don't you dare, asshole!"

The barkeep scowled as he watched the swaying tourist turn several shades of green.

Guidry whistled sharply. From out of nowhere materialized a hairy, shirtless, ex-biker type in a leather vest. But he was too late: The party animal made it only as far as the men's room door before he bent double and barfed up a foaming streamer.

"Christ, he's pukin'—somebody keep him off his back!" screamed the corpulent bartender. Guidry shook his head. *"Laissez les bons temps roules!"* he called out cynically as the bouncer escorted the reveler toward the door. "Let the good times roll, ignut coonass!"

"Now, now," soothed Breaux. He tried to look wise and pious. "It's better to light one candle than to curse the darkness."

"You don't have to clean it up, pilgrim!"

Beside them, Jernigan tuned the commotion out, riveting his attention on the velvet-voiced singer. Her music always ignited pleasing pyrotechnics in his head. Her voice shot galvanic currents up the back of his neck.

She shunted back and forth among reggae, zouk, blues, soul, and pop, as effortlessly as a bee sampling flowers. The versatile voice radiated emotion, fun, a carefree sexual energy.

Definitely talented, Steve thought.

Definitely beautiful too.

He watched her eyes glitter like chips of bright crystal, scintillating even through the murky pall of smoke. She finished her number and the audience broke into applause, cheers, whistles, and urgent pleas for more.

Steve Jernigan frowned, his brow corrugating slightly.

For a moment, at the peak of the applause, it almost seemed as if the singer had . . . winced with pain, he told himself, puzzled.

Something else occurred to him, though less force-fully. Ever since the old street performer with the white-painted face had arrived, he'd tried his damn-dest to blend in with the woodwork. But now he was applauding so enthusiastically that several people turned to stare at him. Even the demure Sabrina met his gaze to acknowledge him.

Again pain seemed to flare up briefly in her daz-zling eyes, passing so quickly it could have been an optical quirk caused by the lighting. But something about the moment troubled Jernigan. Something he had read, maybe, or told his students, or written down during a lecture . . .

(at the peak of the applause)

Guidry's brash voice abruptly derailed the train of his thoughts.

"Not only can that woman sing, check out them garbanzos. D-cuppers, f'sure!"

Breaux tipped the brim of an imaginary Stetson. "Slap your brand on my filly, pard, and you'll be shoveling coal in hell."

"Listen to this shit! She's already got a grandpa, pilgrim."

Steve watched as Guidry and Breaux slapped palms in a high-five, a smile easing his lips apart. They recited in a fast, perfect chorus:

Eity-ditey, Christ Al-mighty,
Who in the hell are *we*?
Zim-*zam,*
God-*damn,*
We're the *var*-sity!

11

Across the room, Sabrina finished a brief consultation with the keyboard player and whirled back around to her mike. The Ragin' Cajun erupted in cheers and whistles when the combo broke into the Caribe beat of "Delta Fever," her first tune to hit the national Top Forty.

Even the still-disgruntled C. J. Guidry joined the enthusiastic applause when she finished. But again Jernigan felt something oddly out of place, something indefinably wrong. It was more visceral than intellectual, a conviction that some vaguely pernicious quality tainted the atmosphere.

He couldn't remember ever having a headache in his life, but he was sure he had one now—a splitting, throbbing ache centered between his eyes like a piercing compass point. It was worse during the applause.

At first he thought it was routine paranoia, perhaps triggered by the bizarre nature of his current research interest. But when he glanced at the middle-aged detective beside him, the other man met his eyes for a moment and almost seemed to nod.

As if he, too, sensed something very wrong.

Sabrina launched into "Tipitina." Her eyes swept the room, paused at the table occupied by the lone, white-faced patron.

Jernigan winced when the velvet voice turned rusty and horribly off-key. But when the unharmonious moment passed, quick as a heartbeat, he wondered if he had actually heard anything wrong. Especially when she finished the set to deafening cheers and applause.

The old mime rose to his feet, applauding slowly but with great force. Her eyes met his across a sea of tables and bodies. She smiled. He smiled back, mouthing a voiceless compliment.

A bead of sweat trickled from beneath Jernigan's hairline and zigzagged down his forehead.

(Whether it involves frightened animals, angry parents, or homicidal psychotics, the nervous but clear female voice reiterated inside his head, *the fixed stare always accompanies hostile behavior.)*

The exchange between singer and fan was brief and few noticed it. Only seconds later Sabrina's huge green eyes were glancing elsewhere and the old man was making his way toward the side door. But several people would later tell reporters that the singer had suddenly looked seriously ill.

In the midst of the crowd euphoria Jernigan again felt that strange, palpable miasma.

On his way out, the Emperor swerved wide and stopped at the Mardi Gras countdown calendar. One trembling, liver-spotted hand reached out to tear yesterday's date off. The mime wadded it up and dropped it to the floor.

Alan Breaux watched this as well. The cop met Jernigan's stare.

"What the hell's going on?" the older man demanded quietly.

Jernigan slowly shook his head. He slid off the barstool. He sensed that, whatever it was, they were already too late.

Sabrina abruptly staggered and clutched the microphone stand. Her expression was dazed, shell-shocked. Her sultry lips slackened into a drug-dulled smile.

She stumbled again, crashing into a second micro-

13

phone and sending it toppling.

The singer looked as if she wanted to ask for help but lacked the vocabulary to describe what she was feeling. Later, at the hospital, she would tell her doctor that all she remembered was a splitting headache, then feeling sleepy and exhausted. She refused to mention the other sensation: the absurd yet vivid feeling that she was having good sex with the wrong man.

"Ladies and gentlemen," she said to her mike, then stopped abruptly.

Her eyes clouded.

Both knees buckled.

"Oh, Mother Mary, *help* me!" she pleaded in a lost-little-girl voice.

Seconds later, an obscene gout of blood erupted in a scarlet rope down her chin. And somebody screamed.

Chapter 2

The Quarter was teeming with tourists and street performers by the time the artist arrived at Jackson Square and rolled back the corrugated-steel curtains of her little sidewalk studio.

She laid out pens and charcoals, mounted her display drawings, and flicked on the portable arc-sodium floodlights.

Finally she hung out the carved rosewood sign: PORTRAITS BY CORINNE.

This flurry of activity gave her a good excuse for not glancing over her shoulder toward the broad, black-marble steps of St. Louis Cathedral. She knew he would be there, surrounded by the usual gaggle of admirers.

Not that she really cared, Corinne assured herself.

The old man was always there. And he always dressed the same: a summerweight black suit with a fresh gardenia in the buttonhole of his lapel, white shirt with a frilly lace jabot instead of a tie. His face, as always, would be painted chalk white, a stark backdrop for the shaggy silver ridge of his connecting eyebrows.

And no matter how often I check, she thought suddenly, he'll be watching me. Never staring, but always aware.

"Aw-ryyye, comin' through, cap! Aw-ryyye, make a hole!"

The raucous voice startled her. A Lucky Dog vendor wheeled his giant tin hot dog past, scattering sightseers as if they were toy boats in a bathtub. Nearby, a group of teenage break-dancers unrolled a strip of waxed linoleum and set up their ghetto blaster. A mule-drawn surrey clopped by, jammed tight with debauching visitors who had scrimped all year so they could blow all their money in three days like sailors on shore leave.

Once again the carnival atmosphere worked its beneficent magic on her. She emptied her mind of thought, ignoring the budding chrysalis of doubt and suspicion incubating inside her.

A faint thin blush behind the cathedral was all that remained of the day's sun. Earlier it had rained, and shallow pools had collected in the hollows of the stone flags in Jackson Square. The entire plaza glowed like a Bakelite floor in the reflection from the shop windows. From here she couldn't see the river beyond the levee. But she could spot the brightly lighted upper deck of the steamboat *Natchez,* boarding passengers for its next cruise.

Several early carousers, obviously conventioneers judging from their plastic name badges, undressed her with bloodshot eyes as they passed.

"Show your tits!" one of them shouted at her. She

16

flashed him the finger, which ignited a chorus of drunken whoops.

Another streetlight glimmered to life. Watching it, she felt a familiar airbrush-tickle of apprehension in her stomach.

Don't even *dare* start that crap again! she admonished herself fiercely.

Other artists in the Quarter had already advised her to set up her studio closer to the fountain, where pedestrian flow was heavier. They also advised her to set up later when demand was brisker. She was ashamed to admit she always arrived so early simply to claim this corner near the cathedral where it was well-lighted.

"Oh! *Damn* it!"

Earlier she had torn a perfectly good sheet of cameo rose paper removing it from the pad. Now one elbow had just upset her equipment tray. My God, she thought, stooping to gather everything up. She didn't normally think of herself as a klutz, but lately she was a walking disaster area.

She arranged everything neatly and moved the tray to one of the two folding-metal chairs which filled nearly half of her open-fronted sidewalk studio. While she occupied herself with this busy work, she idly wondered again if she had picked up a bug of some kind. The downbeat moods lately, the vague depression, the nauseous flutters in her stomach . . . more and more she had to resist the urge to close down early and go home, the temptation to use sleep to avoid everything.

One of the break-dancers was tuning his ghetto blaster to a local rap program. For a moment he picked up a fragment of a news broadcast, and the words drifted out over the square like escaped balloons:

"—inger Sabrina Nash was rushed to Presbyterian Hospital last night after collapsing during a performance at—"

This lately wasn't just the typical blue funk she occasionally slipped into, Corinne decided. The queasy stomach and splitting headaches, the lack of energy, the spacey, strung-out feeling like she was having a rough menstrual period . . . if those B-complex vitamins Maddy swore by didn't do the trick, maybe she'd better see a doctor at Student Health. Maybe she needed a special diet.

She glanced toward the steps of the cathedral. The Emperor was gazing toward her.

Not *at* her—toward her. That was his way. Always, the oblique vigilance.

It's not just him, she realized. The truth was that *all* mimes made her nervous. She admired their talent, but what drove them to their strange profession? Some did indeed actively pantomime. But many just posed absolutely stone still, stone silent for what seemed like hours while rude and drunk tourists tried to ruin their composure with taunts and lewd suggestions. Judging from the bills perpetually overflowing the Emperor's contribution hat, crowds loved the old man's sphinxlike composure.

Still, she could have sworn he was watching her apartment building when she went out for breakfast early this morning.

She reminded herself that he could have been watching for anyone. After all, at least a dozen people

18

lived in the building.

Thinking of her building prompted her to glance down Decatur Street. She could see it, a rose-stuccoed three-story near the French Market. Her peeling wrought-iron balcony was brilliant in the streetlight, resplendent with bright zinnias and jonquils. Two stories below, bold pigeons terrorized sidewalk patrons at the Cafe du Monde.

Next door to hers, she could see the only balcony in sight that wasn't chockablock with flowers, plants, and lounge chairs.

And he was out there right now.

Corinne had been noticing her neighbor for about a month now. Several times she had seen him at Maddy's store, flipping through the old jazz albums. She had also spotted him well after dark, on nights when she couldn't sleep and the crowds had thinned enough to allow her some quiet time on the balcony. Corinne had watched, fascinated, as he practiced the yoga or tai chi or whatever it was he did out there. And sometimes she heard him polishing up speeches or lectures, occasionally referring to a thick sheaf of notes while he paced the balcony.

I never see him with a woman, said a curious inner voice.

So what? retorted another defensive one. *He never sees you with a man.*

She watched the sky deepen from indigo to black, careful not to look toward the crowd on the steps of the cathedral.

Idly, Steve Jernigan watched the girl down below in

19

Jackson Square. From the balcony he saw her only in miniature, but her face was clear in his mind's eye.

She's pretty, he thought. Especially with that new haircut.

Behind him in the apartment, a Wynton Marsalis tune was spewing precision trumpet notes through the French windows. By now the sky had lost the last grainy tones of early evening. Neons buzzed like cicadas above the steady purl of the crowd.

As if his mind were a stereopticon, his view of the girl and the street did a slow fade-out. Instead, he saw Sabrina Nash clutching her microphone stand, eyes catatonic with pain and confusion as blood blossomed on her lips.

(*What the hell's going on?*)

Steve angrily forced his mind back to the present. He reminded himself yet again: Correlation is not causation.

If he hadn't even learned *that* by now, why not just trade his doctorate for a crystal ball and get it over with?

Guiltily, he thought about the stack of student research proposals waiting for him inside on the coffee table. He had to finish evaluating them tonight so they could be handed back tomorrow morning to his nine o'clock class. He had already missed one deadline, prompting some disgruntled remarks.

He glanced at the folded sheet in his hand: a minutely detailed Army map of nearby Honey Island Swamp, developed especially for hurricane evacuation. It had cost him almost fifty bucks, but was proving well worth every cent of it. He hadn't come so far, spent so much money, invested so much time and energy and hope, only to let a giant bog stop him.

But that meant several hours again tonight poring over the map, studying each section of grids for access to every symbol that designated a human dwelling. Tremain had called earlier and said the boat would be available tomorrow afternoon. Considering the rates he was paying, Steve knew he *had* to be prepared to use his time wisely.

Despite his pressing obligations, Steve continued standing near the wrought-iron railing of the balcony, lost in thought and the soothing music.

Barely aware that he was doing it, he raised his hands out to shoulder level in front of him. Alternately, he began clenching each fist tightly, then spreading the fingers wide.

Ten times . . .

Twenty . . .

Forty . . .

At about repetition number fifty, the relaxing monotony of the exercise had slowed his brain waves from Beta to Alpha range. Now a barely noticed detail, which had been prodding at conscious awareness since he first saw his pretty neighbor tonight, took center stage in his mind.

The Emperor had been watching her from the steps of the cathedral!

But by the time Steve thought to glance over to the square again, both the Emperor and the girl were gone.

I am you and you are me. There is no I, but only we.

21

By now the sacred vow was a subvocal mantra as familiar as the searing dagger point of hatred and rage and bloodlust that had burned deep into his guts for thirty years. The words had sounded in his mind as he watched the pretty artist lock up her sidewalk studio. They had provided the cadence when he followed her to the Cafe du Monde.

He hugged the weathered frame facade of a long-shore-workers' bar on Decatur, monitoring the artist and one other woman sitting in the restaurant across the street. Occasionally a chance headlight beam caught him in its sweep, and the stark white face flashed briefly out of the night like a macabre strobe. One eye glittered a deep brilliant blue, the other a murky brown that rivaled the fabric of darkness just beyond the streetlights.

The redhead bent across the table to whisper something, and her young friend laughed, her pretty face scandalized. Watching her, the Emperor felt a sudden flush of murderous rage. Frightened by what he had almost been tempted to do, he quickly averted his gaze. No. It shouldn't be that quick . . . nor that merciful.

Soon, he whispered, addressing the word to himself *and* to the girl.

When the angry blood finally quit throbbing in his temples, the Emperor resumed his vigilant study of Corinne.

Chapter 3

"Doctor Grodner?"

The physician stopped in front of the elevator and glanced at Breaux wearily. "Yes?"

"Any new word on Miss Nash?"

Grodner's forehead was suddenly runneled with annoyance. "The next official press release goes out tomorrow morning at nine A.M."

"I'm not a reporter," the other man hastened to explain. "Name's Alan Breaux."

He showed the doctor his photostat.

Grodner was cautious. "What does my patient's condition have to do with the police?"

There was a long pause while Breaux decided what to say. The elevator doors thumped open, but no one got off. Somebody with a nasal twang paged a Doctor Cleveland. The fourth-floor lobby of Presbyterian Hospital was nearly deserted save for a pair of wilting banana plants on either side of the drinking fountain.

"Actually," replied Breaux, "not a thing. It's just that I happened to be present last night when she . . . collapsed."

"I'll tell her you're concerned," Grodner said curtly. He turned toward the elevator again. "I'm sure she'll appreciate it."

"Doctor Grodner?"

The physician glanced at him sharply. *"Please,* Mr. Breaux. It's nearly eleven P.M. and I've been here since noon. I'm beat, I'm hungry, and I'm due in surgery in ten hours."

"I apologize for delaying you, Doctor. My reason is not official police business, but I promise this isn't just fan curiosity. A minute of your time?"

Grodner's tired, neatly bearded face was still set in a frown. But already he was relenting. For one thing, this was the first cop he could recall lately who didn't call him "Doc" — a word that irritated the hell out of him.

Old habit had already taken over, and Breaux was discreetly but meticulously studying the other man. Grodner *was* tired, certainly. He looked like a prime candidate for the walking-wounded list. But he also had something eating at him inside, something that would not let sleep come quickly this night. Something he just might divulge to someone he trusted.

Breaux made a decision about how to play this one.

"Look," he said, "I promise to level with you, Doctor Grodner. No games, no trick questions, no ulterior motives. Hell, I've got a kid in med school at U.T. Austin."

Breaux paused, making his face look solemn. "You know, I worry sometimes. My wife's a good woman but I still have to wonder whose brains the boy inherited. That kid doesn't *look* like me either."

Grodner finally relented, grinning at this show of

24

cornball humility. "Not exactly the hardboiled gum-shoe, are you?"

"That's why they stuck me on Bunko. I spend most of my time breaking up lotteries and pigeon games in the CBD. I'm such a nice fella, the sharpies are always trying to slip it to me."

"Right now I'm too bushed to con you." Grodner nodded toward the vending machines in a nearby alcove. "But I'll spring for a cup of the lousiest coffee you've ever tasted."

"Thought you'd never offer," said Breaux.

Grodner hadn't lied about the coffee. Breaux only drank it because the physician did. Hopefully, it wasn't toxic.

"May I assume," said Grodner, "that you wouldn't exactly be happy if your superiors knew you were inquiring about Sabrina?"

"You may. Especially if they knew I was flashing my shield for extra clout."

Grodner nodded, satisfied. "Okay. If a broken heart doesn't drive you here, what does?"

"I promised no games, and I meant it. The truth is, I'm not exactly sure what brings me here. I guess I can put it this way: Something—I'm not sure what—was odd about what happened to Sabrina last night."

"Odd? How do you mean?"

Breaux shrugged apologetically. "I told you my kid inherited all the brains."

"Yeah, but something specific must have led to your suspicion?"

"Agreed, but I don't know—or I can't *explain*—what it was. My 'evidence' is too subjective. But the feeling is strong enough that I decided I could at least find out if anybody on the medical team noticed anything . . . well, let's just say 'atypical' about what happened to her."

Grodner stroked his beard with several fingertips and watched the cop thoughtfully.

"You haven't told me a damn thing, yet I have a feeling you're not just coming out of left field with this hunch of yours. Why?"

"Maybe," Breaux suggested carefully, "it's because of the surgery you mentioned — the surgery coming up in ten hours?"

Grodner looked at him sharply, glanced away.

"Okay," the doctor finally admitted. "Maybe it is."

Breaux was silently elated at how deftly he had switched interrogator roles with Grodner. "What's wrong with her?"

Grodner gazed across the lobby, idly swishing his coffee around in the paper cup. It left a grainy brown film on the sides.

"Hell," he said finally, "you'll know tomorrow anyway."

His eyes met the cop's.

"Actually, it's routine surgery to lance a very small perforated ulcer. Her prognosis is good."

Breaux frowned. "A small ulcer caused her to cough up all that blood?"

"According to the theory, the ulcer had started bleeding sometime prior to her engagement at the nightclub. X-rays show that it's a peptic ulcer, unusually high in the stomach, near the esophagus. As the blood eventually worked into the esophagus, it initiated reverse peristalsis."

"Reverse whosis?"

26

"Her gag reflex was tickled," explained Grodner. "She vomited blood mixed with mucus. Looked much worse than it was."

"I take it," said Breaux, "you don't like this theory?"

"In the abstract it's not that problematic, although the amount of blood strikes me as unusual."

"Okay," prodded Breaux. "So much for the abstract. Why don't you like it in Sabrina's case?"

Grodner finished his coffee and wadded the cup. He flipped it into a nearby trash receptacle and said, "You're a cop. Tell me, how's your stomach?"

Surprised, Breaux arched his brows. He wiggled one hand in a so-so gesture. "No major problems. Once in awhile I have to pick up a roll of antacid."

Grodner nodded. "So do I. So do millions of people, including Sabrina."

"You mean . . . ?"

"I mean that once—*just* once, maybe five years ago—she had some complaints about stomach discomfort after eating. At the time I ran her through a complete checkup including upper and lower GI x-rays. We found the beginning, just the beginning, of a small peptic ulcer, maybe half the size of a pencil eraser. She responded well to the usual regimen of Tagament and high-potency antacid. The lesion cleared up, she made some dietary changes, and was fine after that. Oh, once in a while she takes a spoonful of Di-Gel or whatever. Otherwise, fine."

Grodner stifled a yawn, then consulted his watch. "What bugs me," he concluded, "is that ulcers rarely crop up unnoticed and reach perforation stage without symptoms. But Sabrina swears she's felt fine lately. Plus I have x-rays from her last physical, less than two months ago. Two gastroenterologists have concurred with my reading. With the exception of that one small lesion, those negatives are *clean*. The stomach folds aren't even thickened, which always occurs when excessive gastric acid has chronically irritated the stomach lining."

Breaux said, "On the Scale of Medical Weirdness, how would you rate this?"

Grodner smiled. "You kidding? In Korea a baby was recently born with two separate, functioning brains. In New York, during the sixties, a surgeon was performing an autopsy before a group of medical students when the 'corpse' suddenly sat up and seized him by the throat. The surgeon died of shock on the spot. Swear to God I once removed an appendix with a half-carat diamond embedded in it. On a scale of one to ten, I'm afraid I could only give Sabrina's case about a 6.5. But it still bothers me."

Both men were heading toward the elevator as Grodner finished speaking. He looked at Breaux and said, "I've just shot professional ethics all to hell by discussing her medical history with you. You sure you can't tell me something in return?"

"Positive. But if and when I can, you'll be the first to know."

The two men parted downstairs in the main lobby. Outside, the winter night was cool, and the raw edge of a damp wind sliced through Breaux's sport jacket.

A 6.5 on a scale of one to ten, he thought as he headed across the asphalt parking lot toward his car. He had enough to do without wasting more of his own off-duty time on unofficial investigations.

Besides, *what* was he investigating? Bizarre vibes? Already Breaux was starting to feel a little foolish.

Maybe silliness was his answer to the mid-life crisis?

But as he unlocked his Toyota, he couldn't shake the image of that old mime defiantly ripping a page off the Mardi Gras countdown calendar . . . nor the gut-level feeling that the gesture had meant something.

Chapter 4

"A key research problem concerning the brain," said Professor Eric Winters, "is the crucial question of capacity. Precisely *what* is this elusive organic computer actually capable of? According to a consensus of expert opinion, the brain is grossly underutilized. Some even feel that so-called 'psychic ability,' for example, lies dormant in all of us. The challenge for researchers is to discover the catalyst for making a quantum leap in harnessing the brain's potential."

Winters paused, allowing his students to take notes. Remembering his medication, he fished a filigreed silver pillbox out of his suit jacket and shook a small tab into his palm. Excusing himself, he stepped into the hallway and, placing the pill on his tongue, washed it down at a drinking fountain.

"Concerning this thorny question of capacity," he continued, after stepping back into the classroom, "the case of Albert Einstein's brain is particularly instructive."

Winters frowned at the peroxide blonde in the last row who was demurely filing her nails. She withered under the stare of his icy blue eyes and hastily resumed a semblance of note-taking.

"When the scientist died in 1955," said Winters, "his body was cremated, but his brain was preserved for analysis. At first, researchers found nothing to distinguish his brain from any other. Eventually, however, came a discovery that marked a new epoch in brain study."

He paused to relish the suspense.

"To understand that discovery, you must hark back to last month's lecture on the two types of brain cells: neurons and glial cells. Mr. Carr, will you please define the different functions of these cells?"

"Neurons are the primary cells of the brain. They can't divide. Glial cells, however, which nourish the neurons, can increase in number."

"Just so," Winters said approvingly. "Research had already proven that greater mental activity is accompanied by an increase in the ratio of glial cells to neurons. It turned out that Einstein's brain contained a significantly higher number of glial cells. We don't know if this condition was acquired or congenital. But we know now that an increase in glial cells corresponds with an increase in brain potential."

"Professor Winters," said a student in the front, "when you say an increase in brain potential, do you mean simply IQ?"

"Absolutely not. Consider, for example, hypermnesia, which is the opposite of amnesia. Extraordinarily sharp and vivid recall characterizes some persons with a higher ratio of glial cells to neurons."

"But, sir," objected the student named Carr, "isn't hypermnesia also associated with mental illness?"

"Many things we can't understand or appreciate," he responded, "are associated with mental illness, are they not? Society is quick to label the extraordinary as 'deviant.' "

"I'm just not sure," observed Carr, "about the ethics of artificially exploiting the brain."

While Carr spoke, Winters glanced out the window toward the huge crushed-shell parking lot. A blue Mazda RX-7 was pulling into the section reserved for faculty. A half smile glimmered on the professor's lips.

"Perhaps, Mr. Carr," he said, "you might discuss the ethical ramifications with Steve Jernigan. I understand *he* has an interest in such questions."

Delta College was situated near City Park on the south shore of vast Lake Pontchartrain. Nationally recognized for its outstanding premed and nursing programs, it was a pleasant architectural hodgepodge of unpolished red granite and ivy-covered fieldstone. The campus was dotted with chinaberry trees and massive live oaks dripping streamers of Spanish moss.

Jernigan parked and locked his car, then paused to watch the rowing team sculling out on the lake. The I-10 Causeway stretched toward infinity across the water, reflecting like a long white ribbon in the morning sunlight.

The manila folder under his right arm was bulging with the research proposals he had finally finished grading at two A.M. He still had twenty minutes until his first class, so Jernigan dropped the papers off at his office. Then he stopped by the faculty mailroom to check his pigeonhole.

He sorted through a stack of department memos, publishers' announcements, and computer printouts showing the latest enrollment figures. Only one letter was buried in the pile.

He recognized the handwriting immediately, even before he noticed the Ann Arbor, Michigan, postmark.

Tossing the rest of the correspondence back into his mailbox, he tore the envelope open. The greeting card inside depicted a struggling man being dragged away in a straitjacket by two goons in white coats. "Why," implored the message inside, "are you so afraid of commitment?" The card was signed, "Sardonically yours, Lisa."

He stood for a moment, smiling at the card, lost in thought.

Steve had recently returned home to Ann Arbor to visit his family. Lisa, an old flame from his graduate years at Michigan, was now divorced from her dentist husband and teaching anthropology there as an assistant professor. Naturally, in a town the size of Ann Arbor, their paths had inevitably crossed. And just as naturally, considering the ardor of their former relationship, the old emotions had rekindled into a brief but passionate fling.

Despite her beauty and intelligence (or *because* of them? he wondered), Lisa was a contradictory combination of insecurity and headstrong determination. He had essentially told her the same thing this time that he had five years earlier when he left for the South. He was willing to share her life, but on a more loosely defined basis than what she wanted.

33

Besides, he thought now, he was more or less in romantic limbo until he cleared up the mystery surrounding his father's "accidental" death. The tragedy had blighted his mother's happiness, casting a pall over her final years. And it festered inside him every day — a raw canker of doubt and suspicion and burning curiosity.

And fear.

He headed back down the hallway toward his office. A knot of students emerged from a classroom, followed by Eric Winters carrying a calfskin briefcase.

"What a coincidence," Winters greeted him. "My class was just discussing the amusing contributions of pop psychology."

The way his colleague was dressed made Steve feel like one of the students in his own jeans and pullover shirt. French cuffs even, he noted with wry disgust.

"Well," he responded, keeping his tone light, "we can't all lay the genetic groundwork for the next Aryan Superman, can we, Herr Professor?"

He and Eric Winters had formed a mutual-hate society almost from the first moment Steve was hired last semester as an adjunct lecturer. Winters, a neurosurgeon and tenured professor, had nothing but disdain for the "software faculty," as he termed any teacher who dealt with social or psychological issues and did not wield a scalpel to the exclusion of all else. Steve had taken his doctorate in psychobiology, a relatively new academic discipline in which his father had been a pioneer. Winters had once succinctly termed it "phrenology masquerading as science."

"Actually," Winters said now, sticking the knife in

and twisting it, "you're *good* for Delta College. Students, being nefariously lazy creatures, love classes like yours. It brings their GPA up without causing any stress. You're good for enrollment."

Steve felt warm blood creeping up the back of his neck. He resisted a sudden impulse to cold-cock the smarmy bastard on the spot.

Instead, he reminded himself it wasn't just Winters. He was also catching flak from the department chairman and others because he wasn't getting involved in committees, department meetings, and professional publishing. And to some extent he knew their criticism was justified. His obsession with the search that had lured him south—actually, his father's search, which Steve had inherited like a family curse—was occupying more and more of his time.

"Pardon me all to hell," he replied finally, "for being liked by my students. Now if you'll excuse me, I have to go give away some more cake A's."

The interaction with Winters left an acidic taste in his mouth for the rest of the morning. Something else about the man troubled him, too, something he couldn't quite identify. But Steve soon occupied himself with the reminder that he was going out to Honey Island Swamp later today.

Today, his mind repeated in a hopeful litany. *Today you'll finally hit pay dirt.*

Corinne paused for a moment in front of her apartment building, watching as workers backed a huge papier-mâché float out of a warehouse across the street.

Getting it ready for Carnival, she thought. Carnival season had already officially begun. It was not quite three weeks until Fat Tuesday. Soon the secret krewes would be rolling their parades throughout the city, luring visitors by the millions. She would make more money doing portraits during the peak two weeks of Carnival than she normally would in three months.

She crossed the street and headed toward Maddy's shop on Toulouse, her shadow lengthening in the afternoon sun. The winter day was breezy, but warm enough for shorts. The smell of seafood and Lucky Dogs blended with the musty-rope tang of the nearby Mississippi. This kind of weather usually put her in an upbeat mood, but today she still felt dull as dishwater.

Preoccupied, she realized too late that she had forgotten to bypass the construction gang that was erecting parade-viewing stands next to the Jax Brewery. Knowing what was coming, she steeled herself.

One of them whistled to alert the others.

"Where yat, babe?"

"Who dat? *Oooo!*"

"Need it bad, *cher!*"

Within seconds the entire crew was coming on like mafioso muscle, whistling, shouting, and gesturing. She had encountered this type of reaction for years, but things had gotten ridiculous since she let Maddy talk her into this new haircut.

Feeling her face flame up at the harmless but unwanted attention, she cut around the next corner and took the shortcut through Pirate's Alley.

Instantly she regretted it.

Though the day still had plenty of light to offer,

this block-long, deserted alley was surrounded by tall brick buildings. Already the cobblestones were painted in tenebrous shadows like the gloom of a forest night.

That familiar gnawing in her stomach returned.

Dammit, she admonished herself, *stop* it!

Twenty-five years old and still afraid of the dark, still afraid of bogymen hiding under the bed.

Still afraid because of a past she could never change. Afraid because . . .

A warning sounded deep within her, and she carefully sequestered her mind from further thought. As if to punish herself for such foolishness, she slowed to a leisurely stroll. But she expelled a long sigh of relief when she emerged from the alley into the comfort of bright daylight and milling crowds.

Two blocks later she reached Bourbon Street.

Despite the relatively early hour, it was already seductively garish. Blinking lights and gaudy window displays drew attention away from the mounds of garbage bags and refuse lining the gutters. Jazz and blues strains leaked through the jalousies. Hawkers prowled in front of the topless joints, promising there would be no cover if you slipped in now before the show started. Glassy-eyed drunks jostled each other and sloshed their drinks over the edge of plastic cups. A juggler on a unicycle told an interfering bible-thumper to fuck off.

Ahh, the glory that was Dixie, she thought, smiling.

Maddy's souvenir shop was at the corner of Bourbon and Toulouse—a little shotgun house with narrow louvers flanking the huge display window. A former slave quarters, it now featured a woodburned sign over the front door: A LITTLE LAGNIAPPE.

Corinne paused for a moment in the street to admire the display window. Again she felt a little bubble of pride form in her throat when she saw, ensconced among the sweet pralines and Cajun cookbooks, the handsome volume titled *An Illustrated History of New Orleans*.

The cover of the book, a silver-point drawing of the old Napoleon House, was her *magnum opus* so far. The original illo hung in her little studio at home beside the Louisiana Council of the Arts Award it had won the year before.

She was still gazing at it when a tourist couple wandered up beside her.

"Look how pretty!" exclaimed the woman. She pointed to the *Illustrated History*.

A moment later the woman added in a scandalized tone, "My God, it's almost *forty* dollars!"

"Let's wait for the flick to come out," wisecracked her companion.

They lost interest and strolled on past. Corinne felt the little bubble in her throat burst.

Okay, she thought, trying to assuage the disappointment.

O-*kay*.

So it wasn't exactly selling like a Danielle Steel novel. And so what if right now she *was* only a fast-buck portrait artist? She was a damn good one. How many people were able to survive (*scrape by,* amended an inner voice) doing something they passionately

38

loved? Not only were her portraits and the increasing commissions from small-press jobs keeping her alive, they were slowly but surely financing her MFA.

As if timed to underscore these thoughts, her eyes focused through the window on the placard Maddy kept next to the cash register: HAPPINESS IS POSITIVE CASH FLOW.

Undaunted by the unexpected irony, she stepped inside.

A woman was dawdling at the postcard rack; two teens were chuckling as they sorted through the bawdy-message T-shirts. Maddy, straightening a display of voodoo dolls near the counter, turned when the bell over the door tinkled.

"Hey, babe!" she greeted Corinne. "How you makin' it?"

Maddy's eyes were huge and apple green, her red hair brilliant. She wore long crystal-drop earrings, several huge rings on each finger, and bright bangles on her wrists and ankles. When she smiled, Corinne noticed a smear of lipstick on her front teeth.

"God, I love that haircut!" Maddy said, reaching out to pat Corinne's asymmetrical bob. It was layered on one side only, leaving a luxuriant mass of curl. "Hon, I swear, if I had your looks I wouldn't be paying income tax."

"Speaking of income . . ." Corinne aimed a rueful glance at the stack of unsold books on the counter. "I take it my royalties won't be flying us to Paris?"

"Don't you be whining at me, girl!"

Maddy lowered her voice so the customers couldn't hear. "I told you, go commercial. The bestselling stuff in the Quarter is sex novelties and dirty T-shirts. You know that. Go with the flow, at least until your cash base is stable. Crank out some racy poster illustrations, I'll get 'm printed. With your talent and my business greed, we'll be snorkeling in hot tubs, puss."

"My big dream in college—to be a snorkeling pornographer."

Maddy shook her head and began straightening another row of dolls. Pointedly, she said, "Just another jerk taking pride in her work," but her tone was affectionate.

"Hey," Maddy added, "you know that hunk-and-a-half who lives next to you—the one who exercises practically naked on his balcony? He was in yesterday to pick up an album. You find out his name yet?"

"Why would I want to know his name?"

"Why? Babe, it's time your old Aunt Madora took you out back for a little talk."

"Even if I did want to meet him, I'd hardly just waltz up and ask his name. Around here he'd probably assume I was a hooker."

"Well, hey, if you could turn a little *profit* too . . ."

They both laughed. "Seriously," said Maddy. "I think you two'd hit it off great. He's a culture-vulture, just like you." She made her voice deep. " 'Excuse me, Miss, but do you have any recordings by R. T. Williams?' "

"I don't have time for all that relationship stuff right now," Corinne protested.

Maddy wagged a finger at her. "Babe, I mean it. I'm worried about you. You get more and more antisocial every day."

"Antisocial? By your definition, a woman is antisocial if she doesn't carry condoms in her purse."

"F'sure! Get the ones with the little pickle bumps."

Corinne laughed again, already shaking off the bad mood that had plagued her for the last few days. "To tell you the truth," she finally admitted, "he *is* kind of cute."

"I knew it! I *knew* it! You *do* like him! I saw the way you were looking at him last week. And he was looking right back."

Corinne flushed when one of the teens glanced over, curious. "Keep it down, mouth," she warned her friend.

The woman browsing through the postcards had selected a handful and now was approaching the register. The bell tinkled as several more customers drifted in.

"I better go," said Corinne. "Time to set up for the night."

"Okay, hon. But what say we go out and do the major oink-oink when you finish?" Maddy grinned and added, "I'm in the mood for oysters."

Corinne rolled her eyes. "That's carrying coals to Newcastle, woman! Okay. Come on by around ten."

The moment she stepped out into the sunlight Corinne spotted the Emperor on the other side of Toulouse Street. He was just standing there, gazing abstractly toward Maddy's shop.

Or toward me? thought Corinne.

All she knew about him were the stories heard throughout the Quarter. One story held that he was a former billionaire whose banking empire in Texas had bottomed out with the plummeting oil prices. Another claimed he was a Wall-Streeter on the lam from an insider-trading indictment. No one knew any of this for certain, of course. But in the *Vieux Carré*, a romantic rumor was preferable to a mundane fact.

He wore the familiar black suit, a stark contrast to his moonstone-white visage. She was still watching him when it happened.

An elderly black woman was coming down the sidewalk toward the Emperor, carrying a sack of groceries. As she passed the mime, she glanced into his face, then quickly averted her glance. Corinne saw her raise her free hand and extend the index and little fingers, bending the others inward so the raised fingers resembled horns. Then she made the sign of the cross and hurried to get past him.

Her eyes squinting with momentary curiosity, Corinne watched the old woman scuttle away.

Corinne remembered reading about the gesture in her folklore class, and seeing it in *Dracula* or one of those old Hammer horror flicks. It was a protection against evil, but she forgot exactly what kind. Maybe . . .

She glanced across the street again. But the Emperor was gone.

Chapter 5

"Check it out, cap!"

Tremain "Tree" Dominique slipped a cassette tape out of his shirt pocket and handed it to Jernigan.

"All right! The new Chick Corea!"

"O-yay, o-*yay!* Nuthin' but the best on the Pontchartrain Express!"

Jernigan, a huge jambox in one hand, unlooped the painter while Tree stepped down into the launch and started the Johnson outboard purring. Steve tossed a couple of flotation cushions to him, then stepped down off the dock and centered the ghetto-blaster between their seats. He popped the cassette in and hit the play button. Tree levered the engine into reverse, easing them away from the dock.

Minutes later they were skimming the placid surface of Lake Pontchartrain, the city and the south shore gradually receding behind them. Tree pointed the bow northeast toward a distant point where the East Pearl River emptied into the lake, providing access to the remote region known as Honey Island Swamp.

Traffic on the lake was light today. To their left, toward the I-10 Causeway, a lone boater was putting an agile catamaran through its aquatic paces, its white sail glistening in the sun. Closer at hand, several fishermen tried their luck from a twenty-five-foot cabin cruiser. The skipper waved from the bridge and Steve waved back.

The competing clamor of the engine and the jambox made conversation impractical. Steve unfolded his map of the swamp and pinned it against his knees to study it. Tree slapped the wheel with both hands, keeping time to the music. He wore tatty sneakers, Army fatigue pants, and a New Orleans Saints T-shirt. His jet-black hair hung in shiny dreadlocks. Around his neck was a small wooden gris-gris on a gold chain.

Tree's employer—the man who owned the launch and the smaller dinghy they would soon transfer to—operated a marine salvage outfit out of nearby St. Bernard Parish. When Tree wasn't hauling valuable ship propellers and other parts up from the bottom of the Mississippi and the Gulf, he ran a charter service for visiting hunters and fishermen. For a month now he had ferried Steve Jernigan into the remotest headwaters and the bayous of Honey Island. A mutual love of jazz and blues had blossomed into friendship.

Steve glanced up from the map, and finally spotted the hazy land mass of the north shore. The sun momentarily ducked behind a scud of clouds, turning the surface of the lake into a flat sheet the color of cement.

The momentary gloom also cast a pall over his good mood.

Again he glanced at the map. He had carefully divided it into dozens of sectors. By now he and Tree had covered nearly half of the swamp. So far, no soap. Locating one reclusive person in that dank jungle was like trying to catch a fly with chopsticks.

Especially when that one reclusive person might not even exist.

She *has* to exist, the rebellious inner voice which had first prompted this long, arduous search insisted—the same voice which would not permit him to accept the official malarkey about his father's brakes failing, plunging him to his death against an overpass.

It just wouldn't hang. His father killed in a car wreck, his father's research partner drowned in a "boating accident" on the Pearl River. And both men searching for the same thing.

Steve had no kick against coincidence. Life was seldom neat and orderly and safely predictable, despite the assurances of statisticians and actuarial tables. But in this case the chain of events did not point toward coincidence. The bold theft of a priceless specimen from their laboratory had led his father and his partner on a long, convoluted trail that ended here in the Mississippi delta. And it was here both men had died, only weeks apart.

Hardly coincidence.

Lost in rumination, Steve was surprised when Tree gave the launch a short burst of reverse to slow it. A moment later they gently bumped into a line of tires roped to the edge of a dock.

Tree glanced at him, giving Jernigan his snake-swift, gap-toothed grin. "Where yat, brah? That music got you cruisin' on the 'L' train?"

Steve grinned back and hopped up onto the dock, grabbing the painter and securing it to a stanchion. It took the two men only a few minutes to haul a small trawling motor down to the lake from a nearby boathouse owned by Tree's boss. They secured the motor to a clinker-built dinghy advertising CRESCENT CITY MARINE SALVAGE in black decals on the bow.

Fifteen minutes later they entered the lazy brown mouth of the East Pearl. Its current was so weak that the little craft made steady progress against it.

The Pearl's headwaters formed in Choctaw County, Mississippi, and twisted and turned for 485 miles down to the Gulf coast. Thirty miles from the Gulf it formed two branches—the East and West Pearl Rivers. Between these two branches lay the fecund, isolated area known as Honey Island Swamp. It had once served as a haven for Indians, runaway slaves, bandits, pirates, and Confederate and Yankee Army deserters, as well as for the bootleggers whose hidden white lightnin' stills had been known by locals as "blind tigers." Today its only residents—besides a host of alligators, water moccasins, black bears, opossums, and hundreds of species of birds—were a handful of diehard Cajuns.

And, Steve hoped, the mysterious woman rumored to dwell all alone somewhere in its junglelike depths. A woman his father had hinted about in the very last diary entry of his life.

Now the dense foliage overhead formed a thick green canopy. Sunlight leaked through here and there in slanting shafts, stippling both men with quivering specks of gold. They were surrounded by a seemingly impenetrable forest of cypress, magnolia, tupelo, sweet gum, and massive oaks draped in Spanish moss.

"There," said Jernigan, consulting his map and then pointing off to the left. "See it? The inlet next to that cypress head. There's a dwelling marked on the map."

Tree nodded and leaned on the rudder, edging them toward the muddy strip of water. Here there was no current at all and they made even better time.

By mutual consent they left the music turned off to enjoy the mausoleum stillness of the swamp. Even the steady putt-putt of the little motor was quickly absorbed by the lush wall of growth on either side.

It was Tree who first broke the silence.

"What you lookin' for, brought you all the way to Nawlins from Michigan?"

The sudden question surprised Steve. So far Tree had been content to collect his pay and keep a lid on his curiosity.

"I'm trying to locate something that was stolen," he answered finally. "I have reason to believe it ended up somewhere around here."

Tree kept his eyes carefully averted, pretending to watch a half-submerged log near the bank.

"Stolen? What? Money?"

Steve hesitated.

"Lawd — *law*dy!" said Tree, breaking into his shuffling-Negro routine. "Hush mah nigger mouf for axin' dem questions! *Please* don' whup me, boss man!"

Steve grinned. "You asshole, knock it off. No, it's not money. It's a laboratory specimen. A body part," he added reluctantly.

Tree stopped his routine, but the astonished stare was suddenly genuine.

"You talkin' like . . . *human* body?"

Steve nodded.

"Shurnuf?"

He nodded again.

"O-yay, o-*yay!* And you're thinkin' maybe this old woman you been lookin' for is the one's got it?"

"Not really. But she might . . . I don't know, be able to tell me something about what happened to it."

"Hoooo!" Tree shook his head. "Forget I opened my mouth, awright?"

Ten minutes later Tree negotiated a dogleg turn in the bayou and a dwelling came into view—an old flyblown shanty on stilts. Lazy plumes of cooking smoke curled out of a tin chimney. A raft was tied to one of the stilts.

Tree killed the engine and they drifted alongside. The man who stepped outside to meet them was somewhere in his late thirties, dressed in kersey trousers and a patched broadcloth shirt. His grizzled face was friendly but wary.

The two men greeted him from their dinghy, craning their necks to look up at him.

"We're just wondering," said Steve, "if there's any more places besides yours in this direction?"

In fact his map showed two more dwellings before the bayou formed another switchback and connected with the East Pearl River again. But experience with the taciturn, cautious locals had taught him to approach his real question obliquely.

"Couple," the man finally answered.

"We're looking for a woman who's supposed to live

around here somewhere. I don't know her name, but she lives by herself. I just want to ask her a few questions."

Whatever emotion glimmered for a moment in the man's eyes passed quickly. A moment later they were carefully veiled again.

"You trow your time away you go dat way, garontee. Ain't no womans."

"You're sure? One maybe a little older than you?"

But now the other man's blank expression shut them out as effectively as a brick wall. Steve watched his eyes fasten for a moment on the gris-gris around Tree's neck.

"Just trow away your time," the Cajun repeated stubbornly.

Before Steve could ask another question, he nodded at them and stepped back into the shack.

"Shit," Steve muttered under his breath. Then he expelled a long sigh and glanced at his watch. "All right, Tree, let's hit it. We'll finish out this sector and then head on back for today."

Chapter 6

Alan Breaux stopped in front of the fourth-floor nurse's station. Self-consciously, he shifted a bunch of long-stemmed roses to his other hand.

"Is Sabrina Nash receiving visitors this evening?" he asked the duty nurse.

The woman was instantly wary. "Are you a relative?" she asked.

Breaux watched her face closely and saw something he definitely did not like.

"Not exactly, but —"

"I'm sorry. Unless you're a relative, I can't —"

"The heck of it is," explained Breaux with a congenial smile, "my wife is normally a very mild-mannered woman. But she used to babysit Sabrina, and if she finds out I didn't at least drop these off to her in person . . ."

His voice trailed off and he arched his eyebrows hopefully, letting the nurse envision the scene of domestic horror which awaited him if he failed in this mission.

But it was no use. She shook her head adamantly.

"I'm sorry. If you'd like to leave them here, I'll see that they're delivered to her room."

Breaux studied her face some more and decided something was *beaucoup* off-kilter here. She projected a good professional veneer, but experience told him she was a lousy con artist.

He said, "Is Doctor Grodner around?"

"Yes he is, but he's not available at the moment."

Breaux considered for a minute, and then reluctantly made up his mind. He produced his NOPD photostat and flashed it at her.

"Police business," he said brusquely, hoping he was a better liar than she was.

She gave it a tight-lipped glance before meeting his gaze. "I'll page Doctor Grodner," she said, relenting finally.

Breaux paced up and down impatiently in front of the elevators. Evening visiting hours had just begun, and a steady stream of arrivals kept the elevator doors whumping open and shut. An elderly patient in a skimpy hospital johnny shuffled past, his paper slippers rustling against the tile floor.

Finally the elevator doors eased open and Grodner stepped out, his face drawn tight with nervous strain. He spotted the cop immediately. His eyes flicked to the roses. No explanations were necessary.

"Logging some overtime again tonight, I see," Breaux said, greeting him.

Without a word, Grodner led the older man to a pair of unoccupied chrome-and-vinyl chairs in the far corner of the lobby.

The physician spoke woodenly. The glaze over his eyes reminded Breaux of the battlefield stare he had seen too damn often in Korea.

"Sabrina's dead," Grodner said bluntly.

"She's . . . *what?*"

"She died forty minutes ago."

"But that can't be! You said it was routine, she—"

"I *know* what I said," Grodner snapped. One hand nervously worried his neat beard.

"But how—"

Grodner raised the other hand wearily to stop him. "We don't know how. We opened her up this morning and found no perforated ulcer. No ulcers period. I don't know what in the hell showed up on those x-rays, but her stomach was as clean as Mother Teresa's conscience. It was a routine incision, we closed her back up without complications. But a couple of hours ago her blood pressure started to fall rapidly and she went into shock. We did everything we could, she just . . ."

Grodner's voice trailed off and he sank back heavily into the chair. "Jesus Christ," he said softly, as if fully realizing for the first time what had happened. "Jesus Christ Almighty, I still can't believe that beautiful woman is *gone.*"

The roses were suddenly dead weight in Breaux's hands.

"What . . . what's the official cause of death?"

Grodner shook his head. "We'll have to wait for the autopsy. The best theory now is a delayed allergic reaction to the anesthetic, but she exhibited none of the usual symptoms."

Grodner met the policeman's shocked stare. "That Scale of Medical Weirdness you mentioned last night? It's gone up from a 6.5 to at least a 9."

Corinne stripped to the skin and reached for the sleep shirt that was hanging from the screw-on finial of the bedpost. She paused then, instead, stepping in front of a full-length mirror covering the closet door.

Seeing herself naked always forced her to admit that she was too harsh in appraising her own looks. She had a nice body. And Maddy was right — she *was* pretty. Except, she thought, her eyes narrowing for a more critical look, that her teeth could maybe be a little straighter. But then, orthodontics hadn't been a high priority with her parents.

That little warning sounded deep inside. But she had imbibed one glass of wine too many during dinner tonight with Maddy, and failed to heed it.

She slipped into the long knit shirt, then stepped around a portable shoji screen that divided her studio apartment into a bedroom and atelier. She couldn't stand the acrylic furniture and Masonite end tables that had come with the place, and had asked the manager to haul them out. Now it was sparse on furnishings. Now there was only a pleated armchair, a brocade settee, a camelback sofa, and the huge burl walnut table where she worked.

As if tugged by invisible strings, her eyes shifted to the wall where a gold-framed five-by-seven photo hung next to her Council of the Arts Award.

Why had she kept it all these years? Maybe, she decided, for the same reason that soldiers kept pinup photos in their lockers. Fantasies were free — and an illusion was better than nothing at all.

But at least a soldier's fantasies were untainted by

reality. She wished the same were true about her memories of that couple in the photo.

What did *she* have to cherish that she could thank them for? A childhood of deprivation and neglect. A brutal, alcoholic father and a selfish, neurotic mother who habitually left her alone in their rural home miles from nowhere, ensuring that she would never outgrow her childhood fear of the dark.

Her mother, especially, was merely a blur in memory, as foreign as that pretty, quietly desperate face staring out of the photo. Corinne was only eight when her mother had finally given full rein to her irresponsibility and run away with a salesman who frequented the highway diner where she waited tables. Corinne could forgive her for taking off, but couldn't she at least have taken her only child with her? How could a mother desert her own kid? Even her drunken, mean-spirited father had at least tried to stick it out — until he finally drank himself into an early grave.

She spent the rest of her childhood in an orphanage run by the Sisters of Mercy in New Orleans. They were strict, but good to her, making sure she developed her natural artistic talents, which won her a highly coveted scholarship to Tulane. At college she was bright, never missing a semester on the Dean's List. But she had never fit in at the "Harvard of the South." She never had the clothes, the cars, the wallet full of credit cards, the sunlamp tan cultivated by exotic semester breaks in Cancun or the Bahamas. Other girls were rushed by sororities while she waited tables at the student rathskeller and dreamed of other places she'd rather be.

A sudden thumping noise on the balcony made her

heart turn over.

For a long, frozen moment she couldn't move. Then, her heart hammering fiercely, she slowly turned and stared at the French doors leading outside.

They stared back, challenging her to come closer.

Beyond their mullioned, curtainless windows the night sky was a murky blue-black void. She forced herself to take the first step, then the second, considering the possibility that someone had hidden out there, waiting for her to go to bed.

Maybe she should get out now? But that meant getting dressed, going out alone at this time of night.

Another step. Now a spasm of fear set her insides churning like overworked digestive gears.

(*The old black woman raised her free hand and extended the index and little fingers, bending the others inward so the raised fingers resembled horns. Then she made the sign of the cross and hurried to get past him.*)

Crying out in fright, Corinne seized one of the doors and flung it open.

She spotted it immediately.

One of her macramé plant hangers had tumbled a few feet to the floor of the balcony. It had spilled a little soil, but the terra-cotta pot hadn't even cracked.

Corinne stood there for a long moment, letting her heart slow down.

Below, the peach-colored lights of Decatur Street glowed reassuringly. She immediately felt like a fool.

Even so, Corinne made sure two lights were burning before she went to bed. Two, in case one burned out during the night.

There was one other nocturnal ritual that she

couldn't skip.

Right before she slipped between the sheets, she picked up a bright yellow tennis ball from the top of the dresser. Standing well back from the bed, she bent down and rolled it under. As always, it shot through on the other side and ricocheted off the wall.

All clear . . .

Despite the little flush of shame she always felt after her nightly "bogeyman check," she heaved a sigh of relief.

Like a junkie experiencing shame after his latest fix, she promised herself again that soon she would break herself of this stupid habit.

Chapter 7

"According to a theory advanced by myself and others," said Professor Eric Winters, "behavioral capacity — a broad label more comprehensive than mere 'intelligence' — is not contingent on the *size* of a brain. Rather, it is an index of what is called cephalization: the quantity of brain tissue beyond that necessary for relaying impulses to and from the brain."

Winters paused in his lecture, listening to pens scratching as his class dutifully took notes.

He was about to continue when the peroxide blonde in the last row shot a hand up.

The eyes he turned on her were hard blue gems. "Yes, Ms. Rutherford?"

"Are you saying, it's not just how much you've got, but how you use it?"

The researcher winced slightly, nonplussed. "Yes," he replied finally, "I suppose that *would* qualify as a crude layman's translation."

A couple of brown-nosers sniggered. Winters continued.

"Equally critical, at least in determining human

57

behavioral capacity, has been the progressive evolution of the forebrain. This highly convoluted mantle not only coordinates the understanding and production of language, it permits higher conceptualization and abstraction. It is responsible for what we call 'judgment,' and thus enables humans to contemplate and influence their own behavior."

Again he paused to allow his students to catch up their notes. Outside, over Lake Pontchartrain, the sun blazed in a morning sky as blue as a butane flame.

"Last class," Winters resumed, "we discussed the relationship between glial cells and neurons. Recall that the higher the ratio of glial cells to neurons, the greater the increase in mental activity. And recall also that we defined 'mental activity' much more broadly than mere performance on standard IQ tests. We cited the case of hypermnesia, or accelerated recall and memory."

Winters thought of something and frowned. He tugged the sleeve of his natty blue suit jacket up and glanced at his watch, deciding he could take his medication after class.

"These three factors," he summed up, "cephalization, the forebrain, and the ratio of glial cells to neurons, are interconnected in the critical problem of utilizing the brain at or near its full potential. Now, how does all this relate to today's reading on the electroencephalogram or EEG?"

"An EEG," promptly responded a student down front, "records oscillating electric currents from the scalp—so-called brain waves. These are classified according to frequency bands in cycles per second, and they correspond to the level and type of behavioral activity. Thus you can tell what 'mode' the brain is in by analyzing the EEG pattern."

Winters beamed. It was precisely the type of response he liked—factual information untainted by subjective interpretation.

"Very good. Common frequency bands include alpha activity from 8 to 14 Hertz, beta activity above 14 Hertz, delta activity below 4 Hertz, and theta activity from 4 to less than 8 Hertz. Each is associated with different activities—alpha with relaxation, for example. But most critical, from the standpoint of increased brain utilization, is beta activity. Beta corresponds to intellectual cognition and excitement. Rest assured that Einstein was functioning in beta when he formulated his famous Theory of Relativity—as was Descartes when he wrote the *Discourse on Method*."

Pens scraped furiously. Winters paused, his brilliant azure eyes glancing through the window and focusing on some distant point past Lake Pontchartrain.

"In a nutshell," he concluded, "the problem is this: How do we manipulate the physicochemical properties of the brain to induce what we might term Maximum Beta Mode or MBM? Only then will we achieve a quantum leap not only in intelligence quotient, but in the entire range of human psychic activity."

Except for the fast scritching of pens, the silence in his classroom was almost palpable. Until the young man named Donald Carr raised a tentative hand. Winters steadied himself.

"Mr. Carr?" he said icily.

"Professor Winters, this is all very fascinating. But

most of us are going into some branch of applied medicine, not research. The catalog description of this course implied that we would be dealing with such practical problems as gross lesions of the brain, epilepsy, the diagnostic use of CAT scans, and so forth. I wonder if—"

"High-tech diagnosis," Winters cut in dryly, "is fully covered in Delta College's course on introductory radiology and axial tomography. As for the rest, the specific content of this course is determined by the professor teaching it."

Carr obviously had further objections, but the period mercifully ended. Winters assigned another reading chapter, then dismissed the class until Monday.

In the hallway he set his calfskin briefcase down and paused to remove the silver pillbox from his suit jacket. He placed a tablet on his tongue and washed it down with a drink from the fountain.

Winters stalled as long as possible. He detested keeping office hours, but Delta required all instructors to offer a minimum of three a week. Unable to avoid it any longer, he unlocked his door at the end of the hallway and slapped at the light switch.

The small room was as ascetic as a monk's cell—a gunmetal filing cabinet and a bare blondewood desk with a spring-backed chair were the only furnishings. A full-color chart on one wall illustrated the vivisectioned quadrants of the human brain.

Winters settled into the chair and opened the top drawer of his desk to remove a Greater New Orleans phone book.

Randomly he flipped it open to a page and scanned

the four columns of names, addresses, and phone numbers. When he was sure that his eyes had passed over all of the approximately three hundred entries, he closed the book again.

With a confident smile he put it back in the drawer. "Godwin," he recited, "Martha H. 1040 St. Charles Avenue, 861-8290. Godwin, Morris. 2208 River Ridge, 821-1554. Godwin, Nathaniel P. 430 Gretna Highway, 273-1595. Godwin, Paul E. 9905 Loyola Avenue, 394-8126. Godwin, Robert C. 716 Constantinople Drive, 866-1330. Godwin, Sylvester M. 1147 One Shell Square . . ."

His smile widened as he progressed down the list, effortlessly ticking off names, addresses, and telephone numbers.

Ten minutes later, he was still reciting.

Chapter 8

"How you makin' it, gents?"

C. J. Guidry plunked a pair of foaming schooners down, then leaned across the bar on both elbows and added, "Know why the Cajun stuck rubbers over his ears?"

Jernigan and Alan Breaux exchanged bemused glances. Breaux finally shrugged and said, "I'll bite."

"Hell, he didn't wanna catch hearing aids!"

The two men groaned in chorus while the barkeep hustled back to the kitchen. Despite the fact that it was Friday night, the crowd was not too festive. News of Sabrina Nash's death had muted the party mood of her hometown fans, especially here in the Quarter where she had made her start.

Again the two customers at the end of the S-shaped bar lapsed into reflective silence. Breaux's glance eased sideways to study the younger man's face. Once more he was struck by the brooding intensity of those eyes, the complete absorption in some atypical problem that couldn't be solved by a good binge, a good shrink, or even a good woman.

He stuck his hand out toward Jernigan.

"Excuse me," he said, interrupting Jernigan's thoughts. "I've seen you around here before, but I never caught your name. I'm Alan Breaux."

"Steve Jernigan." The two men shook hands.

Breaux raised his schooner. "To the memory of Sabrina."

They clinked glasses and took sweeping deep swallows.

"Twenty-four years old," said Steve, shaking his head. "I still can't believe it."

Their eyes met and held. "No," agreed Breaux. "Neither can I."

Both men glanced away self-consciously.

C. J. emerged from the kitchen, carrying a steaming plate of red beans and rice. He set it down on the bar and rubbed his palms together briskly. "Overfed and underloved," he said happily.

Breaux glanced at the man's ample paunch. "I hear your wife lost 250 pounds of ugly fat when she divorced you."

"Go fuck yourself sideways, pilgrim!" C. J. barely got the words out around a mouthful of food.

"The Emperor been in lately?" said Breaux. From the corner of his eye he saw Jernigan glance at him.

"Nahh. Ain't been in since . . . since Sabrina collapsed."

For a moment C. J. stopped eating, scowling at his plate as he thought about the singer. "Ulcer surgery, my sweet aunt! Goddamn ignut doctors."

He attacked his plate again.

"Funny thing," Breaux persisted casually. "I've been

63

coming here for years. I can't recall seeing the Emperor around here before."

"No shit, Sherlock," Guidry shot back. "That's because he never came in until Sabrina started singing here."

The waitress called out an order and the bartender reluctantly deserted his supper.

"I understand you're a cop," remarked Steve.

"During the day," said Breaux, and both men laughed. "How about yourself?"

"In a way we're both in the same business. I'm a sort of physiological detective—a psychobiologist, to be exact. I teach out at Delta."

"Psycho-*who*sis?"

Jernigan grinned. "Just think of it as psychology from a biologist's perspective. We're more interested in the state of your pituitary gland than we are in your relationship with your mother."

Breaux seemed genuinely interested. Over a couple more beers, he plied Steve with questions about his work. In the face of Breaux's subtle but remarkable talent for drawing people out, Steve found himself opening up as he hadn't in quite some time. He explained how he had inherited his father's interest in explaining psychic and occult abilities from a physiological standpoint.

"My father's work really began to take off in the late seventies," he explained. "Have you ever heard of a guy named Mario Townsend?"

Breaux shook his head. "Doesn't ring a—wait, take five. Isn't he the guy who was supposedly able to move stuff around without touching it? Went on the

64

Johnny Carson Show once or twice?"

"That's the guy—or was. He died in 1977. And it wasn't just telekinesis he was known for. He was also credited with powers of ESP, clairvoyance, and so-called thaumaturgy—miracle healing. Anyway, Dad's break actually came when Townsend died, because he willed his brain to my father and his partner for extensive analysis. He was familiar with their hypothesis that Townsend's abilities could be explained—physiologically—on the basis of unique chemical transmitters in his brain. He left them a rare chance to prove their hypothesis."

Breaux was fascinated. "Were they able to do it?"

Steve moved one shoulder slightly, gazing into his beer. Breaux saw the brooding absorption in his eyes again.

"Unfortunately, the question is moot. Somebody broke into the university lab in Ann Arbor and stole Townsend's brain. A lot of publicity had surrounded the acquisition, so in theory it could have been anyone. But my father and his partner came to the conclusion that another brain researcher was behind the theft. Dad's partner, a professor of neurosurgery named Dale McGinnis, took a semester-long sabbatical to follow up some leads they had put together with the help of a private investigator."

Steve knocked off the rest of his beer before he continued.

"The trail led McGinnis here to New Orleans. Two weeks after his arrival he was found dead, floating in the Pearl River. My father took an emergency leave of absence and came down himself. It was their second mistake. He was killed in Jefferson Parish, his rented car totaled against an overpass."

"Both of them died?"

Steve nodded. "Yeah, I know what you're thinking—somebody should've cried murder most foul. But both deaths were ruled accidental. And conveniently, the missing brain never turned up. Almost everything I know comes from my father's journal, which was in his hotel room among his possessions. He believed another researcher was after that specimen. But unfortunately, if he had someone in mind, he never mentioned a name. He did refer to a woman he thought was somehow connected to the case. So far, I haven't been able to find her."

Breaux considered asking more about this woman. Instead, he was silent for a long moment.

"I take it, from your last comment, that it's no coincidence you ended up teaching here?"

Steve shook his head. "I passed up a tenure-track position at the University of Minnesota to come down here and teach for half the money. But right now I don't give a shit about money."

He lapsed into a brooding silence. Breaux signaled C. J. to bring them two more.

"Jesus," the cop finally said. "It sounds like some weird sci-fi scenario. A stolen brain, two mysterious deaths. And I thought this *other* was weird."

His voice trailed off, as his eyes veered toward the Mardi Gras countdown calendar hanging between the dartboards.

Steve seemed to return from some faraway place. "I heard you ask C. J. a couple of questions about that

66

old mime. Does that mean the police are looking into Sabrina's death?"

Breaux glanced at him quickly. *"Should* they be?"

Steve raised both hands helplessly. "That's your ball game, not mine."

"Yeah, I'm the pro."

Breaux sighed, took a long draught of beer, and wiped a foamy mustache away with his index finger. His face was the picture of innocence as he added, "My wife—she's a fine woman, but she thinks I should spend more time listening to others. Says I might learn something that way."

Steve grinned. "Seems I hear a lot about this wife of yours."

"God love her. Woman's a saint."

"Others might open up more," Steve volunteered cryptically, "if they thought that all your cards were on the table."

Breaux scratched at one of his silver-tinted sideburns. "Sometimes," he said finally, "showing your hole card can amount to a serious breach of confidentiality. Understood?"

"Understood."

"But maybe it's all right to speculate—just speculate, mind you—that a certain doctor might be extremely puzzled right about now. Perhaps more puzzled than he's ever been in his career. So puzzled, let's say, that he doesn't really expect an autopsy report this weekend to clear anything up."

"You mean—"

"I'm just tossing this out," Breaux said, cutting him off. "Informal probing, really, to find out if someone besides me *might* have thought there was something a tad . . . odd about the events surrounding Sabrina's collapse. About this rare appearance of the Emperor, about the way he behaved, the way he got up and split so suddenly."

Steve nodded slowly. "Maybe this someone else you're looking for . . . *felt* something too — something hard to describe. Something very subjective — but definitely out of the ordinary."

Breaux glanced at the carnival countdown calendar again, then back to Jernigan.

"If there *was* someone like that," he said, "and he happened to be an intelligent, well-educated guy who obviously knows shit from apple butter . . . well, I'd be quick to let him know how much I'd appreciate any thoughts he might come up with concerning the matter. All in an unofficial vein, of course."

"Of course," said Steve.

"You two queer for each other?" demanded C. J. Guidry, interrupting them to slap two shot glasses down on the bar. He poured them each a knock of Crown Royal. "This one's on the house 'cause f'sure you cheap bastards'll never buy one."

The two men clinked glasses.

"To your wife," said Steve, meeting the cop's eyes.

"A paragon of womanhood," Breaux said piously, returning the glance.

"Corky, you little brat! I'm telling Professor Wiggle-Wobble on you!"

"No, Pepe, please don't!"

"Oh, but I *will,* you . . . you dumb little chunk of driftwood!"

"Pepe! Please don't!"

"I will, I *will!* Professor Wiggle-Wobble will carve you into toothpicks, you sawed-off little tree stump!"

"AHHARRG!"

At the corner of Chartres and St. Peter, the kids clustered around the puppeteer's booth howled with delighted laughter as Corky rained a fusillade of blows on Pepe.

"Take *that,* blockhead!"

"Help, Professor Wiggle-Wobble, HELLL-P!"

Parents too smiled with delight as they watched the animated faces of their youngsters. The pretty girl who was deftly manipulating the control paddles was around twenty—her long, stunning chestnut hair capped by a beige tam-o'-shanter cocked at a jaunty angle.

"Hear, hear!" she roared in the mock basso-profundo voice of Professor Wiggle-Wobble offstage. "What's all this racket? Mark my words, kids, if I have to come out there . . . !"

The children roared again, recognizing the age-old hollow threat of all parents. A few moms and dads grinned sheepishly.

Only the Quarter's arabesque street lamps held off the black encroachment of the night. A single arc-sodium floodlight illuminated the hand-carved set where the two puppets danced and capered. Their graceful choreography helped the kids forget that strings were attached to the wooden limbs.

"Damn, she's *good!*" a man from Corpus Christi

said to his wife, tossing several bills into a silk top hat near the stage. The bottom of the hat was already covered with bills and change.

Cheers and applause split the night as Pepe and Corky took their final bow and capered offstage. More money rained into the topper.

One spectator in particular applauded with wild enthusiasm. He stepped out from the murky shadows beyond the streetlight. Some of the tourists recognized the alabaster face of the old mime they had seen on the steps of nearby St. Louis Cathedral.

Several persons — including the young puppeteer — noticed the portrait of Andrew Jackson on the bill he tossed into her hat.

She met his eyes, her face beaming with pride and gratitude.

She was still too high on applause to notice how both of his shaggy, silver-white brows knitted together, forming one line. Nor did she observe that one of his huge, piercing eyes was blue, the other brown.

Still clapping the loudest, he held her gaze while he mouthed the silent word "Bravo!"

Spectators were starting to peel away from the throng, wandering toward the bright lights and music of Bourbon Street. The old man blended into their group.

Only a few of the tourists noticed the subtle thrumming of the air — as if the atmosphere were suffused with radioactive motes. For a moment the pretty puppeteer looked as if the wind had been knocked out of her.

She uttered a pathetic mewling sound, like a small

70

animal in pain.

The girl staggered into the puppet stage, almost knocking it off its sturdy oak table.

Somebody gasped.

A little girl down front screamed.

"Dream about this *forever,* kids!" the puppeteer commanded in the deep, resonant tone of Professor Wiggle-Wobble. Then she collapsed. She was dead before she hit the cobblestones.

Chapter 9

Corinne slept fitfully and woke up on Saturday morning with a pulsating ache behind her temples.

For one long moment — her consciousness still trapped in the limbo between sleeping and waking — the throbbing pain seemed to pin her rigid to the mattress. She experienced the disquieting impression that the ceiling had been replaced by a giant peering eye studying her like a germ under a microscope. But when she opened her eyes, she saw nothing overhead but the nubby white stucco of the ceiling.

A long, hot shower eased the headache somewhat. But sudden flutters of nausea during breakfast in her tiny kitchenette prompted Corinne to toss away a half-eaten brioche.

I've picked up a damn bug of some kind, she thought idly as she sponged the formica counter clean.

Normally Saturday mornings were reserved for homework due in her Monday night art class. Today, however, she felt an incipient case of cabin fever coming on and decided, instead, to open up her little sidewalk studio early.

She arrived at Jackson Square by ten o'clock, blissfully ignorant of the previous night's tragedy only a half block away. The morning was coppery with sunshine, though dark tatters of cloud over the Gulf were starting to weave a leaden pall far out on the horizon. Beyond the edge of the French Quarter, across Canal Street, granite and glass office buildings thrust their spires into the soft blue belly of the sky.

She had just finished rolling back the metal curtains of her studio when it suddenly felt as if a glove of ice had been laid across the back of her neck.

Her heartbeat quickened slightly.

Corinne glanced back over her shoulder toward the long marble steps of St. Louis Cathedral. Except for a pigeon or two scavenging for crumbs, they were deserted. The old mime was nowhere in sight.

Judas Priest, woman, she thought with a grim little smile. *Precisely what is your problem?*

The arrival of the day's first customers quickly dispelled her pensive mood.

They were a middle-aged couple from Rochester, New York. The man explained that he wanted this rendition of his wife as a twentieth anniversary present to himself.

Corinne had long ago discovered that, almost invariably, her customers were somewhat diffident about posing for what was often their first portrait. Despite her own natural shyness, she always enjoyed the confident stream of patter with which she set them at ease. Any trace of her own insecurity would vanish as she set about doing what she did best.

She showed them her display drawings in various mediums, and they decided on charcoal. The woman was not a beauty by any stretch of the imagination.

But she had a pleasant, open face and strikingly handsome eyes. Corinne rendered her faithfully, using bold strokes to capitalize on the woman's good features.

She turned the easel so the woman could examine her progress. Corinne could tell, from her relieved, genuinely pleased expression, that she was glad the young artist hadn't tried to turn her into Ingrid Bergman—as a few of Corinne's talented but more jaded peers on the plaza might well have done.

They paid, tipping her generously, and asked if she'd be around later so they could send two friends by. As Corinne was flipping her pad to another sheet, the new page ripped nearly in half.

*"Damn*it!"

That was twice now in the last couple days. And this stuff was one-hundred-percent cotton fiber at ten bucks a pad, not the el-cheapo rag contents she used for practice. Since when had she become such a klutz?

(*since the headaches started*)

(*since the "morning sickness" began*)

(*since the sudden spells of sleepiness and the abrupt blue funks took over*)

(*since . . .*)

Involuntarily, she glanced back toward the steps of the cathedral.

Still empty.

(*like the space under your bed?*)

Despite the increasing number of tourists, Jackson Square now seemed much too vast and lonely. Corinne suddenly decided she could use another cup of coffee. She took in her sign, swung the metal curtain down, and snapped the heavy brushed-chrome Yale padlock shut. Then she headed toward the Cafe du Monde on Decatur.

Corinne glanced warily about her as she crossed the cobblestone plaza.

No one seemed to be paying her the least bit of attention. But she couldn't shake the vulnerable feeling that she was being closely scrutinized. It reminded her of that recurring dream which had plagued her in junior high and high school—the one in which she was hurrying down the crowded halls at school, when she would suddenly glance down and realize she was naked.

On the far side of the square she paused to watch one of her colleagues, a dapper old French Canadian named Georges Lagacé, who'd been doing portraits in the Quarter for decades. Now he was whipping up a likeness of two lovers posed arm-in-arm.

He glanced up and winked at Corinne.

"Good morning, *ma jolie!* Please may I draw that lovely face today?"

As always she smiled and shook her head no. Again, watching his deft hands, she felt a stab of envy at his adept hatching technique for background shading—one technical aspect of drawing that still seemed to elude her at times. But she was almost chilled by the way Georges worked with the assembly-line indifference of a fry cook creating a Big Mac. She prayed that art would never become that humdrum for her.

As if he could read her face, Georges winked again and said, "I am fast, and I am efficient—like a car wash, nuh? But *this*"—he indicated the plaza with a careless flip of his free hand—"is where I belong. You?"

He lifted his pen from the paper for a moment and pointed heavenward.

"You are a great *artiste!* I must have your portrait for my private collection, *ma jolie,* because that burning in your eyes is true greatness!"

Warm blood seeped into her cheeks at the compliment.

"That 'burning' in my eyes," she responded lightly, "is probably starvation. See you later."

"Pouf! Always the great ones are modest."

He rolled his eyes tragically and blew her a kiss.

The weather had lured tourists out earlier than usual, and she found Decatur Street teeming with late-morning activity. A mule-drawn surrey clopped by; the animals looked festive and silly in their floppy, flower-studded carnival hats. Everywhere, visitors were aiming camcorders like fat ray guns, recording life in the Big Easy.

The open-air Cafe du Monde sprawled for nearly half a block, a vast confusion of wrought-iron tables and crumb-strewn terrazzo flooring. She shooed a few pigeons away and selected a table near the sidewalk.

A harried-looking waiter scuttled over and Corinne ordered *café au lait.* While she waited for her order she once again admired the series of framed lithographs lining the pillars of the covered patio. They depicted life along the bayou, and one in particular always arrested her attention—an old Creole couple fishing from a dory, their faces radiating a peace and contentment so real that Corinne always felt a stab of envy when observing them.

On a sudden impulse she stood and crossed to the lithograph, examining the artist's signature: Katerina Zverkov, 1957.

Idly, Corinne wondered what had become of her. She was extremely talented. Had the fingers that had once coaxed such crisp lines and forms, such a three-dimensional illusion of texture into being, gone on to desert art and wring out diapers instead?

Corinne was on her way back to the table when she spotted her handsome neighbor.

He sat only three tables away, raptly watching an old man at a neighboring piano bar bang out the "Maple Leaf Rag." He hadn't spotted her yet. She watched him stand and push his chair aside to let an overweight couple squeeze by. Again she noticed how fit and lithe he looked, how his every movement seemed so economical and sure. He radiated an aura of quiet confidence that she herself felt only when she was working.

And crude Maddy was right: He definitely qualified as a hunk-and-a-half.

The waiter returned with her coffee and a plate of warm sugar-sprinkled beignets. She nibbled at the corner of one, frowning when a little loss-of-gravity rush of nausea again tickled her stomach. With a frustrated sigh she shoved the plate aside and settled for her coffee.

She glanced around again. The old pianist had taken a break, and now her neighbor was busy writing something, his own coffee remaining untouched.

Part of her wanted him to look up and spot her. Another part of her hoped he wouldn't.

The man at the next table left, abandoning his morning *Times-Picayune*. Corinne grabbed it and spread it open before her.

The double-deck headline seemed to leap off page one at her:

FRENCH QUARTER STREET PERFORMER
COLLAPSES BEFORE HORRIFIED CROWD

Blood pulsing tight in her temples, Corinne scanned the frustratingly vague story. She didn't recognize the girl's name—Jeanette Manders—but she was positive, from the location mentioned, that she knew her.

My God, she thought, her mind a riot of confused thoughts. My *God,* they'd been greeting each other for almost a year now, and several times Corinne had stopped to watch her show—actually, to enjoy the magic on the faces of the kids in her audience.

The cause of death, she read, had not yet been determined.

Just like Sabrina Nash, she thought woodenly.

(*I've picked up a damn bug of some kind, that's all*)

She uttered a little cry of dismay when her pottery cup suddenly seemed to leap from her fingers, shattering on the polished chips of the floor and splashing hot coffee on her new white Reeboks.

Several people stared at her, causing a hot blush to paint her cheeks sanguine.

You stupid little klutz, she admonished herself angrily as she bent to pick up the jagged fragments of

78

the cup. What in God's name is *wrong* with you?

She was still scooping up pieces when the back of her neck began to throb with warning insistence.

Corinne abruptly sat up and stared beyond a bright low border of hydrangea. She felt a trembling shock as her veins iced over.

The Emperor's moonstone-white face was watching her from the other side of Decatur.

No, not watching her, she corrected herself. He never stared directly at her. It was as if he stood watch over some wider sector—a sector which always just happened to include her.

She was still gazing at him when a bus with INTER-NATIONAL TOURS, INC. on the side pulled to a stop near the mime and began unloading. Japanese, Hispanic, European tourists streamed from the coach, speaking a confusing medley of tongues. Several pointed excitedly at the old mime and snapped his picture. He stoically ignored them, still gazing in Corinne's direction.

Abruptly, a stooped old woman being helped by a younger couple began to protest loudly. She pointed at the mime and spoke rapidly in what Corinne guessed was Italian.

"Jettatore!" the old woman shrieked. *"Jettatore!"*

The Emperor executed a spry 180-degree turn and blended into the flow along Decatur's busy sidewalk. A moment later the young couple managed to hush their companion's outcries.

Corinne's brow furrowed. What did it mean? And a couple days ago, that black woman who had—

A shadow fell across her table and Corinne almost cried out in fright.

Chapter 10

"Hey, I'm sorry," said Jernigan awkwardly. "I didn't mean to startle you. I just thought you could use a hand."

He performed a deep-knee bend and finished picking up the pieces of the broken cup.

"I could use *some*thing," she admitted helplessly. "Maybe a seminar in physical coordination. Lately I'm a walking disaster area."

He dropped the pieces in a nearby trash container. A moment later he surprised her by snatching a couple of napkins out of the holder on her table and kneeling once again, this time going to work on her sneakers.

"I think the stains'll wash out," he announced, swiping at the coffee on her toes.

She felt foolish sitting there like a helpless girl while he cleaned up her mess. But she also realized she was enjoying the unaccustomed feeling of being fussed over.

He rose again, and she found herself looking squarely into his steady, gray-green eyes.

"By the way, I'm your neighbor. My name's Steve Jernigan."

"I know. I mean," she amended, flustered, "I know you're my neighbor. I'm Corinne Matthews."

He stood before her, unsure what to say or do next.

"Would you mind," she said quickly, "if I join you at your table? I've destroyed this area."

He grinned. "Good idea. I'll order you another *cafe au lait* too."

"Ask for a straw," she added, and they both laughed.

She followed him to his table. Corinne couldn't help noticing, as she sat down across from him, a stamped, still-unsealed envelope addressed to a Professor Lisa somebody, Department of Anthropology. She glanced away before she caught the name of the school.

"I'm writing to a friend in Ann Arbor," he explained. He gathered the envelope and his unfinished letter up and slipped them into a paper bag beside his chair.

"Are you a teacher too?" she asked. Immediately she regretted the "too." Now he knew she had been snoopy and read the envelope.

"Uh-hunh. I teach out at Delta. And you're an artist."

It was a statement, not a question. She nodded confirmation. A moment later she gaped in astonishment when he pulled a copy of *An Illustrated History of New Orleans* from the bag at his feet.

"You *bought* a copy!" she blurted, staring at her silver-point cover illustration of the old Napoleon House.

He smiled at the undisguised delight in her face. "Had to, it's too big to steal! I stopped by your friend's shop this morning to look for some albums. I was admiring this when your friend—Maddy?—told me my very own neighbor had done the cover."

"But it's so expensive," protested Corinne. She glanced guiltily at the $39.95 price tag.

Jernigan shrugged. "Quality costs. Maddy told me about the award you won for this cover."

Corinne glanced away.

"Knowing Maddy, I imagine she told you plenty." Steve grinned. "She's not too shy, is she?"

They locked glances. Abruptly, they both laughed again.

"Anyway," said Steve, sliding the book and a pen across the table, "I definitely want an autograph. Right here—right next to your credit line."

"So," he added while she signed her name, "I'd guess, from that charming accent of yours, that you're a homegrown Looziana lass, not an import like me?"

She smiled. "I'm from Shaylor. It's about twenty miles north of Baton Rouge. Two gas stations, four bars, and a motel that features porn cable. The kind of place that looks great in a rearview mirror."

He was about to ask another question when a horn tooted nearby and a woman called out, "Professor Jernigan!"

They both glanced toward Decatur. A sleek bronze Jaguar XJ6 nosed into the curb and parked. The chrome was polished so smooth it sent off dazzling heliographs when the sun caught it. A bumper sticker proclaimed: WHEN THE GOING GETS TOUGH,

THE TOUGH GO SHOPPING.

"Oh, Christ, *no,*" muttered Steve as the driver hurried toward them.

She was dressed to the nines, in a sable cape, a high-slit skirt, and silver shoes with string-strap heels.

"Professor Jernigan, I just wondered—did you ever receive my note regarding a possible change of grade?"

Corinne winced. The woman's exaggerated Southern drawl grated against a raw nerve.

"I got it," Jernigan said.

The young woman, Colleen Pritchard, bestowed a smile on her former instructor.

"I know that, because of grandmother's horrible brain embolism, my performance on the exams was disappointing, but—"

"Guilding the lily a bit, aren't we?" he interrupted. "I'd call three F's and a D-minus a disaster, not a disappointment."

Now her smile was strained but held its own. "I turned in an excellent paper," she pursued doggedly.

"You *turned in* an excellent paper," he agreed. "It's too bad you didn't also write it."

"You can't prove that!" Her voice was snippy.

"No. But I can prove that your mail-order paper was nowhere near the assigned topic. And that you hadn't read even one of the works cited in your footnotes. That's good enough for the Honors Board."

The smile reappeared as she decided to change her tack.

"Perhaps I could give you my address and you could . . . stop by soon so we could discuss it?"

"Don't flatter yourself," he said quietly. "Anyway,

last semester is a *fait accompli*. I never change a grade unless a student can prove a mathematical error in my final computation."

Now she shot a poisonous glance at Corinne. "I see. Well, perhaps you'll change your mind after my daddy's law firm contacts the Dean?"

Corinne watched coals suddenly smolder behind those cool gray-green eyes.

"And perhaps," he suggested in a deceptively gentle voice, "you and your 'daddy' can both go piss up a rope?"

Red leaped into Colleen Pritchard's cheeks. Without another word she whirled around and flounced away in high dudgeon.

Steve glanced at Corinne. "Look," he began in an embarrassed tone, "I'm sorry, I—"

"Don't be," she said, cutting him off. "I loved it. I spent four years at Tulane watching a few arrogant bitches like her buy a college degree. Except I didn't know they blushed."

She grinned and added, "But you *do* know you overreacted, don't you? All she wanted you to do was . . . stop by."

Once again they found themselves sharing a laugh with the unself-conscious ease of long acquaintances.

"You know," he said abruptly, "you're awfully nice company. Why don't we have dinner together tonight? I know a little place on the Esplanade that serves up a decent shrimp remoulade. Or would you prefer a po-'boy up at Riverbend?"

She hung fire for a moment, alerted by a little inner stir of defensive apprehension. The feeling had nothing to do with not liking him—in fact, just the opposite.

"Hey," he added quickly, misinterpreting her hesitation. "I'm sorry for being so pushy, okay? As if a pretty girl like you wouldn't be booked up on a Saturday night. It's just that I never . . . that is, I've never noticed you with a guy," he finished weakly, adding sheepishly, "Open mouth, insert foot."

She watched him for a long time, her face revealing nothing.

"Shall I stop by your place," she finally asked with mock formality, "or will you be sending your carriage by for me?"

God was once wise, thought the Emperor, but man has made Him mentally ill.

He watched the young couple on the patio of Cafe du Monde. Watched them laughing together, watched them sneaking glances at one another with the flirtatious curiosity of the young. Water brawled noisily as it splashed down the cement tiers of the fountain behind which he was hiding. Inside, rage burned like a hot knife twisting into his guts.

And because God is mentally ill, he thought, His children could now be created in His perfect image, yet be sick and deformed beneath the surface.

The invisible worm that flies in the night in the howling storm . . .

Sick like *her* . . .

He caught the flash of Corinne's strong white teeth, saw her eyes seem to throw off sparks at something the man said to her.

Yes, he admitted, she was a beauty, and he had

always been sensitive to powerful physical beauty such as hers. But it was her even more powerful insight he most envied — the quiet, confident, emotional insight that differentiated her work from mere talent.

Just like the others.

Just like that singer.

Just like the puppeteer he had fascinated with last night's *jetta*.

God had been kind to them — healthy, fecund young beauties with talents envied by millions.

Again the rage of intense jealousy boiled inside him, forcing him to clench his jaw so tightly the muscles bunched like goiters.

Why should *they* be allowed to enjoy what others had not?

He stayed in the shadow of the fountain to attract as little attention as possible. His face was painted white as chalk, and a fresh gardenia adorned his lapel. In the dim light it was difficult to notice the shaggy, unbroken line of his eyebrows or the fact that one eye was a brilliant blue, the other a deep brown.

So far, he told himself, this one was different from the others. She was more private, more self-sufficient, less dependent on public praise. All of which of course made the *jetta* more difficult. It was most challenging to peel back the defensive layers of her psyche. He sensed a strong carapace of mistrust and strength, but also of fear and insecurity.

Unlike the others, she had never, since he began his attempt at fascination, appeared with a man — until now. She had been aloof, distant around them. And perhaps that was a clue to her greater resistance?

She seemed particularly difficult to influence this

86

morning. And now he realized why. It was the table and chair.

Tuccari ferru, he thought with frustration.

Touch iron . . .

But the thought drifted crazily on the storm-tossed sea of his mind, whirling, swirling, eddying into the violent maelstrom beyond the firm shores of sanity.

The rage rose within him again, an acidic geyser erupting up his esophagus.

With an intense clarity that wrenched a sob from him, he again suffered the hell-spawned kaleidoscope of images—the masked, drunken revelers; the brilliant floats like papier-mâché dragons; hands groping for the cheap trinkets tossed to the spectators.

The screams . . .

The shouted warnings . . .

His hands reaching out, but too late . . .

Now all was confusion, shouts, the shrill, mad whickering of the wild-eyed horses. . . .

And the blood.

Oh, yes . . . everywhere, the obscene scarlet blood. Never would he forget the blood. . . .

"No!"

He staggered against the fountain as another sob hitched in his chest. For a moment tears filmed his eyes, and the day seemed to melt and blur like an image through a wet windowpane.

He whispered the words with a caressing softness: "I am you, and you are me. There is no I, but only we."

Then—again—the rage. Molten lava burning inside, purifying him for what lay ahead.

For years he had patiently sought to hone his limited powers of *malocchio*.

Now he was a full-fledged master . . . a fascinator. And the power increased almost daily. The first time, he had induced only eventual death. But last night? Ahh, last night he had succeeded in mental domination. He had willed the dying woman to speak.

Again he gazed at the couple happily losing themselves in each other.

They too would eventually succumb to his *jetta*.

He thought of the carnival countdown calendar at the Ragin' Cajun, and his alabaster face creased in a blissful smile. Many must suffer for God's mental deviance, for the Divine Perversion their behavior had caused.

. . . *and his dark secret love does thy life destroy!*

Chapter 11

Madora Hill glanced up when the bell over the door gave out its musical little tinkle.

"Hey, babe! With you in a jiff."

While Maddy finished ringing up a purchase, Corinne wandered over to a display of bright satin Mardi Gras masks. Early afternoon sunlight slanted through the narrow louvers flanking the front window and laid delicate gold pin stripes across the display rack.

One of the masks, the smiling face of Greek comedy, stared back at her, bright spangles glittering in the sunlight. For a long moment Corinne fixated on the vacant, almond-shaped eyeholes.

Behind her, Maddy said something and a customer laughed.

What was the word that old lady shouted earlier? the mask seemed to challenge her. *The one that made you think of a Volkswagen?*

Abruptly, Corinne crossed to the bilingual dictionaries beside the postcard rack. French-English, Spanish-English, German-English . . . there it was: Italian-English.

But what was the word that tourist had shouted at the Emperor? She thought it had started with a J or maybe a *ch* sound. Hesitantly, Corinne picked up the dictionary and thumbed through the J's. But it was no use, nothing jogged her memory—

A hand fell on her shoulder and Corinne started, dropping the book.

"Good Lord, girl!" Maddy exclaimed. "Did I catch you shoplifting or what?"

Corinne grimaced sheepishly and stooped to retrieve the dictionary.

"Guess what?" Maddy added mysteriously. Her green eyes were pregnant with some secret.

"Let me see." Corinne's brow furrowed in mock concentration. "It's starting to form a gestalt now . . . yes . . . I know! You sold a copy of the *Illustrated History* earlier today?"

"F'sure I did! How did *you* know that?"

"Because I'll be having din-din tonight with the customer who bought it."

Maddy beamed like a game-show contestant who had wisely chosen the prize behind the curtain. "I knew you couldn't pass that hunk up! You're the only reason I haven't eaten him alive by now!"

"My God," snapped Corinne. Her tone was harsher than she meant it to be. "Is sex *all* men are to you?"

Maddy stood with arms akimbo, staring at her. *"Ooo*—I see the bitch lamps are lit today."

Corinne relented with a frown of annoyance at herself. Maddy's harmless remark hadn't rated such a peppery outburst. "Sorry."

Maddy patted her shoulder. The movement set the half-dozen bangles on her wrist clicking like the beads of an abacus. "Lovey, take it from your old Aunt Madora. You've been pushing yourself too hard. You're gonna burn out before thirty if you don't loosen up."

"I spoze."

Corinne dug a kleenex out of her purse and handed it to her friend. "Here. You've got lipstick on your teeth."

Absently, Maddy dabbed at the smear. She squinted slightly as she studied her friend. "You okay, hon? For a gal who's going out with Mr. Macrocharm, you sure look down in the dumps."

Again the irritation flared up, the abrupt mood shift surprising Corinne. "When you aren't man-starved," she replied testily, "a date isn't the solution to all your problems."

Instead of angering her, this second verbal thrust only caused Maddy to scrutinize her closer. "Maybe I am 'man-starved,' " she finally conceded. "Damn few of 'em are worth a shit. But babe, you know good and well I'm ninety-percent mouth. Besides, maybe you're man-*shy*. I worry about you, that's all."

This time Corinne remained silent, admitting to herself that Maddy was right. She *did* have a basic mistrust of men, at least when it came to getting close to them. Though Corinne was sometimes intrigued by them, occasionally attracted physically, she also felt an instinctive fear of them.

It hadn't helped matters when the one who *had* seemed right for her, for whom she had felt more than a fleeting physical compatibility, had turned out to be a "bachelor" with a wife and family stashed away back in L.A. He was a visiting art professor she had

91

met during her last year as an undergrad. From that romantic disaster, she had emerged wearing an emotional suit of armor to keep men at bay.

Corinne's tone was contrite. "I'm really sorry, Maddy. I guess I'm just . . ."

She gestured helplessly, unable to finish the sentence.

"There's *nothing* wrong with you that lightening up a little won't help. See, that's where the opposite sex can be handy."

The bell tinkled as a customer wandered in. Maddy lowered her voice a couple octaves, adding, "True, most of a man's brains are between his legs. But what's wrong with *useful* knowledge?"

Corinne rolled her eyes in surrender. "You should put that one on a T-shirt."

"Check the rack by the door. It's right next to the one with the caterpillar trying to screw the French fry."

This time they both laughed so hard the customer glanced over and flashed a curious grin.

"Well," said Corinne, "miles to go and promises to keep. See you later?"

"F'sure. Toodle-oo, babe. You just relax and pass a good time tonight, hear?"

"I hear," promised Corinne. And for the first time in weeks, she even believed.

"Feel like music, brah?"

Steve Jernigan shook his head, not bothering to look up from the map spread out on his knees.

"I guess that's it for this sector," he decided reluctantly. "Might as well hang it up for today."

Tree nodded and turned the rudder. The trawling motor coughed as they began to reverse course on the brackish surface of the bayou. A curious raccoon watched them from a half-submerged log on the near bank. Along the far side, a wall of live oaks dipped green-velvet banners of Spanish moss into the water. It was only mid-afternoon, but the thick canopy of oak and tupelo and sweet gum brought a gloomy false dusk to Honey Island Swamp.

Tree aimed a discreet glance at his employer. All day Steve had been quieter than usual, brooding over his map.

"Knockin' off kinda early today, ain't we, cap?"

Steve nodded. "I've got a date this evening."

Tree flashed his quick, gap-toothed grin. "O-yay, o-yay!"

Steve grinned back, but only halfheartedly. Two hours of aquatic prowling, and the only sign of human life had been a lone fisherman in a johnboat.

Secretly, he was beginning to wonder if he had spent thousands of dollars, traveled thousands of miles, and placed his career on hold, just to come a cropper in this godforsaken swamp. Maybe it was time to give this search up as a bad job and get on with his life.

Tree, sensing that his boss's dejected mood was worsening with the preternatural silence of the swamp, said something about an upcoming Neville Brothers concert at the Lake Front Arena.

But Steve wasn't listening. A section of the far bank had caught his attention.

He took the rudder from Tree and steered them

93

across the nearly dead surface of the water. They nosed in closer to the dense green curtain of Spanish moss.

Nearly hidden by an overhanging deadfall of branches, an inlet yawned open like the mouth of a long-obscure cave.

"That's definitely not marked on my map," said Steve. "Can we get back there, you think?"

Tree killed the outboard and a heavy trap of silence settled over the swamp. Both men hefted an oar and swiped at the worst of the dead foliage. Then they used overhead branches like tug ropes, pulling the dinghy further into the waterway. Branches raked at their faces, and once the boat grounded on a mud flat. But ten minutes of sweating exertion and they emerged into a relatively clear expanse of water. Tree tugged the little outboard to life again.

The uncharted waterway proved to be a sluggish brown crinkum-crankum winding its way past trees marching on exposed, stilt-like roots. As they advanced, frogs and cooters—huge homegrown turtles—cleared a swath before them. At one point a grunting alligator scuttled up onto the bank and disappeared into the saw grass, grinning sinisterly.

Later, when they had reason to discuss it, both men would agree that they spotted the shack at the same time.

It loomed up quick as a darting bird just when they came around a bend, a tatty split-slab structure squatting on a hummock about twenty feet back from the water. Though it currently sat high and dry, a thin watermark surrounded it like an indelible bathtub ring about a foot above its foundation.

"Kill the engine," said Steve.

Tree cut back the throttle and they drifted toward the rounded bank, bumping it gently. Steve grabbed a steel auto rim tied to a rope and dropped it overboard to anchor the dinghy. Then he stepped ashore and dragged the boat up a few feet behind him. Hesitating every few yards, he moved closer.

"Anybody here?" he called out.

His voice was quickly absorbed in the surrounding growth. He waited a few moments and called out again. Still no response from inside. The silence seemed to press in on them with vengeful weight.

He glanced around. A tin-pipe chimney poked through the roof. No smoke trailed out of it, but a pile of logs had been chopped into stove-lengths and stacked against one side of the shack.

"Somebody's staying here," he remarked to Tree.

"Could just be a hunter's shack."

Tree stepped out and stood near the dinghy, dubiously eyeing the building.

"Maybe." Steve shouted again. But all was deathly still and quiet except for the susurrant breath of the wind in the trees.

He moved to the door, his soles making sunction-cup sounds on the spongy ground. Steve pounded on the weathered gray wood with the side of his fist.

"Anybody in there?"

His question was answered by a silence so thick it was almost palpable. He tried the rusted knob. It turned an inch or so each way, but the door refused to budge. There was no keyhole anywhere in sight.

Bolted from the inside? he wondered.

He knocked again. Waited. Still there was no response from inside.

He bent forward and squinted, trying to see between the chinks of the fat hinges. Steve made out nothing but fathomless darkness inside.

But for a moment he thought he felt excited currents of air tickling his face. He was surprised when the back of his neck tingled, as if some instinct more primitive than thought was warning him of danger.

He circled the shack. There was only one window, in the back, and it had been nailed over with a rust-pitted metal sign advertising Jax Beer. He tried to pry one corner back but it wouldn't budge. Steve considered forcing it with a stick but decided against this. A breaking-and-entering charge was hardly likely to further his cause.

Today, he thought bitterly as he returned to the boat, had turned up the same thing as every other day he'd spent on Honey Island: a big fat goose egg.

"To hell with it," he said to Tree. "Maybe we'll come back down here sometime and waste another day."

Tree had left the boat to squat over something by the water. When Steve drew nearer, he saw the young black poking into the soft ground with a stick.

Steve glanced down. A jagged shard of charred pottery protruded from the dirt.

"What is it?"

Tree continued staring for another ten seconds. Finally he glanced up at his friend. "Prolly nothing," he answered.

Steve watched him gaze absently toward the shack. Unaware that he was doing it, Tree lifted his right hand up to the wooden gris-gris suspended around his neck. He touched it lightly with three fingertips.

"Prolly nothing," he repeated as if he'd forgotten he had already spoken once. "You ready?"

Steve shot him a puzzled glance. He turned and cast one last, lingering look toward the dilapidated gray shack. It hunkered atop its swollen hummock, almost seeming to stare back at the two interlopers.

A delicate feather of fear tickled the bumps of his spine.

No maybe about it, he abruptly resolved. We *will* be back.

"Yeah, I'm ready," he replied. "Let's hit it."

Chapter 12

The sun was only a ruddy afterthought on the western horizon by the time Alan Breaux joined the traffic logjam on the Greater New Orleans Bridge.

Years of commuting to the city from his suburban home on the West Bank had taught him patience. Now, as he crawled at a snail's pace behind a growling city bus, he gazed idly out over the long looping crescent of the Mississippi. Opposite the jutting promontory of the Algiers peninsula, the French Quarter huddled against the water like an 18th Century stage set. Out on the channel a fifty-ton Chris-Craft churned up a foaming wake.

He daydreamed and smoked, stretched and sighed while pondering the relationship between coincidence and death. Life went on all around him, heedless of the fact that another beautiful young woman had recently — and inexplicably — been snatched from its ranks.

The bus finally picked up speed, huffing great black clouds of diesel smoke. A minute later Breaux followed it off the bridge and turned right on Magazine. He headed toward the Quarter.

He parked in the public lot on Decatur and hoofed it toward Jackson Square. As he wove his way through the human ebb and flow of tourists, his mind stirred back to life like a snake emerging from a cold sleep.

Now he concentrated on the death of Jeanette Manders.

He had read the routine report filed this morning at precinct headquarters, as well as the newspaper accounts. But he had also managed to talk with the prowl-car cop who'd been on the scene last night. Not surprisingly, the uniformed officer had supplied a few details which hadn't made it into the final report or the media versions.

Neither was Breaux surprised at the "sanitized" reports. The French Quarter Merchants League sometimes managed, in the name of tourism and positive cash flow, to keep the lid on certain unflattering angles of a negative news item. And the media usually cooperated by becoming a little myopic around carnival time.

Breaux understood this, even accepted it. Money was the great flywheel of society, and for New Orleans, the slightest drop in tourism meant a sputter in the great engine of civic progress.

Still, if he was careful, he might tinker a bit with the works.

At the intersection of Chartres and St. Peter he spotted the man he was looking for—at least he hoped it was the same man—the Lucky Dog vendor who had been present at Jeanette Manders's death, and who the uniformed cop claimed to have overheard talking to a reporter.

The vendor was leaning on his forearms against the giant red-and-yellow tin hot dog from which he dispensed his wares. A cigarette hung down from one corner of his mouth. A dirty white paper hat slanted over his forehead like a barracks cap.

"Lucky Dogs!" he brayed listlessly. "Getcher red-hot Lucky Dogs *he*-ah!"

He was around forty, with a thin, vulpine face and an Adam's apple that looked like a bony knee. His cigarette bobbed with each word, dropping ashes into the steam table.

Breaux moved closer and nodded at him, raising one finger. While the vendor speared a pink-bloated frank with his tongs, Breaux said conversationally, "How's business tonight?"

The vendor shot him a sidelong, street-wise glance. When he spoke, he revealed teeth like two rows of crooked yellow gravestones.

"You the heat?" he demanded suspiciously.

Breaux was caught off guard. As a Bunko Division officer assigned to the CBD beyond Canal Street, he had no jurisdiction in the Quarter. The last thing he wanted was for the precinct captain to hear that some unauthorized cop was stirring up a potential PR flap.

"Do I *look* like a cop?"

"No, but they usually don't anymore. And the last time I got busted for . . . whatever, the cop started out by buying a red-hot and asking me how business was. Now I'm a little touchy. Know what I mean, Vern?"

Breaux grinned. "That's pretty good. My wife, she loves that guy's commercials."

The vendor grunted and laid a bright red racing

stripe of ketchup down the middle of the frank.

"Listen," said Breaux. "I swear I'm not here on police business. But I'd like to ask you some questions about what happened last night. The Jeanette Manders thing. Were you around?"

The vendor glanced at him shrewdly. Absently, he picked something from his face and rolled it between thumb and forefinger.

"If I was, and assuming you ain't the heat . . . what's the percentage for me?"

Breaux reached for the alligator billfold in his back pocket. He slipped a ten-dollar bill out and handed it to the vendor. He added a couple of dollars for the hot dog.

The other man eyed the ten happily, then lifted his grungy apron out of the way and slipped the bill into his hip pocket.

"All right," said Breaux. "Let's have it."

The vendor explained that he had caught only the last fifteen minutes or so of Jeanette Manders's act, having wheeled his tin Lucky Dog into Jackson Square around 8:30 P.M. Most of his account dovetailed with the official report Breaux had read this morning—with the exception of the final, grotesque message the girl had supposedly uttered before she dropped dead.

"You're *sure* that's what she said?"

"If I'm jokin', I'm chokin'! She said, 'Dream about this forever, kids.' Think a guy'd forget a thing as spooky as that?"

Breaux agreed it was unlikely. "Think carefully," he urged. "Did you see any blood?"

The vendor shook his head adamantly. "None."

"How did she look? I mean did her face screw up with pain? Did she cry, clutch at any part of her body?"

The vendor thought about it a minute. "She looked . . . surprised, I guess you'd say. Like maybe somebody just punched her in the gulliver and knocked the wind out of her."

"You say," continued Breaux, "that you told the reporters about those words she said. Why do you think they left that part out?"

"Why should a bunch of reporters listen to me?" he asked derisively. "I'm just a coonass weeniemonger."

"Didn't anyone else tell them?"

"Why, hell yeah, cap! And at least one of the newspaper types wrote it all down. Then they just took a few pictures of the EMT's loading her into the meat wagon."

Breaux nodded. He had finally reached the question he'd been pondering all day. "Besides the Manders girl, were there any other street performers hanging around nearby?"

The vendor mulled it over. "Naw, I don't think so."

"You're sure? Think about it."

"If I'm lyin', I'm dyin'! Hell, you think I pay attention to every two-bit juggler and musician around here? Don't never buy anything from me, anyway, cheap bastids. They all eat at that arty-farty yogurt shop on Royal."

"Think," repeated Breaux patiently, like a pediatrician coaxing a recalcitrant child to swallow a pill. "How about, say, that old mime who usually hangs around here — the one who always wears the flower in his lapel?"

"What, the Emperor? I don't think. . . ."

He hesitated, puckering his eyes in concentration.

"Shit-fire, maybe he was. *Seems* like he was, but you see that old kook everywhere. It's like asking me if I remember seeing a tourist carrying a cup from Pat O'Brien's."

"The usual yellow flower in his lapel?"

"Yeah. Wait—no! White, I think."

He glanced at Breaux suspiciously, realizing he had just been tested. "You *sure* you ain't the heat?"

"Friend of the family," Breaux replied evasively. "Listen—thanks for your help."

The detective was about ten feet away before the vendor shouted behind him: "Cap!"

Breaux spun around. The vendor raised the Lucky Dog he had just assembled. A fat dollop of ketchup leaked free and splattered the cobblestones. "You forgotcher red-hot!"

"Have one on me . . . I'm a vegetarian."

The vendor bared his crooked tombstone teeth. "Sounds like a wiener. Know what I mean, Vern?"

Breaux retrieved his Toyota and began driving aimlessly.

He didn't spend much time consciously thinking about what the vendor had just told him, or about anything else for that matter. Instead, he just drove and watched the city go about its nocturnal business. He had long ago achieved a working compromise with his intellect. He gave it plenty of free rein. In return, it sometimes gave him valuable insights, usually when he least expected them.

103

He was cruising Esplanade Avenue when he saw Steve Jernigan emerge from the Creole Kitchen. Jernigan said something to the girl with him, and she smiled.

The lass was sure some looker, Breaux told himself.

For a moment he tried to remember where he had seen her. He had an uncomfortable conviction that he knew her from the Quarter—currently the home of that endangered species known as talented, beautiful, young women.

At Rampart Street he was forced to detour. A city crew was working overtime under portable floodlights to erect a barricade, readying the street for the first of many parades that would roll daily between now and Fat Tuesday. Tomorrow the Krewe of Isis would kick things off.

It wasn't just media hype, Breaux thought with a little glow of pride in his hometown. Mardi Gras in New Orleans really *was* the world's biggest free party. In spite of the omnipresent profit motive, in spite of the millions of frenzied visitors, it was a hometown gig from the ground up.

It was the natives who would go the craziest, in a Bacchanalian ritual that evoked the ghost of ancient pagan orgies. And it would all culminate in the tumultuous madness of Fat Tuesday, when even the cops would close their eyes to everything short of murder. The city would collectively thumb its nose at "propriety" as mild-mannered men screamed, "Show your tits!" and perfectly respectable women obligingly lifted their blouses.

And the parades. Over the decades, following them had been raised to an art form. There were dozens to watch, and they would stretch over the next two weeks. Spectators would set up ladders so their kids could sit topside and compete for the perenially popular "throws"—the beads and doubloons and gaudy plastic cups that the masked krewe members (maintaining their sacred vows of secrecy) tossed from their floats. And later, after the frenzy of the parades, drunken licentiousness would hang in the air like a salty fog.

Christ, thought Breaux as he waited for the light at Canal Street to change. He'd lived here all his life, the only Mardi Gras he'd missed being during the stint he knocked off in Korea when he was eighteen. It was the same every year, but he never grew tired of it.

So why did he have this feeling, nagging him like the throb of an abscessed tooth, that something *was* going to be different this year—terribly, horribly different?

The Emperor watched as night settled over the city like a dark camlet cloak. His disappointment was acid bitter when the girl failed to show. But the crowd spread fanwise at the foot of the cathedral steps saw nothing mar the steady, enigmatic gaze of the talented old mime.

Spectators came and went, some chucking money into his hat. A few—mostly children or drunks—asked him questions, one or two of the more impertinent even reached out for a brief touch. Nothing fazed him. His stark white face remained impassive, his odd two-tone gaze remained focused on some distant point behind the crowd.

"Hey, gabby!" shouted a florid-faced tourist with a hurricane punch in each hand. "By now you must hafta pee worse 'n *I* do!"

Laughter rippled through the crowd. Somebody shouted, "Tickle him!" Now and then a camera flashed, leaving anemic afterimages to fade like wraiths. For each person who finally became bored and drifted on, another soon took his place.

The Emperor tuned all of them out, riveting his malevolent gaze, the full strength of his formidable will, on the third-floor balcony of the familiar rose stucco building.

Soon, he promised the girl.

Soon, he promised the gawking crowd.

Soon, he promised this city spawned by God's unholy madness.

Chapter 13

Corinne sat with her feet tucked up under her in the pleated armchair, leafing through a volume titled *Concepts of the Great Masters*.

The book, presented by the Faculty of Art upon her graduation with honors, included conceptual sketches by virtuosos ranging from da Vinci to Picasso. Three nights a week she studied them faithfully, memorizing balance and linear clarity and tonal values the way a lit major memorizes quotes.

Corinne wore her long knit sleep shirt and white fur slippers. Behind her, beyond the shoji screen dividing the efficiency, the French doors stood open against a Prussian blue sky. It was an unusually warm evening, and the pedestrian traffic on Decatur had gradually migrated toward the more boisterous sections of the Quarter. The only sound Corinne heard was the faint background medley of live jazz and Dixieland—and the rustling whisper of turning pages.

Somewhere in the old building a board groaned, and she glanced up from the page she was studying.

Her eyes fell on the gold-framed photo of her parents.

They seemed to be staring at her, their eyes malevolent with hatred.

She shifted her glance to the nearby settee. For a moment she had the ridiculous impression that it was inching closer to her, stalking her across the living room like a stealthy predator.

A rush of nausea fluttered in her stomach. She poised on the edge of the chair, ready to rush into the bathroom. But in a few moments the sensation passed.

That tears it, she decided.

Tomorrow she would go to her class early and make an appointment at Student Health. This bug or whatever the hell it was had persisted too damn long now.

She closed her book and laid it on the walnut table on which she sketched. Then she rounded the screen and crossed to a triple-mirror vanity beside the bed.

Corinne studied her reflection carefully, looking for signs of illness.

"There's *nothing* wrong," she told the pretty girl in the mirror fiercely.

No, of course not. Just a chronic feeling that her energy was being sucked through a straw; just a perpetual nausea and restlessness and loss of appetite; and now, worst of all, a growing sense of insecurity about her work—the one aspect of life where confidence had never been a problem. Lately, she had been forced to make several false starts before she could complete even the simplest preliminary sketches.

Yes . . . everything was just peachy.

She thought about last night and her dinner with Steve. She had practically resorted to force-feeding, then hurriedly excused herself and rushed off to the toilet to vomit. My God, he must think she was some kind of space cadet!

Corinne studied her eyes closely. Tiny flecks of gold accented the soft copper of her irises. If the eyes were truly the mirrors of the soul, she thought, then she must have an awfully vulnerable soul.

She recalled something she'd read in a folklore class about a remote tribe in India. They believed in something they called the *ahmaw,* a "vampire soul" who enters through the eyes of happy people and makes them ill.

For a moment her skin was nubby with goose-bumps.

(that word . . . starts with a J and made you think of a Volkswagen)

"Girl," she admonished the reflection in the mirror, "I'm beginning to wonder if you're stashing some toys in the attic."

She shook off her mood and turned toward the French doors leading to the balcony.

Alternately, Steve clenched each fist so tightly that the knuckles turned scarlet and white. Then he opened his hand and spread the fingers fanwise. Below his balcony, Decatur made its nightly changing of the guard as merchant marines and longshoremen gradually replaced the tourists deserting the seedy waterfront bars for the safety of Pat O'Brien's and Maison Bourbon.

He and Tree had started for Honey Island Swamp well before mid-morning. But the rapid onsweep of ominous black thunderheads had sent them retreating

109

to the safety of Lake Pontchartrain's south shore. Now all that remained of the all-day rainstorm were huge, mirror-finish amoebas of water on the streets and sidewalks below. Rain still gurgled in drainspouts and left a glaze finish over the bricks and dull-green wrought-iron lampposts.

Steve gradually succumbed to the numbing repetition of the exercise until the clutter and confusion of his mind quieted to a harmless mental hum. Now the cursor of memory spelled out the words as clearly as if he held his father's leatherette diary in front of him:

In this, as in all things momentous, I now have reason to believe a woman is involved—if not behind it all. Information, unfortunately, is extremely hard-won down here. Not only am I an outsider, but one who is asking questions about things the locals don't even discuss among themselves. Still, I believe I've narrowed one player in our quest down to a woman who goes by no name (I suspect she had a name, though, but I'll not record it until I have more reliable evidence). Maddeningly, I have learned nothing definite about her location except that she lives somewhere in Honey Island Swamp. Years of lab research have left me too sedentary—won't be able to search without the assistance of a local. Still, I won't mind the hardships. I only pray to Our Lord that she is not the same woman my instincts hint at. If so, an unnatural ability is being augmented by an unnatural hatred.

From his apartment behind him, a throbbing Cab Calloway tune escaped into the night, migrating toward its musical clan melding in the air three blocks away over the midway madness of Bourbon Street.

110

But even the music was below his threshold of awareness now. He was not surprised when the mental cursor spelled out the thought in letters as stark as klieg lights:

The fixed stare always accompanies hostile behavior.

The Emperor.

The Emperor was watching Corinne. Not now, not tonight, but lately, off and on, day and night, dogging her like a persistent shadow.

Why?

Corinne. Steve was intrigued by his neighbor — why wouldn't the old man be as well? Besides, was he really dogging her, or just watching when she happened to be around? Christ, the old dude was spotted all over the Quarter. For that matter, so was Corinne.

Steve was intrigued, yes. But something bothered him about her. It was as if she was constantly distracted. If some sixth sense didn't convince him otherwise, he'd think she was high all the time lately. Or . . . going slightly mental?

His thoughts scattered like chaff winnowed in the wind.

His fists stopped clenching.

He stood perfectly still, his arms still extended before him like a sleepwalker in a campy horror flick.

A silence so thick it was almost palpable. He tried the rusted doorknob. It turned an inch or so either way, but the door refused to budge. For a moment he felt excited currents of air tickling his face. . . .

"Somebody *was* inside!" he now said out loud, surprising himself with his own outburst.

"Inside where?" said a puzzled female voice from

the balcony beside his.

Jernigan started, then glanced quickly sideways.

Corinne's laughter was musical and light in the quiet night air.

"Looks like it's my turn to apologize. I guess we like to sneak up on each other."

He grinned and doffed an imaginary hat. "That could be bad for our health. We've got to stop meeting like this."

The peach penumbra of the streetlights limmed both of them in its glow. For a long moment they were silent, as if mutually realizing the intimacy of their appearance—he, stripped to the waist, taut muscles cording his chest and shoulders, she, the long knit shirt outlining the deep-sweeping curve of her hips, clinging to her breasts where the nipples protruded under the fabric.

She said, "But seriously, folks . . . sorry for interrupting your meditation. I don't usually come out here this late."

"Believe me, you did me a favor. What brings you out?"

"I've been sitting on my duff all day," she confessed. "Although I did get a lot done for my class tomorrow."

"Wish I could say the same. I blew the whole day off listening to music."

He didn't add: *And thinking about my pretty neighbor.*

"I've seen you doing those exercises before," she volunteered. "I like watching you. It looks so relaxing."

"Used to be. Now it's just another addiction."

"That's funny. You don't impress me as the type who gets addicted easily."

"Oh? How *do* I impress you?"

"Favorably," she replied cryptically.

"Guess that's better than a poke in the eye."

"Much better," she agreed with a smile.

"I want to ask you something," he said, his bantering tone gone now. "Last night—you didn't agree to go out with me again *just* to be neighborly, did you?"

For a moment she was nonplussed. She busied herself fussing with a pot of jonquils that didn't need attention. Then she replied carefully.

"Doesn't it occur to you that I might like your company?"

"Sure it does. And I realize you hardly know me. I guess what I'm saying is, I already know I don't want to be just another one of those 'nice guys' pretty girls always manage to collect as pals."

His meaning was clear enough. "So far," she said after a short silence, a fluid smile on her lips, "there's no danger of *that*."

She added a hasty goodnight and disappeared inside her apartment.

A wan quarter moon the color of fresh Swiss cheese rode high over the city.

The Emperor finished his coffee and left Cafe du Monde, angling across Decatur toward Jackson Square and the St. Louis Cathedral. It was nearing ten P.M. and traffic was light. He could hear the river rhythmically licking at the levee. The storm earlier had not cleared the humidity from the air. Now the

113

gardenia in his lapel hung as limp as wet laundry on a windless day.

He cast a long glance toward *her* balcony as he neared the three-story stucco.

All was still now. Nothing visible but her gay profusion of plants. He had spotted her earlier, but the presence of her neighbor had dissuaded the mime from hanging around in the blue-black apron of shadows across the street.

He glanced with distaste at the black licorice twists of the wrought-iron balcony.

Tuccari ferru.

Touch iron.

It was difficult to influence her when she stood out there.

He reached the public restrooms between Cafe du Monde and the Jax Brewery. The Emperor was about to dart across the damp cobblestones when a sound stopped him in his tracks.

He listened intently, his head cocked like a wary bird's.

The sound came from within the slanted-open restroom door marked with the pictograph of a woman — the steady, unmistakable tinkle of someone urinating.

His lips parted in disgust.

The rage flared up before he could contain it, an infrared rage that blurred his vision until the street turned into an old tintype photo. The better, lessravaged part of his mind cried out to him, pleading with him to hurry away. But that voice was now as remote as a childhood promise.

The degenerate Babylonian whore! Was she so inured to her pathetic humanity that she took no pains to disguise her bodily functions? God was once good and wise and pure, he reminded himself. But men had driven Him mad, defiled Him. Now madness and filth ruled. . . .

He cautioned himself. No, not here, not right now. He could not jeopardize his plans.

(our plans . . . for I am you, and you are me. There is no I, but only we)

But a moment later the woman emerged, and he felt his resolve weaken like a fist unclenching.

She was beautiful, well-heeled, the model of yuppie success. An attractive, bright-eyed creature with soft, feathercut hair the color of ginger. The infant girl in the stroller was a delicate porcelain replica of the mother.

The woman started in fright. Then she relaxed when she spotted the man's white makeup.

"Look, Allegra! See the mime?"

The little girl watched the funny man with a mixture of awe, delight, and fearful mistrust.

"What a lovely, *lovely* little baby!" the Emperor exclaimed, bending forward. "Hello there, sweet love!"

The mother beamed with fond pride. The Emperor brought his face even closer. *"So* lovely," he said softly. "A happy, lovely child!"

"Who is that, Allie?" said the woman, speaking in a clipped East Coast accent. "Who is that nice man, hmm? Is that a mime? See . . . a mime, honey. You made him talk!"

"You are a beautiful little girl," the Emperor cooed.

In her maternal pride, the woman downplayed the odd fact that his stare, his tone of voice, actually seemed to convey a different impression than his words. He abruptly straightened, bid her a good stay in New Orleans, and disappeared into the shadows.

"C'mon, sugar. Let's go meet Daddy."

The little rubber tires of the stroller thrummed steadily against the sidewalk. After a half block or so, something struck the woman as odd — Allegra seemed strangely still.

The little blonde-curled head slumped to one side, and her mother smiled.

Asleep . . .

She bent down to adjust her daughter in the seat. For a moment the overhead mercury-vapor lamp caught the tiny white face in a stark shaft of light.

"No," breathed the woman, her voice wooden with sudden shock. "Oh no, no, no, *no!*"

Her scream shattered the night, an hysterical siren repeating itself over and over until finally it became a long, keening wail of unutterable grief and loss.

Corinne made sure two lights were burning. Then, after a brief attempt to forgo the ritual, she gave in with a sigh and grabbed the tennis ball off the top of the dresser.

She dropped to her knees and prepared to roll the ball under her bed.

Somewhere down below, a woman's scream split the silence and raised the fine tawny hairs on Corinne's forearms.

She poised, frozen, until the screams finally subsided. She was about to call the 911 emergency police number — but now she could hear sirens racing from the direction of the French Quarter precinct headquarters.

She tossed the ball under the bed. It shot through unimpeded and caromed off the opposite wall. She retrieved it and sent it through one more time before finally slipping between the sheets.

"All clear," she assured herself as she burrowed in among the pillows. But those hideous screams seemed to chase her down the long tunnel toward sleep.

That night she dreamed about eyes watching her out of the dark, silent depths of the night.

As the first screams erupted behind him, the Emperor ducked into a littered alley beside a Vietnamese takeout.

There, amidst the stink of rotting fishheads and rancid vegetables, he fought to control his breathing. For a moment, still hearing the ear-piercing cries of grief and pain, he felt sharp digestive cramps of guilt.

But then he remembered *other* screams of terror and pain. And he remembered that the God of this world was now an unbalanced God.

O, rose, thou art sick . . .

Trembling as if suffering an attack of DT's, the Emperor reached into the inside pocket of his black jacket. He fumbled the filigreed silver pillbox open and shook one of the tabs into his palm.

Chapter 14

Soon, when madness and murder and unrelenting terror became his daily lot, Steve Jernigan would recognize the significance of this second visit to the shack.

For now, as he watched Tree drop the steel-rim anchor into the bayou, his curiosity was impelled by the powerful momentum years of searching had produced. He also had a disturbing hunch about this place. Overshadowing everything was the growing conviction that nothing good would come from poking around here—nor could he claim a legal or moral right to do so.

As for Tree, Steve had never seen him show any feelings one way or the other about their task. His attitude throughout had been that of a stoical observer, not a hired jobber. Steve knew his helper had developed a detached curiosity about the purpose of this search. If anything, he seemed to welcome this diversion in the month-long tedium of navigating Honey Island Swamp.

Steve had to admit that the weathered split-slab

shack didn't look too sinister just now. As before, it thrust its cold tin-pipe chimney into the sky like a dead limb. An unbroken mantilla of spiderwebs proved that the stove-lengths stacked neatly on one side had not been disturbed recently.

Their feet made sloppy-kiss sounds until the two men reached the slightly higher ground near the shack. Something small and quick rustled off through the saw grass, disappearing a moment later into the dank, junglelike depths of the swamp. Behind them, a gloomy morning sky reflected the color of cooked oatmeal on the surface of the bayou.

Steve tried the door. Again the rust-pitted knob twisted an inch or so, but the door refused to budge.

He nudged it with his shoulder. Again, harder. It was definitely locked or nailed, he decided, not just stuck. Meaning it had been done from the inside? But then how—

"Hey, brah? Check this out!"

Steve joined Tree at a charred clearing about thirty feet behind the shack. Someone had made a burning-barrel by poking ventilation holes into an empty fifty-gallon oil drum. Around the drum the ground cover was burned off, leaving a blackened circle roughly four feet in diameter.

Steve puckered his face in disgust. What he smelled made him think of the dead cat his father had dragged out from under the front porch the summer before Steve started junior high.

"Look."

Tree stirred the charred circle with a stick. A fragment of burnt pottery fell away, dead ash flaking from its sides. He jabbed with the stick a few more times. Charred objects the color of neglected teeth stirred among the shards of blackened pottery.

"Bones," said Steve, nudging one with the toe of his boot.

He squatted to peer closer. "Animal bones," he added a moment later. "At least, this piece is."

The putrid smell caught up with him again, distorting his face.

As Steve reflexively backed away, he remembered his father's grim frown, his struggle to control his bile as he had knelt and guided a rake past the flower trellis. "Get back in the house!" he had ordered his son. And Steve had eventually obeyed him—but not before he saw what his dad raked out from under that porch. The gas-swollen, infected carcass of the diseased tabby was twice the normal size . . . swollen with poison gas and maggots . . .

Now Tree moved the stick a few inches and poked again.

"No!" warned Steve.

The point of the stick punctured something Tree had mistaken for scorched burlap. The swollen animal carcass belched loudly as it released its trapped pus and gases. The sulphrous death sigh assaulted their nostrils with a physical, brutal stink that Tree later compared to snorting tiny fishhooks smeared with shit.

For at least thirty seconds both men were wracked by convulsions as their gag reflexes took over.

"Sorry, cap," gasped Tree, still bent forward over a bush. "Why the hell'd I *do* that?"

Steve waved it off with one hand, not quite able to speak yet.

"Fuck," said Tree. "This ain't no rada—it's a pe-tro!"

Reacting to his friend's puzzled stare, Tree explained, "Saturday, when we found this place? I figured somebody was messin' around with *vaudau* when I found the burnt pots out front by the water."

"We're talking voodoo?" said Steve. He barely recognized the Cajun French word Tree had used.

"Shurnuf ain't Greek Orthodox, cap."

Steve let it sink in, finding it difficult to conceive of this strange folk religion as anything besides the campy gimcrackery sold all over the French Quarter. "I thought the voodoo doctors, or whatever they called them around here, died out last century."

Tree flashed his gap-toothed grin. "They did . . . bunch of winos and reefer heads. But that stuff's still a good 'no trespassing' sign if there's somethin' you wanna keep hid from the rubes."

Both men glanced toward the shack.

"What do you mean? Think it's for show?"

Tree nodded. Steve glanced toward the festering remains in the charred circle. He said, "Since when does *vaudau* involve sacrifice?"

"Usually it don't. But most people around here that really messes with it are rada cult. That's the church-service stuff that don't hurt nobody. The big boogie there is for the worshippers to be what they call mounted by the loa—the spirits of the dead, or some shit. But this stuff here with bones and burnt pots and dead animals? That's petro cult. They the ones that hang around the cemeteries. You heard the warnings about cemeteries around here?"

Steve nodded. Cemeteries in New Orleans, as all

visitors quickly learned, were to be carefully avoided. No one was actually buried in them because the city was literally built over a swamp, and a few feet of digging invariably struck the water table. Consequently, the deceased dwelled aboveground. Some were entombed in expensive granite vaults, others in mere concrete frames where the coffin was covered over with crushed shells and earth. Many of the larger tombs provided excellent cover for muggers and rapists.

"Some people stays out 'cause a' thieves," said Tree. "Other people stays out 'cause a' petro cult."

"Sounds like you know a little about it." Steve glanced at the wooden gris-gris suspended around his friend's neck. "What do you think?"

Tree shrugged one shoulder. His pullover featured a smiling oyster and the upbeat advice to KEEP ON SHUCKIN!

"*I* don't think much about it at all. My gran'mama is in pretty tight with a buncha them old wimmens that go to the church. One time I checked it out? That ol' *mambo* that ran the gig was a mean motorscooter, brah. F'*sure* she had gran'ma and the rest of them old biddies jerkin' and workin', jumpin' around like they had bugs in their bloomers."

Tree nodded toward the burning barrel. "But this sitch? I'm thinking it's all for show. *Vaudau* spozed to be a big secret, right? So look how quick I found that burnt pottery last time. If *you* was heavy into it, cap, would you be doin' all your sacred shit right down by the water where people can spot it right off?"

Steve shook his head.

122

Tree stared at the shack. "You ax me, somebody don't want people snoopin' around that old building right there, that's all it is."

Monday afternoon turned cold by four o'clock, the Gulf breeze raw with a knife edge of humidity. Corinne dressed warm in jeans, stack-heel leather boots, and a thick cableknit sweater. She packed her drawing materials into a canvas tote and caught the St. Charles streetcar on Canal. Her watercolor class wasn't until seven, but she had a 5:15 appointment at Student Health.

The car bumped and swayed from stop to stop, doors banging open and shut like clumsy cattle gates. The cold weather and overcast sky did little to mute the architectural splendor of St. Charles. Corinne watched for some of her favorites: the little two-story beige stucco, near Constantinople, with its leaded windows; the public library, a donated mansion of stately fieldstone and black oak; the perfectly restored shotgun house near Roberts, a former slave quarters now refurbished in a spirit of yuppie elegance.

The dreamy pleasantness of sightseeing was accompanied by a welcome inner glow when she thought about her neighbor. She savored the feeling like a child with a new Christmas toy, pulling it out now and then to validate its reality.

But she wasn't a child, and Steve was more complicated than a new toy. Corinne wasn't sure exactly when that inner glow began to fade. One moment she was gazing across the avenue at a gleaming white

Greek revival with Doric columns. Its high wrought-iron gates stood open to reveal a courtyard of moss-carpeted flagstones and a classic Daimler Sovereign touring car parked in the cul-de-sac. The next moment she lost interest, feeling herself withdraw into the tough carapace of her defensive shell.

Doesn't it seem unlikely, whispered a pesky mental voice, that a guy as attractive and charming as Steve is also free of emotional entanglements?

After all, he had another life up north in Michigan—one about which he had not been very talkative at dinner Saturday night. Not that he had to spill his guts on a first date. Still, Corinne remembered the letter she had glimpsed at Cafe du Monde.

Another life . . . like Wayne's secret wife and family back in California, making a mockery of her passion for the noble young professor who stood for *lux et veritas*.

Warm blood surged into her cheeks. Corinne huddled closer to the window, her forehead bumping the glass with the rocking and swaying of the old streetcar. Men are masters, she thought, at lying by omission. No wonder they dominate politics.

True, she admitted. For her, once burned meant twice shy. Maddy was right, she was afraid of men.

Still, Steve *was* holding something back.

But what?

"There. That should do it for today."

Doctor Sarah Hanchon loosened the blood-pressure cuff and slipped it off Corinne's arm. She made a note on the patient-history file lying open in front

124

of her on the desk.

"You *may* have some slight lymphatic swelling. I confess I'm not sure. If so, I suspect a mild bacterial infection. We'll get you started on antibiotics. As I mentioned, we'll run more complete lab tests on the blood and urine samples and have them back with your Pap smear results. But don't hold your breath worrying. Frankly, I suspect the symptoms you described are mostly subjective."

The Student Health wing was nearly deserted, and the physician had left her office door slanted open. Corinne could see the pea-green plastic sofas and chairs scattered about the waiting room, the double-glazed windows now turning the view of Tulane's campus into a greenish-brown blur as the day waned.

"Is that good news?" Corinne tugged her sleeve back down.

Springs squealed in protest as the doctor shifted in her chair. She was in her early fifties, a plain, businesslike woman with steel-gray hair cut in short bangs.

"Physically, yes. Psychologically . . . I'm not so sure. That's not my turf."

Her brusque manner seemed to add: *thank God.*

"Psychologically?" Corinne paused until the first flush of indignation had passed. Then she said, "I don't understand. Are you suggesting that I'm not controlling stress adequately, or what?"

Doctor Hanchon continued to write in the patient-history file. The jalousies over the west windows were open at a forty-five-degree angle, laying a shimmering gold grillwork of sunlight on the tile floor.

"Please don't put words in my mouth, young lady.

All I suggest is that you might make an appointment with a counselor."

"Yes, I gathered that much," said Corinne defensively. The angry words rose in her throat like tight bubbles before she could stop them. "I'm just curious. Was it my drool or my psychotic smile that tipped you off?"

The doctor glanced up sharply. But her annoyed frown disappeared when she saw Corinne's angry, hurt glare.

"I apologize, Ms. Matthews. I don't mean to make light of your complaints. I'll be candid with you. It's been a terrible semester for me. Last week I had to tell a nineteen-year-old freshman and his parents that he had AIDS. Only three weeks ago another student tested positive for leukemia. I *know* it's unprofessional, but sometimes I run a little low on empathy. You just caught me between recharges."

"I understand, Doctor. And *I* apologize, for being so thin-skinned. Maybe I just don't want to admit that maybe you're right."

Doctor Hanchon seemed glad to make amends. "You know, we didn't discuss your sexual activities. I know from your form you aren't married. But is there a fiancé or some other steady sexual partner . . . or partners?"

Partners? thought Corinne with a twinge of irony. *Maddy thinks I don't get enough. Are you suggesting I get too much?*

Sarah Hanchon saw her patient's pretty face close against her.

"I ask," the doctor persisted, "because the simple truth is that most of the young women I see here have sex-related worries and they're hesitant to discuss them. If you have any questions about venereal disease or birth control, we can—"

"Thank you, Doctor," Corinne cut in, keeping her voice neutral only with extreme effort. "I appreciate your time, and I'll consider what you've told me."

She gripped her canvas tote and stood up. Again Corinne realized why she had such mixed feelings about doctors. Maybe it was just her bad luck, but she'd met precious few who didn't condescend to her as if she were a child—and not a particularly bright child, at that. And the female medicos were just as imperious as the men—as if three years of carving up cadavers turned them into little tin goddesses or something.

Sarah Hanchon rose with her and handed over a prescription. "Your lab results should be back by Wednesday morning. I want you to take the Erythromycin every six hours until they're gone."

"Thank you again."

Corinne was halfway to the door when the doctor's voice stopped her.

"Ms. Matthews . . . Corinne?"

Corinne turned around.

"I'm sorry," said Sarah Hanchon, "that we didn't get along better. Whatever is troubling you, I hope you work it out."

The physician seemed momentarily vulnerable, her face a network of worry lines. Corinne watched her thumb reflexively clicking the ballpoint pen in her hand.

Corinne flashed her a smile. "Thanks. Maybe I will if I can stop being so bullheaded."

The parting exchange seemed to lift a weight off her shoulders. Corinne decided to grab coffee and a sandwich at the Student Union before her class.

But halfway across the main diag, she felt a familiar flutter of nausea. Again it was followed by that feeling as if cold fingers had been laid across the back of her neck.

She paused in front of the library and whirled around.

"Oh!"

"Watch out!"

The bicycling professor managed some last-second acrobatics, his veering ten-speed missing her by inches.

"Excuse me!" she shouted behind him.

"Quite all right!" he groused over his shoulder.

No one was watching her. Still, she couldn't shake the feeling that the Emperor was nearby holding her in his gaze, monitoring her.

The doctor's words reverberated in her mind like an accusatory litany: *Frankly, I suspect the symptoms you describe are subjective . . . subjective . . . subjective . . .*

Weirdest of all, she couldn't stop thinking about Volkswagens.

Chapter 15

"That was quite a lovely little *jeune fille* I saw you with on Saturday," said Alan Breaux. "And here I thought you were in the South solely to appease scientific curiosity."

Steve grinned. "Hasn't that venerable wife of yours warned you about all work and no play?"

"She has," agreed Breaux. "She certainly has."

As if to prove it, he drained his schooner and banged it down on the bar. "Innkeeper!" he shouted. "More of your stoutest ale for meself and the laddie buck!"

C. J. Guidry, busy demolishing a roast beef po'boy near the kitchen door, flipped him a middle finger. He wiped his hands on a grungy apron, then grabbed a cigar from the display beside the register and slipped it out of its cedar wrapper. Lighting up, he took several ostentatious puffs. Only then did he amble down to refill their glasses.

"Tell me, pilgrim," he said to Breaux, thumping the pair of foaming glasses down on the bar. "Ever considered suing your brains for nonsupport?"

Guidry raised his right hand over his head. Breaux slapped it in a high-five, and both men chanted:

Eity-ditey, Christ Al-mighty,
Who in hell are *we*?
Zim-*zam*,
God-*damn*,
We're the *var*-sity!

Steve said, "I take it you clowns played ball to-gether?"

"Belle Chasse High," said Guidry proudly. "City Triple A champs in 1951."

"Would you believe," put in Breaux, nodding at the bartender, "that this fat schlep standing before you was our leading receiver?"

"And would you believe," retorted Guidry, "that this nancy-boy nebbish sitting beside you was our star quarterback? Blew off a full-ride scholarship at LSU just to play grunt in Korea. Ignut fuck."

"Good old Guidry," said Breaux fondly. "Every other inch a gentleman."

C. J. blew smoke at him, then wandered back down to resume the attack on his po'boy.

It was Monday evening and business was slow. A hard-core alky at the opposite end of the S-shaped bar stared like a comatose zombie at a 60-inch pro-jection TV, watching Newhart through a murky alco-hol fog. In a back corner, a group of trendies in mock hospital scrubs and Banana Republic T-shirts were singing theme songs from sixties sitcoms.

"Autopsy results on Sabrina Nash were released this morning," Breaux remarked to his neighbor at the bar. "Zilch—no official cause of death."

"Medical incompetence?"

Breaux shook his head. "Just won't factor in. She had the best medical attention. Complications related to the anaesthesia have been ruled out."

"How 'bout the other girl, Jeanette Manders?"

Breaux folded his fingers together and rested his chin on the cradle formed by his knuckles. He glanced sideways at the younger man.

"So you've been wondering about her too? Well, so far it's right off the same shelf as Sabrina's death—a pretty, young, talented girl dies for no apparent reason. The only difference is that Jeanette Manders was pronounced dead at the scene."

"Pretty, young, talented," repeated Steve thoughtfully. He lapsed into silence, thinking about Corinne. And about the Emperor. He could almost swear the old mime was spying on her.

As if surmising the thoughts reflected in Steve's brooding eyes, Breaux said, "Might be one more common factor. A witness *thinks* that the Emperor was present when the Manders girl collapsed."

Steve paused with his schooner halfway to his lips. Breaux went on.

"Which brings us to an interesting little item that appeared in today's newspaper on page 4 of the *Metro* section. You notice it? About the little girl?"

Steve shook his head.

"Didn't think so. It was buried under a story about a ninety-year-old nun who plays frisbee. Anyway, seems a New Jersey couple split up for an hour or so last night. You with me? The husband's a commodities broker, apparently the workaholic type.

131

Spent the time in their hotel room hacking on his computer while the wife and six-month-old daughter took a stroll along the riverwalk. On the way back to meet her hubby, the wife stops to take a whiz at the public johns on Decatur. The daughter is fine when they come out. A couple blocks later, Mom discovers the kid is dead."

Steve winced. "Jesus."

"Woman was still in shock this morning at Charity Hospital. But understand, the thing is — she distinctly remembers stopping to speak with an old mime wearing a gardenia in his lapel, right before she discovered that her kid was dead."

Steve had forgotten his beer now. Behind them, the tipsy habitués in the back corner were launching into the theme from *Gilligan's Island*.

"Correlation is not causation," Steve finally said, as if debating an imaginary opponent. But there was little conviction behind the words.

"No," agreed Breaux. "But when two relatively intelligent, rational observers both smell something rotten, it's probably because something stinks."

Steve combed his hair with his fingers while he thought it over. Finally he nodded.

Breaux averted his eyes. "You had any more thoughts about all this since we hashed it over last time?"

"Some. But what I'm playing with is still too far out in left field to mention. I've decided to contact a lady in Ann Arbor who might be able to give me the information I need. Give me a few days."

Thinking about Lisa caused a tight steel spring of guilt to wind even tighter inside Steve. Contacting her now, even with the simple motive of picking her considerable brain, would be a move open to other interpretations by Lisa. She had already made it clear she was waiting to see what, if anything, he had decided about their future. He found such a decision impossible right now, especially with the strong attraction he felt for Corinne.

Breaux noted the long silence. "Ahh, when I wore a younger man's clothes," he muttered in a stage whisper.

Grinning, Steve gladly abandoned the reverie. "You can scrap the salty-old-timer bit. I don't buy any of your bullshit acts."

"Your cynicism cuts me to the quick. Say, made any progress in that little search of yours?"

Steve formed a giant zero with both thumbs and index fingers.

Breaux signalled C. J. for another round. He paused a few seconds, his salt 'n' pepper brows puckered in thought, then asked, "What if I said to you, explain in twenty-five words or less, to an audience of laypersons, what was the nub of your father's scientific work?"

Steve thought about it. "I'd say basically it was this: Much of the weird but documented phenomena we call paranormal or psychic can be explained, perhaps even reduplicated, once we know their physico-chemical basis."

Breaux nodded. "Very good," he said, maintaining a poker face. "I think that was only twenty-four words."

But a few seconds later, musing out loud, Breaux said, "You're helping me. Maybe I can return tit for tat. I've got some files to pull anyway. How about I get some dates from you and have a look at the reports about the death of your dad and his partner?"

" 'Preciate it," said Steve. "And I'll get moving on that call to Ann Arbor."

"Six more fun-filled hours," groused C. J., plunking two fresh beers down in front of them, "and I'm *out*ta here."

It was just after nine P.M. when Corinne emerged from the Fine Arts Building, her tote slung over one shoulder. All around the campus milky moonlight filtered through live oaks in patches like luminous fog.

She hung around on the brick steps for ten minutes or so, chatting with a few other members of her watercolor class. As usual, Regina Davis offered to give her a ride back to the Quarter. Also as usual, Corinne resisted the strong temptation to accept.

This weekly trip home after dark was the only real-world "therapy" for her lifelong nyctophobia. She had tried everything she could—psychotherapy, self-help books, logical argument, prayer . . . nothing seemed to alleviate this morbid fear of darkness. Taking a night class was as close as she'd come, so far, to confronting her phobia. Every yard of her route had been carefully laid out during the days prior to semester opening, from the initial streetcar stop downtown at Canal and Carondelet to her midcity stop at the arched green gates of Audubon Park, across St. Charles Avenue from Tulane.

Now the campus seemed oddly deserted, until she remembered that many of the students were partying at the parade on nearby Henry Clay Avenue. The night was humid, and the few dead leaves under her feet were too limp to crunch. She followed a shell path that wound toward the streetcar line, trying not to think of the circles of lamplight as stepping stones in a piranha-filled moat.

She passed a twelve-story high-rise dorm, drawing comfort from the thousand glaring eyes of the windows, the schizoid medley of music spilling through open windows. The reassuring racket faded behind her as she reached the last block of campus before the streetcar line.

She was crossing a flower quad between two administration buildings when a gaggle of skinheads and Road Warrior clones veered toward her.

One, his dope-wired eyes mocking her, whipped out a switchblade.

"Cut out her heart!" cried one of his droogs.

Corinne's legs stopped moving, though she knew she should run. A ball of ice imbedded itself in her stomach.

The kid snicked the "switchblade" open and a comb popped out. He ran it over his shaved head while his companions hooted and whistled.

"You little assholes!" Corinne exploded.

They hooted louder, but gave her wide berth as they swarmed past her. She waited in the soft yellow glow of an overhead globe until her heart eased back down out of her throat. Three minutes later she reached St. Charles, trying to pretend it was no big deal.

She didn't understand why the usual cluster of commuters was absent from the stop, until she remembered the parade tonight. It had halted streetcar service on this side of Henry Clay. Either she waited here a couple of more hours, or she walked a few blocks up the line to the next stop.

Corinne glanced down the line. Several of the overhead lights had burned out—or had been broken.

But auto traffic was brisk on St. Charles, she reassured herself. Headlight beams swept the velvet darkness on both sides of the wide neutral ground reserved for the streetcar.

Not allowing herself more time to debate the matter, she headed into the shadowy stage setting of the night.

She knew what they were, of course.

They were mundane realities, turned sinister in the crucible of darkness: bushes, birdbaths, fences, trees, unlit buildings. That lurking presence ahead was only an oleander, that crouching figure to her right merely a litter can. But something was moving along the periphery of vision, almost tracking her. Put a name to it, she commanded herself, then forget about it.

But for a brief moment all her mock confidence receded. In the hostile unknown darkness, time and place lost all meaning. She was a ten-year-old again, waking at two A.M. to a dark, silent, and empty house. Her father was out commiserating in some hole-in-the-wall bar with other unemployed workers whose fortunes had gone belly up with the advent of new oil-patch technology. And her mother was playing her own variation of the same game, careful only to avoid the bars he frequented.

Of course Corinne hadn't filled in so many details. Not then. All she knew was that it was late and there was no one home—no one, except that amorphous white shape floating beside the bed like a ghostly nova.

It turned out to be her blouse, hung neatly on the chair where she had left it when she went to bed. But the house was *still* empty.

Like this street now.

At least the tracking motion along the periphery of her vision proved to be only a waist-high hedgerow.

She heard the distant clang of streetcars as she approached Webster Street. The slipstreaming whisper of traffic reassured her. Only another half block. But now footsteps were approaching behind her out of the night, a hurried, disembodied cadence. Corinne quickened her own steps.

The footsteps behind her gained.

She glanced over one shoulder and felt the hair draw tight over the nape of her neck. A ghostly patch of white like that long-ago childhood memory was drifting toward her!

Barely restraining herself from breaking into a panicked lunge, she finally jutted across Webster— triggering an angry explosion of horns and brakes— and joined the others waiting in the reassuring glow of the stop's overhead lamp.

Corinne watched the amorphous-bedsheet shape

draw nearer, then take recognizable form as a white merino sweater. The harried-looking young man wearing it carried a thick volume tucked under one arm. He edged past Corinne, and she read the book's gilt-lettered leather spine: *Cases in Real Estate Law*.

Her relief was more physical than mental, as if her muscles had been stretched taut on tenterhooks and someone had just loosened the pressure. This time she was easy on herself as the rush of warm shame flooded up her neck and into her cheeks. All things considered, she thought, she had kept it together reasonably well.

A streetcar rumbled to a stop, and she rummaged in her tote for two quarters and a dime. For a moment she stared at the back of the plump neck ahead of her in line, then she was feeding her change into the coin receptacle.

She sighed with weary contentment and ignored the gawking, red-eyed tourists. The car lurched suddenly forward, and she stumbled. But as she spun around and plunked ungraciously into the nearest empty seat, she glimpsed something. A millisecond later her mind processed the image, and shock slammed into her like a body-blow.

Three seats back, staring toward but not at her, was the waxen visage of the Emperor.

After all these years it had almost seemed like a voice from the grave.

Congressman Clinton J. Pearlman lay wide awake in the small hours of the morning, mulling over the recent phone call which had sent him scurrying from his Washington, D.C., condo to the family estate just south of Baton Route along Bayou Duplanier.

Be ready, were his only instructions so far. *Your assistance might be required again.*

Be ready . . . but for what?

Beside him, his wife's face — blank and innocent in sleep — sheened with a patina of aloe vera lotion. It was a cloudless night, and buttery moonlight spilled through the open French doors leading to the second-floor terrace. Outside, an owl hooted, bullfrogs bellowed their eerie bass rhythm down by the banks of the bayou. Now and then the old house settled with a groan of an exhausted joist.

A voice from the grave, thought Pearlman again. After all these years of silence since *he* had first enlisted Pearlman's aid while the politico was still a police chief.

Don't return to Washington for the rest of Mardi Gras, the voice had told him. *Stay close at hand until Fat Tuesday.*

For a long, uncomfortable moment, the night seemed to press down on Pearlman with palpable weight, making breathing difficult for him. Everything disappeared from the screen of memory except those mismatched eyes, probing into him like surgical instruments, trapping his will like a culture smeared in a petri dish. He could recall little of what he had actually done so many years ago in New Orleans, but he remembered those eyes commanding him to do it.

Your assistance might be required . . .

After all that time. A voice from the grave.

139

Still . . . hadn't the caller fulfilled *his* end of the bargain long ago? And a bargain was a bargain, after all.

Especially a bargain with the devil.

Chapter 16

"I *don't* question your authority, sir," Donald Carr was protesting at the moment Steve entered the hallway reserved for faculty offices. "You are obviously a brilliant man."

"Thank you for the encomium," Winters shot back sarcastically. "May I list you as a recommendation?"

Carr's face went stony with anger. "The question is not your knowledge or qualifications, Professor Winters. I'm familiar with your books and articles, your many contributions to chemical-learning theory. Nor do I agree with that animal-rights activist at LSU who claims you 'torture' lab animals with your experiments. It's valuable research that ought to go forward. My complaint is more basic. I still think you've taken too vast a liberty in defining the parameters of our class. It simply isn't practical enough for our needs."

Trying to blend in with the woodwork, Steve slipped past the arguing pair. Winters stood with his back to his office door. It was slanted partway open, and a bunch of keys dangled from the lock. Carr stood in the middle of the hall. A crushed-ice denim backpack rode awkwardly high on one shoulder.

Steve instantly felt his sympathies going out to Carr. The kid was an excellent student, one of only three who had aced the psychobiology seminar Steve taught last semester. He was intelligent, down-to-earth, and curious. Steve only hoped that cynical egotists like Winters wouldn't discourage him. So naturally he was as surprised as Carr when Winters replied pleasantly enough.

"Very well, Mr. Carr. Perhaps you're right. Next class, give me a list of topics you'd like to hear addressed."

Carr thanked him, said hello to Steve, then hurried off to his ten A.M. class.

Watching his colleague now, Steve got the distinct impression that he had only given in to get rid of Carr. Something else was on Winters's mind as he stepped into the office and started to pull the door shut behind him.

"Turning into a student-lover, Eric?"

Winters flinched and turned around. His eyes met Steve's across the empty hallway. They were blue shards of ice.

"Jernigan!" Winters pumped his voice full of false bonhomie. "Missed you at the department meeting."

"I'll just bet you did." Steve unlocked his own door.

Winters poured on an unguent smile. "Not that your presence was necessary, of course. We discussed forthcoming articles and lectures by department

142

members. You would have been bored."

Steve observed him for a long moment before he slapped on the light switch.

"You know something, Winters?" he replied finally. "Your asshole's screwed on too tight. Why don't you go out and get laid or something?"

The startled hatred that flared briefly in Winters's eyes was reward enough for Steve. For a moment he tried again to figure out what it was about the academic's appearance that bothered him. Giving up, he grinned in his colleague's face and pushed the door shut.

Score one for us unpublished peons, he gloated.

But his moment of triumph was fleeting. His eyes fell to the bulky black institutional telephone on one corner of the desk.

Lisa. In her card she'd said mornings were a good time to catch her in her office. But should he call? Was there a "good" time for calling an ex-lover?

He ignored the chair and perched on one end of the desk. Unaware he was doing it, Steve began to alternately clench his fists, then spread wide the fingers.

Ten times . . .

Twenty . . .

Thirty . . .

His mind downshifted. For a moment he imagined the remote, weather-rawed shack hidden in Honey Island Swamp. There was also a fleeting image of Corinne, her copper-tinted eyes big and vulnerable . . . exaggeratedly so, the sad, pop-eyed stare of a famine victim.

(The old mime rose to his feet, applauding slowly but with great force. Her eyes met his across a sea of tables and bodies. She smiled; he smiled back, mouthed a voiceless compliment.)

When he knew he was ready, Steve reached for the telephone.

"In summation," said the pretty woman lecturing to the auditorium full of students, "aggressive behavior cannot be adequately analyzed without considering the critical interaction between eye contact and gaze aversion. Remember that the fixed stare always accompanies hostile behavior. In contrast, tension is reduced by gaze aversion. Also remember that most of us have mastered the 'fractional glance,' the game of peeking at others to see if they're peeking in return."

The speaker paused to consult her note cards stacked neatly in front of her on the podium. She was in her late twenties with straight, honey-blonde hair and milky blue eyes that gave her a deceptively dreamy look. Her tall, supple body was disguised by the conservative clothing.

Outside, snow caked the sills of the auditorium's tall, lancet-arched windows. The vine-covered stone of the classroom building next door looked brittle with cold.

Lisa Berman checked her watch, then dismissed the class. The steps at the end of the hall were covered with filthy slush, so she opted for the elevator.

The phone started ringing while she was keying the

144

lock of her office door.

Lisa snatched the handset up on the third ring. "Professor Berman speaking."

"Always pulling rank on us lowly instructors, aren't you?"

The voice caused a smile to split her face. "Steve?" Immediately the smile wavered. "Okay, wisenheimer. Give me one good reason why I shouldn't tell you to take a hike."

A sigh filled the silence at the other end. Then he said, "I take it you got my letter?"

"Oh, was that a *letter?* I wondered. I thought maybe it was a masculine declaration of independence. Is this an accurate paraphrase: 'Steal the horses and screw the women'?"

"Get off it. I didn't say anything I haven't told you before."

"True. But the bold devil-may-care tone is something new. I didn't seem to detect it last summer during your visit."

"As I recall, you—*we*—had other priorities."

Lisa felt her breath quicken slightly as she too remembered those priorities. "Fair enough," she conceded. She cleared her throat. "I hate to dash cold water on our fun, but something tells me you didn't call just to confabulate with your Yankee sweetie."

"No," he confessed. "I have a favor."

"Let me guess. You have business in Ann Arbor, and since I'm the only guaranteed game in town on such short not—"

"Maybe," his exasperated voice interrupted, "I should call back after you climb off your high horse?"

Her tone softened. "Sorry. I just dismounted. What's the favor?"

"Do you remember that lecture you presented at the folklore conference in Lansing? *Mal Ojo,* I think it was titled."

"I used that term, but the lecture was titled *Malocchio,* and how could I forget? You were in the audience. I was so nervous I was ready to have kittens."

"Were you serious with that business about how carefully documented the effects of the Evil Eye are?"

"No." She sounded miffed. "I made it all up just so I could ruin a budding career in front of three hundred Ph.D.'s."

He laughed. "Sorry I questioned your integrity."

"As I recall, *you* were the one who cavalierly fudged a footnote or two. So what about my brilliant lecture?"

"Any chance of getting a copy, including the bibliography, so I can track down your sources if I need to?"

A long silence underlined her sudden curiosity.

"Yes and no," she finally replied. "I think I can give you the bibliography. But I received my invitation to participate only a week before the conference, remember? When the guy from Syracuse canceled out? The lecture was never actually typed out as a paper. I winged it from note cards. God knows where they are now."

She hesitated, then added, "Tell me, have you finally freaked out completely? What do you want with that information?"

"I just need it. I can't explain right now. It would sound too off the wall."

"I'm sure it would, if it drove you to call me."

Steve ignored the remark. "You said you could send me that bibliography?"

"I think so. Unfortunately, there are really only about a dozen books on the subject of the Evil Eye that are worth a damn, and nine of them are right here in the Hoyt-Stillman Collection. As rare books, they don't circulate. And all but one are out of print."

"Shit."

"I take it from that eloquent rejoinder that you're in a hurry?"

"You might say that."

"I *could* put together a reading list for you, burn off some articles, type up some notes, and so forth. But that would be time-consuming, and frankly I'm a busy little girl this semester."

"Any other suggestion?"

"If the library can't come to you, you come to the library. If you fly up here, you'll have access to the best folklore collection in the country. Plus you'll have access to me, a certified expert on the anthropology of eye contact. Not too many of *those* around."

He was silent at his end.

"When I say 'access,' " she added, her voice velvety now, "please interpret the word loosely."

"Don't tempt me."

"You love it. Besides, I confess you've got me

curious as hell."

"How 'bout I call you back tonight and let you know?"

"Whatever happened to spontaneity?" She expelled a long sigh, took a deep breath. "Okay. You think about it. And you think about last summer too, okay? We both know it was just starting to get good when it ended. I'll be expecting your call."

She hung up, cutting him off before he could respond.

Alan Breaux paused halfway across the hotel's arcaded gallery. Below him an open court was teeming with lush tropical growth. Couples strolled hand-in-hand along crushed-shell paths. A group of rowdy kids played tag around the marble Cupid who spurted water through puckered lips.

Breaux wrestled with another bout of guilt.

He was supposed to be staking out Lee's Circle downtown, gathering data on a lottery scam operating nearby. Instead, he was about to question two very unhappy tourists and probably make them even unhappier.

At the end of the gallery he paused again to look at his reflection in a Chippendale scroll mirror.

His face looked terrible in the morning, he decided. Baggy and flabby and old, his eyes multicracking at the corners like the crinkled spine of a paperback.

Breaux shook off his pensive mood, ducked into the second-floor corridor, and followed the textured

148

wall to the door of Suite 9.

His knock was answered almost immediately by a big, florid-faced man wearing a chamois-cloth shirt and tan chinos.

"Yes?" he demanded imperiously.

Breaux glanced around him into the suite. The Holmans were staying at a quaint little wrought-iron ripoff on Royal Street. He glimpsed red satin curtains, high-backed Regency chairs, and a fringed canopy over the Louis Quatorze bed.

"Mr. Holman? Mr. John Holman?"

The big man nodded impatiently. Breaux produced his photostat. Holman glanced at it, then scowled.

"The police? We've already talked to you."

Holman had a nervous habit of jingling the change in his pocket. Breaux quickly read the scowling face and recognized the type instantly: a hard-driving executron, one of those petty tyrants who always picked up the tab because doing so left others in his debt. Even grief had apparently failed to mellow him.

"Yes, I understand that," replied Breaux. "I'd just like to ask your wife a couple more questions."

"Why?" demanded Holman. "Are questions going to bring our little girl back? Why don't you people eliminate the redundancy in your operation?"

"Who is it, John?"

The woman who stepped into view behind her husband was pretty but haggard, her eyes pouchy from grief now muted by tranquilizers. Soft, ginger hair framed a pale and oval face.

Instead of answering, Holman swore and reluctantly moved back, allowing Breaux to step inside.

The detective glanced from one to the other. "I'm sorry about what happened to your daughter. I wouldn't be bothering you like this if it wasn't important."

He looked at Sheila Holman now. "As I was reviewing the officer's report, I noticed that you mentioned someone who spoke briefly with Allegra just before she . . . before you discovered what had happened?"

Sheila Holman gazed at him in confusion for a moment. Then some memory momentarily drove the torpor from her eyes.

"That's right," she said firmly, as if he had challenged her. "An old mime."

Breaux nodded. Beside him, John Holman was furiously jingling his change.

"Mrs. Holman, did the mime touch Allegra in any way?"

"The other cop already asked that," Holman said, cutting in.

"I know that," Breaux said mildly. He looked at Sheila again and repeated his question.

She chewed her bottom lip. One hand rose to her throat in a vaguely protective gesture.

"No," she finally replied. "I remember it so clearly. He bent his face close to hers, but he never took his hands off his knees."

Again Breaux nodded. He took a deep breath. "Mrs. Holman, the report didn't mention anything else about the mime. Why did you feel it was important to bring him up?"

She said nothing, refusing to meet his eye. Breaux remembered something Jernigan had mentioned.

"The air?" he prompted. "Anything feel unusual?"

Sheila still refused to look at him, but his question had widened her eyes.

"There was *some*thing," she conceded, searching for words. "Something wrong. Right before he left, it was like . . . I don't know, like for a minute the air around us wasn't fit to breathe."

Breaux nodded. "Fine. But that's something you just now recalled, isn't it? Please tell me, *why* did you feel it was important to mention the mime the first time you told your story?"

This time her eyes fastened on his as if searching for a kindred soul. "Because," she said slowly but clearly, "he *did* something to my baby!"

"What did he do?" coaxed Breaux. He aimed a warning glance at Holman, who was about to protest again.

"I . . . I don't know. He . . . he said she was beautiful, he called her sweetheart. But . . . something was wrong with his voice, the way he looked at her. For a second I thought, I don't know . . . I thought he actually *hated* her."

Tears formed quivering crystal dollops on her eyelashes, then fell zigzagging down both cheeks.

"That does it!" snarled Holman.

For a moment the bluff, ruddy face bloated with rage and his skin stretched knuckle-tight over his cheekbones. He pointed a stubby forefinger at Breaux.

"*You!* Get the hell out, or I'll by God put you out, cop or no! Can't you see she's crazy desperate with grief? Why encourage her paranoia?"

Breaux had a couple more questions, but saw it would be dicey to push his luck. Especially since it was becoming clear that city officials and the media had consciously decided to soft-pedal the recent, atypical string of deaths.

He thanked Sheila Holman and turned toward the door. His eyes met her husband's. For a moment Breaux glimpsed beyond the bullying, arrogant exterior and saw the grief and confusion fueling the man's rage.

"Sorry, guy," Breaux said sincerely. "I'm only trying to help."

Holman just nodded once and turned away, waving Breaux out of the room.

Chapter 17

Don't even *think* about getting sick now, Corinne admonished herself fiercely.

More by habit than volition, she headed toward Maddy's shop at the corner of Toulouse and Bourbon. She still felt numb and lightheaded from reading the letter that had just arrived in the noon mail.

Her. Belgard Davis had selected *her!*

Braking tires screamed, an angry horn blared. Corinne jumped back to the curb just in time to avoid being clipped by a Firebird.

The driver's brutal, pissed-off face glared at her like an image from *Bigtime Wrestling*. "Watch where you're going, stupid cunt!"

"Sorry," she called back distractedly, too full of her good news to be offended.

The letter was brief, businesslike, and written in his own hand. Davis, a nationally acclaimed local sculptor who specialized in outdoor works on a large scale, had been commissioned by Loyola University to execute a sculpture for their new Fine Arts Center. Loyola's Faculty of Art had also submitted five names as candidates to assist him in the numerous drawing phases of the conceptual sketches. He had reviewed the work of all five and selected her. The project wouldn't actually get underway until late spring, he explained, but if she was interested, would she please call him sometime soon?

Interested? she thought. My God! But was her body going to freak out on her?

She crossed Decatur, mindful of traffic this time, and headed toward Jackson Square. The day was warm and she wore an off-the-shoulder knit pullover and tight black leggings.

Corinne felt herself coming back to earth as she thought about her health woes.

Earlier this morning the chronic nausea had escalated to an outright stomach ache. And she felt physically sapped. Last night, while brushing her teeth, her right arm had begun to tremble weakly after only a minute of brushing—as if she were hefting a heavy sack of groceries, not wielding a mere toothbrush.

(*Frankly, I suspect the symptoms you describe are subjective. . . .*)

A young female mime was posed statue-still on the steps of St. Louis Cathedral. The crowd had scattered out fanwise around her. Corinne paused and watched her for at least five minutes. The girl's bright-painted clown's face gazed back at the crowd without so much as a muscle twitch. Even her eyeblinks seemed imperceptible.

"Is she *real*, Mama?" demanded a child's fascinated voice, and laughter rippled through the crowd.

She's good, thought Corinne. It must take incredible talent to maintain such poise. Still, that detached yet piercing gaze disturbed Corinne, made her feel vulnerable, somehow violated.

She tossed a dollar bill into the young entertainer's hat and angled across the square toward Toulouse. Corinne tried to submerge her thoughts in the busy noon-hour stream around her.

But it was no use. Watching one mime had made her think of another.

Was it just a coincidence, she thought, or had the Emperor been waiting for her last night at the streetcar stop? After all, he could easily have slipped on just ahead of her, she hadn't paid any attention to the line of people.

But if so, why?

The question prompted an ominous gnawing of terror in the pit of her stomach and she quickly shooed the thought back under the lid of her subconscious.

"Good morning, *ma jolie!*"

Georges Lagacé, his face half in shadow under a jipijapa, waved to her from his little open-fronted sidewalk studio. Several tourists were admiring the display drawings. He ignored the potential customers with cool indifference, comfortable under his canvas awning.

Corinne waved. She was about to round the corner of the cathedral when she remembered something. Georges could tell her, she thought. He'd lived here since the end of World War Two.

She retraced her steps. He rose gallantly at her approach, lifting his hat and bowing forward slightly from the waist.

"Today, *non?* Today you permit me to capture this

155

lovely face?"

Corinne smiled, flattered and embarrassed at the same time. " 'Fraid not. Just came over to ask a question."

"Superb," he approved after a prolonged gaze at her exposed shoulders. "Such a sensual blend of delicacy and strength."

He sighed, then enjoyed the rest of her in a lingering glance. "I make no apologies for staring," he added. "Old men still *think* like young ones."

Now he assumed his dickering face and said, "A question?"

"Yes. You know those lithos that are scattered around the Cafe du Monde? The ones by Katerina someone?"

He blinked a few times, but said nothing. She thought he hadn't heard her. "The lithos that're mounted at Cafe du Monde? They—"

"I know them well," he assured her quietly. "By Mademoiselle Katerina Zverkov. She was beautiful, a great *artiste*. Perhaps even as talented as you."

"Was? What happened to her?"

Georges smiled evasively, dismissing her question. With a tone that was almost brusque, he replied, "You are an artist, not a detective! Develop the talent God has given you, and the Devil take the rest! Now you must excuse me."

With a sudden conviviality that made her suspicious, he approached the small group of tourists and launched into a bantering patter she'd never heard him use before.

"Hey, babe!"

Madora waved from behind the counter, a half-dozen bangles slip-clicking down to her elbows when she raised her arm.

"How 'bout dinner tonight," said Corinne. "On me this time. I've got a letter to show you."

"Good news?"

"Very."

"Don't tease, you little shit! What is it?"

"You'll see," said Corinne mysteriously. She turned to scan the paperback rack.

Maddy started to object again, then paused to frown as she studied Corinne closer. She came around the counter.

"Corinne? Look at me."

She glanced up, startled at hearing Maddy use her name.

"My God, puss, those eyes're gonna give me macronightmares! When's the last time you ate something heftier than a granola bar?"

"I'm eating okay, Mother."

Maddy's frown became more thoughtful. "Really, hon, you feeling okay?"

"I'm fine. I'm just fighting off the flu or something. It's going around."

Neither one looked up when the bell over the front door chimed.

"Been to a doctor?" persisted Maddy.

"Good gravy, woman, set it to a tune! *Yes!* I checked out fine, honest."

"Maybe," said Maddy doubtfully. "Anyway, f'sure I'll have dinner with you tonight. And you're gonna eat good, lovey, or Aunt Madora will beat your little

157

ass black and blue."

"Good luck," cut in a masculine voice behind Corinne, startling the two friends. "I couldn't get her to eat much either."

Maddy glanced up. Corinne whirled around.

Steve grinned at them, brashly unapologetic about eavesdropping.

"I just can't guess what's happened to that girl's appetite," said Maddy innocently. She started to wander away. "Maybe you could help her, Mr. Jernigan?"

Maddy crossed to the bawdy T-shirts and pretended to straighten up a few of them.

"I was hoping I might run into you here," Steve told Corinne.

She felt him studying her face with concerned eyes. My God, she thought, was Maddy right? Do I look *that* bad?

Steve continued watching her. "This weekend— that date we still haven't finalized?"

She nodded.

"Is it okay if we make it for Saturday instead of Friday?" he continued. "Something's just come up. I'll be out of town for a few days. I'm flying to Michigan tomorrow."

For a moment his last word hung in the air between them, a confession of sorts. Corinne looked away. Her eyes fell on the bright satin Mardi Gras masks. Their hollow sockets watched her from the display rack, silently mocking her for feeling so vulnerable and jealous—and for being so damn naive about men. She glanced down at the paperbacks again.

"Of course," she replied lightly. "Business before pleasure, right?"

The Emperor watched the Krewe of Hiawatha begin rolling down Carrollton Avenue shortly after 8 P.M.

A U.S. Marine Corps Reserve band led the parade, belting out a rousing John Philip Sousa march. They were followed by local high school marching bands playing jazz and Dixieland variations of the same march. Next came a group of drunken World War Two vets in a shambling, makeshift formation, most of them carrying plastic cups of beer.

After the vets passed by, the first of the huge, papier-mâché and foam floats appeared. The theme this year was "Demons of Ancient Greece." Giant fire-breathing dragons, huge bat-winged harpies, and a basilisk-eyed Cyclops glared down on the carnival revelers. The drivers of the tractors pulling the floats revved their engines, creating convincing angry-beast roars.

Revelers, thought the Emperor with an inner flexing of tight disgust. As if these drunk, happy, tenderhearted spectators were capable of a true revel! A friendly, drunken bash, yes. But a true orgy in the spirit of Bacchus, complete with the purgation and atonement of bloodlust?

No.

The carnival spirit now wore the tawdry hide of commercialism. And something even baser. As the Emperor watched the lead float, his thin cracked lips parted in disgust. Several politicians were out on the hustings, flashing their reflex smiles, while tossing out campaign flyers instead of the usual beads and frisbees and gold-painted aluminum doubloons.

The Emperor's eyes were attracted by a platoon of baton-twirling majorettes separating the first and second floats.

Graceful young things, he thought. And pretty . . . especially that petite, lissome creature in the first rank, the one wearing the jewelled coronet and the gold lamé leotard.

Watching her, he felt hot tears abruptly welling up in his eyes. For a moment — as the unbidden images of madness and mayhem captured his screen of memory — it felt like a spiked heel was pressing into his abdomen.

The screams . . .

The shouted warnings . . .

His hands reaching out, but too late . . .

No one near him in the frenzied crowd paid any attention to the white-faced old mime with the oddly colored eyes. He was just one more costumed celebrant. All were absorbed in drinking, screaming for attention, copping quick feels, and leaping for the trinkets tossed down from the symbolic gods on high.

The last glazed vestige of grief melted from the old man's eyes, leaving only two burning points of murderous rage.

He waited impatiently until he saw the first of the mounted police.

There were two of them — a man and a woman wearing neat Smokey Bears. Both rode huge, magnificent sorrels, their iron-shod hooves clopping on the pavement as the cops paced one of the floats and patiently nudged the raucous crowd back. Now and then one of the horses started at a misthrown trinket.

The Emperor raised his eyes beyond the riders to the float. Quickly he scanned the masked members of the krewe. All were watching the spectators intently, tossing great bunches of "throws" into the outstretched hands of the prettiest or most enthusiastic contenders.

He found the one he wanted, a ridiculously robed figure now looking in his general direction. An empty Corona beer bottle rested beside his huge box of throws.

The krewe member wore a masked hood with exaggerated eyes represented by painted concentric circles. The weird disks flashed in his direction when the Emperor suddenly shot both hands up, pleading for throws.

The two men exchanged brief glances. For a split-second, some in attendance would later claim, they remembered noticing a sickly sweet septic-tank smell. A moment later a purple bead necklace snaked through the air, and the Emperor caught it in one hand.

"You're most kind!" he shouted to the anonymous rider, his words instantly lost in the din.

The secret benefactor nodded. Only the Emperor saw all of what happened next.

The masked krewe member reached down as if to grab more throws from his box. Instead his hand shot down to palm the long neck of the Corona bottle. He picked it up and snapped it into the air in one smooth motion.

It flipped neatly end-over-end, like a boomerang. With a hard, solid *thuck* it caromed off the skull of the near horse and shattered on the pavement.

The woman officer was nearly thrown from her saddle when the sorrel whickered in fright and reared on its hind legs.

Someone screamed, the crowd surged back like a seawall before a tidal wave. Once, twice, again the frightened sorrel's hooves cracked harmlessly against pavement as the well-trained officer fought to gentle him, skillfully buying the crowd time to run.

Then the panicked mob ran out of running room.

Someone tripped, legs flailed, and the sorrel came down one final time, its right hoof rupturing an old man's stomach.

The left hoof landed on wet leaves and skittered into a storm drain. The sorrel fell heavily, crushing a teenage girl and her baby brother and snapping the officer's left leg with a crack like new wood splitting.

Chapter 18

"Here in the Crescent City, tragedy marred last night's Krewe of Hiawatha parade when a policewoman's horse bolted into nearby spectators, killing one and injuring three others, one seriously. Police are searching for a person whom they suspect may have thrown a bottle at the horse, initiating the incident. Dead is sixteen-year-old Amanda Jefferson, who witnesses say . . ."

Alan Breaux frowned as he advanced the microfilm. He paid little attention to the radio broadcast filtering in from down the hall.

He paused and made a brief notation on the yellow legal pad at his elbow. Breaux ignored the styrofoam cup of coffee now growing an oily film as it cooled. He sat at a long table flanked by the drawer-lined walls of the Records & Investigation Division. R & I's drawers housed the miles of microfilmed records generated each year by the NOPD.

He reread the information on the screen, checked his notes, frowned again.

You ever heard of a guy named Mario Townsend?

There were some inconsistencies here, some nettlesome oversights.

He died in 1977. It wasn't just telekinesis he was known for. . . .

The whole did not equal the sum of its parts.

Dad's break actually came when Townsend died, because he willed his brain to my father and his partner for extensive analysis. . . .

But that brain had been stolen from the university lab in Ann Arbor, Michigan. According to Jernigan, the trail eventually led his father and his research associate, Dale McGinnis, to New Orleans. And here both men had died, less than two weeks apart.

A startling coincidence, Breaux thought. Or that was all it seemed if you didn't look too closely . . . and someone had clearly decided *not* to look very closely.

Why?

Again he consulted the screen. Both reports had been signed by the Chief of Police himself. That wasn't SOP. Normally a precinct captain or even the investigating officer certified an accident report.

Even more troublesome, the deaths had occurred two weeks apart, involving men from the same relatively small northern city—two men who taught at the same college and were engaged in the same project that brought both of them south. All these connections, Breaux thought, and the Chief of Police had not ordered a routine homicide investigation?

The questions didn't stop there. First to die was Dale McGinnis, the forty-seven-year-old professor of neurology. A routine boating accident, according to the report. Not so unusual in itself, Breaux mused, except that McGinnis's record included a DD 214 listing four years as a Navy SEAL. Would a former commando be likely to die in a "boating accident" on a river so normally docile as the Pearl?

Then there was the Medical Examiner's note on Robert Jernigan: *Clearly the impact of the deceased's auto against the concrete overpass was sufficient to cause death. However, the dominant skull fracture is of a depressed type, with fragments of the skull having been pushed inward. This suggests a more concentrated impact than the typical comminuted fracture of most vehicular accidents, in which multiple cracks radiate from the center of impact.*

Plain and simple, thought Breaux, somebody might have bashed him on the bean and then staged a wreck.

True, the evidence was far from damning. Despite that fracture detail, whoever did it was no amateur at such things. He had worked quickly, with reasonable efficiency. Hardly likely to have been one of the rival brain researchers Steve had mentioned.

Again he read the signature: Clinton J. Pearlman, Chief of Police.

Breaux had still been assigned to Vice during Pearlman's three-year-stint at the helm. It had been a period undistinguished by either scandal or brilliant policework. Pearlman had been your typical, porcelain-smiled PR flack with political aspirations.

In his case, those aspirations had panned out. Breaux recalled how, not quite a decade ago, the Crescent City had been stunned by former Police Chief Pearlman's sleeper ad campaign for State Representative.

Late in the campaign, when Louisianans were thoroughly fed up with the same old TV spots, Pearlman's political machine came out with its theme that "the eyes of Louisiana are on the future." The approach was textually simple, but visually effective. A sonorous voice summed up the hanging offenses of the current spate of candidates, while Louisianans from every walk of life crossed at a busy downtown crosswalk. Slowly, everything faded to shadow except the eyes of one pedestrian, plaintively staring at the voters while the persuasive voice-over repeated, "The eyes of Louisiana are on the future. Vote Clinton J. Pearlman, State Representative."

Breaux made a face and gave up on the lukewarm cafeteria coffee. He rewound the microfilm and popped it out of the reader, refiling it.

Actually, he thought, Pearlman's ads had struck him as more of the usual political tripe. Breaux had voted for his opponent. But the ads must have helped. Pearlman, hitherto a clear underdog, had emerged with a whopping percentage of the vote. Four years later he had ridden that crest of popularity to the U.S. House of Representatives.

Funny, Breaux thought, pausing for a moment after he shut the microfilm drawer. Even Cindy had voted for Pearlman—the only time in her life, Alan's wife swore, that she had ever defected and voted Republican.

He started watching her sometime around noon.

Corinne had spotted him about an hour ago, frozen in an orator's gesturing pose on the steps of the

166

cathedral. Of course she had no proof he was watching her. But she felt his eyes probing like unwelcome fingers, touching places he had no right to touch.

He looked the same as always: black summer-weight suit, white gardenia, matching face as pale as frosted hoar, eyebrows forming a single silver shelf.

If you know he's watching *you*, so much, she chided herself while she opened her sidewalk studio, that means you're watching *him* just as much.

Fortunately, the influx of Mardi Gras visitors justified her decision to open early, and during the next two nonstop hours she found little time to worry about the Emperor. First a portrait of Australian newlyweds, then four children in a row, all drawn from wallet snaps because the kids themselves were up in Indiana with their grandparents.

Still, in the brief interstices of idleness, other thoughts scampered in and out of awareness. Some were pleasant, such as remembering that she had to call Belgard Davis soon; others were more onerous, such as the realization that her chronic headache was worse this morning. It was centered in her temples, a hard, ringing pain as if she'd drunk something cold too fast.

What could it mean, especially now that Student Health had called earlier today to give her a clean bill of health?

(*the symptoms you describe are subjective . . . subjective . . . subjective . . .*)

A clean bill of *physical* health, she reflected while she gathered up her display drawings and closed for the afternoon. But was she playing some mind games on herself? Lately, she had felt torn by a desperate polarity. It was as if the artist in her were at war with the girl who only wanted to be "normal" and accepted by others. Forget all that, urged the rebellious artist. You were an orphan, for Christ's sake! You'll never fit in. If—

With an abrupt shudder the steel curtain practically leaped down its tracks, startling her as it slammed shut.

She snaked her hand back quickly, staring at the corrugated metal as if it had tried to bite her. I barely touched it, she assured herself.

Corinne's palms throbbed slightly. She glanced around.

People seemed to be watching her, or was it the noise just now that made them look toward her? But it wasn't just people. For a moment *every*thing seemed to be monitoring her: the stained-glass windows of the cathedral, car headlights, even the pigeons were in on the conspiracy.

They all know you don't really belong, whispered an insidious voice that made her flesh crawl. *So does Steve. Why do you think he's visiting a "friend" up North?*

Only then did she remember the Emperor. Slowly, not really wanting to, she turned to face the steps of St. Louis Cathedral.

Chapter 19

The luggage carousel revolved slowly and steadily, a hypnotist's disk lulling him into a welcome trance.

Finally his scuffed tan Samsonite spun into view and Steve grabbed it. He followed the pastel arrow marked CONCOURSE, telling himself it was pointless to continue speculating beyond the facts. But questions and doubts plagued him willy-nilly.

For starters, he hoped he wasn't just overreacting and opening a nasty can of worms with this visit. True, the practical difficulties had been minimal. Earlier today he had announced to his students that his Friday classes were canceled, which didn't exactly reduce anyone to tears. Besides, Tree was busy until early next week helping to salvage a barge down near Boothville. Unless Steve rented his own boat, he couldn't get anything accomplished in Honey Island Swamp until Tree returned.

No, the real problem was Lisa. Or more correctly, Lisa and he together. During the emotional tilt-a-whirl of their grad-school love affair, one factor had remained constant between them—a short sexual fuse. Their bodies got along much better than their minds, which at best had merely tolerated each other.

He watched for her now as the escalator lifted him onto the main concourse. Passengers streamed everywhere, most of them bundled in heavy winter coats. Beyond the bank of pay TV's, the vast windows showed dirty mountains of ploughed snow dotting the borders of a runway like pockmarks. It was only late afternoon, but already the winter sky was bleak with snow-laden twilight.

He remembered that Lisa would be picking him up outside at the five-minute parking lane. Steve crossed toward the door earmarked for westbound street traffic, mentally summing up what he knew.

Perhaps least significant, but most bothersome, was his suspicion that the Emperor was watching Corinne. The Emperor, who was a disturbing common factor in three highly unusual deaths in or near the French Quarter. True, it appeared he hadn't laid a hand on Sabrina Nash, Jeanette Manders, or six-month-old Allegra Holman. But he was always *there*.

All of which suggested that Corinne's risqué girlfriend was right. Something was indisputably wrong with Corinne. He'd noticed the decline in the last few weeks — a gradual, wasting kind of malady that was slowly sapping her energy. That wan, stressed-out girl he had spoken with yesterday at Maddy's shop was *not* the same person he had first noticed out on Jackson Square, charming tourists while she sketched them.

Okay, so what he was toying with here was insane. But a veteran cop had decided to share the delusion with him. That in itself was enough incentive to follow his gut-level hunch on this one.

Electric doors shot open, the sudden cold outside slicing him to the bone.

The crowded streetcar lurched to a stop at Audubon Park, and Corinne barely managed to grab one of the handstraps in time.

Patiently she shuffled forward, stoically smiling at the cranky old ladies and ignoring the creep in the Air Force jacket who was stripping her with his eyes. Just before she stepped down out of the car, she glanced behind her and glimpsed a flash of white.

Her face went prickly cold.

A moment later she realized it was just a nun's habit. Then, herded from behind, she was outside the car and crossing the neutral ground toward the Tulane campus. Her heart continued to race with alarming speed. Twice she looked back to see if she was being followed.

It was only four P.M. when she reached the flagstone walk in front of the library, but she resolved to be quick with her research. Despite her "victory" of sorts against the dark, two nights ago after class, Corinne wanted to make it home before the streetlights came on.

This little fact-finding mission shouldn't take too long, she reasoned. She was determined to find out whatever it was Georges was reluctant to discuss about Katerina Zverkov.

"She was beautiful, a great *artiste*," Georges had claimed. If so, thought Corinne as she angled past a rack of bikes and headed toward the library entrance, then surely some clue to her life and death will turn up in the library.

She wasn't quite sure why she was doing this. Maybe it was Georges's mysterious reticence, or his comparison of Katerina's talent and Corinne's. Maybe—

She paused ten feet from the smoke-tinted glass doors, watching a woman in a fringed poncho feed an armload of books one by one into the outside book repository. Waiting for her nearby was a man in a beige VW Jetta.

The word winked with neon intensity on the inner screen of her mind: *jettatore*.

The word that old lady hurled at the Emperor was *jettatore*. She was sure of it!

Her original purpose was forgotten now as she hurried through the turnstiles and veered left toward the Reference section. She stopped at the card catalog and looked up a comprehensive Italian-English dictionary. She tracked it down, the lugged the massive tome to the nearest table.

Concentrating on her task, she barely glanced at the *Times-Picayune* on the chair next to her, its headline proclaiming ACCIDENT MARS PARADE.

"There's a woman involved in all of this, isn't there?"

Steve glanced up from the note cards and books heaped before him, raising his eyebrows in surprise. Several replies occurred to him. He opted for, "Did I ever say there wasn't?"

"And so quick to volunteer the fact!"

Lisa, seated Buddha fashion near the fireplace, watched him from across the room with a smile hesitating on her lips. A white cotton velour wrapper fell open below her knees, revealing a glimpse of long, sleek calf. Steve realized she was working on her third — fourth? — tequila sunrise.

He laid his pen down, stretched. A glance at his watch startled him. It was almost midnight.

"Don't tell me," Lisa probed, her curiosity finally winning out over her resolve not to pry. "You're rescuing a beautiful young damsel who's in the clutches of some sinister Svengali."

He started, aiming a glance at her. Tongues of flame licked from the fieldstone fireplace, highlighting the blonde streaks in Lisa's hair and casting shadow dancers on the wall. Years of transient fieldwork had not interfered with her love of antiques. An upholstered Hepplewhite sofa seemed to clash oddly with the carved coconut heads and Hopi Indian kachina dolls scattered about. Outside, sleet tapped at the windows.

"Something like that," he replied finally.

"You're serious, aren't you?"

Steve stretched again, kneading the small of his back.

"I was," he said honestly. He thought about everything he had read during the last few hours. "Now

173

I'm not so sure I'm sure."

"Well, hey, I mean, don't give me a clue or anything!"

"I don't get it," mused Steve, ignoring her and riffling through his reading notes. "Some of it fits, but not the most important part."

He glanced at a thoroughly baffled Lisa. "You agree the effects of *malocchio* are objectively verifiable?"

"The effects of *belief* in it are verifiable, no question. They've been amply documented in the Levant, where belief is strongest. Also in Italy, France, Spain, South America, even in the Southwestern U.S. among Latino populations."

He nodded. "In other words, the more people believe, the more susceptible they are to its supposed effects?"

"Bingo, handsome one. Some of them believe so strongly they even come down with psychosomatic symptoms."

Steve frowned. "Then according to that theory, people who *aren't* particularly superstitious shouldn't be susceptible?"

"If you go with science, no. According to believers, anyone is susceptible."

"Some of your notes talk about envy and praise being the keys," he said, encouraging her.

"Envy is probably the reason why belief in the evil eye developed in the first place. Also the reason why it's man's oldest and most universal superstition. To experience envy is literally to 'see against' someone. The mechanics are simple: The fascinator or 'overlooker' speaks enthusiastic words of praise or con-gratulations; but he actually *wills* the opposite of what his words or gestures imply."

Steve was silent for a minute, recalling the Emper-or's spirited applause just before Sabrina Nash col-lapsed.

"Envy," he repeated. He glanced down at one of his notes. " 'The evil eye may blast any person or anything attractive enough to call forth a compli-ment.' "

Lisa watched him, her brow furrowing with curi-osity. "Exactly. Especially kids. In fact, in some places where belief was once powerful—Greece, Tur-key, Italy—it was customary to actually insult, or even spit on, the really good-looking kids. This showed you harbored no ill will. Actually, defensive traces survive even today when we fondly call a kid a rascal or a cute little devil."

" 'Slow, wasting diseases,' " he read from his notes. " 'Nervous or mental disorders for which there is no apparent explanation . . . exhaustion, restless-ness, loss of appetite . . . all manner of ill luck, disease, and death.' "

His glance drifted to a kachina on the mantle. Its bright black eyes gleamed back at him across the room.

"But its victims should be limited to believers only, if you accept the scientific theory. Only to those who attribute validity to the supposed fascinator. Un-less . . ."

Steve's voice trailed off. His eyes clouded with some vaguely formed hunch as the words from his father's diary drifted into memory: *An unnatural ability is being augmented by an unnatural hatred.*

"Unless," he finally resumed, "a fascinator with, say, some very real hypnotic prowess has found some way to . . . augment, to amplify that ability so that a predisposing belief is no longer necessary in victims?"

Steve recalled an article he'd read earlier about fascinators being distinguished by their eyes. They were always somehow different. Squint eyes, eyebrows that knit together, eyes of two different colors . . .

"That fits too," he muttered to himself, recalling the Emperor's shaggy, silver-white brows that formed a single line. He had never gotten close enough to actually see the old man's eye color. He resolved to look.

"That does it." Lisa finished her drink and, somewhat unsteadily, rose to her feet. "In the interest of seducing you, I've been willing to keep my mouth shut. I'm still interested in seducing you. But I confess, all this intrigue has finally gotten to me. What in the hell is going on?"

All night long Steve had been vacillating between a vague, growing sense of dread and the conviction that he was making an utter fool of himself. Her question, bald and demanding, forced him to confront those serious self-doubts.

"I'll tell you," he hedged, "but not tonight. Let me spend some time tomorrow with the Hoyt-Stillman collection, all right?"

"Okay," she agreed. "I'm not all that eager to hear

about the beautiful damsel part anyway."

She crossed to his chair, moved behind him, encircled him with her arms, and leaned against him. The back of his neck rested in the silky hollow between her breasts. Her breath was warm and moist on his eyelids when she kissed them shut.

"You know," she said softly, massaging his pectorals in slow circles, "you should have been a cowboy, grown up riding the high lonesome. You *like* women, all right, and you sure know how to make us happy in bed. But you just don't *need* us, do you?"

Steve tried for his best John Wayne, but it was difficult to pull off now that sudden desire was tightening his throat. "Stretchin' the blanket a mite, ain'tcha, ma'am?"

"I've been good all night," she persisted. "Haven't scared you with messy talk about commitment. Now you have to reward me."

She shucked out of the velour wrapper and slipped, sleek and naked, into his lap. Lisa took one of his hands and guided it to the warm delta between her legs.

"Feel that, cowboy?" she whispered. "I got all wet thinking about us making love right here in the chair."

"No fair," he groaned, his fingers causing lapping noises as they cossetted her love nest. "I was planning on being good tonight."

"You *better* be."

She ignored his weak protest and fumbled his belt loose, then tugged at the zipper to free his straining erection.

"Go inside me!" she pleaded. She spraddled her long legs around his thighs and gripped him, finding the perfect angle. "Please, lover? I need to feel you inside me. . . ."

Heat flowed over him, heralding the mindless oblivion of primal pleasure as their hips found the instinctive rhythm of sex. But even as they thrashed and writhed toward their first greedy orgasm, Steve was aware of the staring black eyes of the kachina on the mantle, watching them.

Much later, entwined with Lisa in a naked tangle of arms and legs in her shadow-mottled water bed, Steve dreamed.

He saw haunting white masks, one of them transforming into Corinne's face twisted in a scream. And like the clue to it all, the gray weathered door of that shack swinging open with a groan of rusted hinges. He could see nothing in the shadowy-cave depths beyond the door.

Nothing but darkness. Until, heart scampering, he stepped further into the shack and the door thumped shut behind him, triggering the brittle, cackling laughter of the foul hell hag who lurked within, waiting just for him.

Chapter 20

On the afternoon Steve was due back from Michigan, Corinne closed the sidewalk studio early and returned to her apartment to nurse a throbbing headache.

One good look at herself in the triple mirrors of the vanity and she made up her mind. She was going to bed, and to hell with everything else.

The plum-tinted half circles under her eyes alarmed her. And the sclera of each eyeball was covered with a crackleware network of tiny red blood vessels. She could thank nausea for that, she thought grimly. She couldn't remember the last day she'd gotten through without vomiting.

What's wrong? her mind demanded again, as if perhaps her body were harboring some secret of its own. She had already considered and reconsidered and mulled the possibilities to the point of frustrated tears. The student health clinic gave her a thumbs-up. She was relatively conscientious about her diet. Vitamins? Maybe she should talk to that girl in her class who was into macrobiotics and nutrition, what was her name? Lynette Boardman. Or could it be some bacteria in the tap water? More and more people claimed city water was far too polluted to drink.

Desperately grasping at straws, she rose from the vanity, stepped around the shoji screen, and went into the kitchenette. A small chalkboard hung from a nail above the formica counter. She picked up a nubbin of chalk and wrote: GET BOTTLED WATER.

As she laid the chalk back down, she felt another spasm of pain, like tacks being pressed into her temples. She paused, wincing. A moment later the pain eased slightly, and she suddenly thought: *Have you really considered everything?*

Jettatore . . . carrier of the evil eye.

A prickling blush crept up her neck. She glanced at the gold-framed photo sharing the wall beside her Council of the Arts Award.

Jettatore, her parents seemed to whisper to her.

God, didn't she have enough hang-ups without adding paranoia to the list? Corinne reminded herself again, with bitter conviction, that she had trapped herself in a vicious circle by looking up that word. Believing in it would perhaps explain her ailments, but it would also make her doubt her own sanity. *Not* believing left her back at square one, in the dark.

In the dark . . .

Unaware she was doing it, she reached for the switch beside her and flipped the overhead light on. An observer would have found the fact curious, considering it was mid-afternoon and the jalousies were thrown wide to reveal bright blue slabs of sky.

Only then did Corinne remember. She had wasted so much time last Wednesday at the library, comparing encyclopedia articles on the "evil eye," that she had completely forgotten her original purpose of researching Katerina Zverkov. She resolved to do it as soon as she felt better.

But right now she wanted nothing more than sweet oblivion, a long dip in that River Lethe known as sleep. She was nearly exhausted, pure and simple, and instinct was warning her to open a psychological release valve. The bizarre paranoia wouldn't go away until her health improved. One was the needle, the other the thread, and she was using both to sew her own straitjacket.

Which brought up the problem of Steve and tonight's date.

She was sure it was just one more ridiculous manifestation of her insecurity these days, but she had interpreted his sudden trip as a personal slight. Men were as fickle as women. Maybe he had decided a sure thing was better than gambling on some spacey klutz who was starting to look as weird as she acted.

To hell with him, whispered a persuasive inner self who startled her. *You're an artist! He's just one more horny male sniffing around.* . . .

A few minutes later she slipped a short note into his mailbox, begging off for tonight, and returned to her apartment. Incredibly, the brief trek up and down two flights of steps had sapped her of her strength. At least her headache was easing. Now she felt only the dull-throbbing memory of pain.

She tugged the phone cord out of its jack, stripped, and slipped into her long knit sleepshirt. Despite the waves of exhaustion threatening to swamp her, she remembered her bogeyman check with the tennis ball. Only when it rolled smoothly under the big brass bed and bounced safely off the wall did she slip between the sheets.

Corinne had almost surrendered herself to sleep when the abrupt thought jolted her wide awake: *You left only one light burning.*

She tried to let it slide this time. But it might be dark when she woke up. Especially, she thought, if that lone lightbulb burned out.

Too tired to berate herself, she rolled out of bed and crossed to her work table, turning on the tensor lamp. The shoji screen would mute enough of its glow to let her sleep. On a sudden impulse she also closed the French doors. It was getting cooler as the afternoon waned.

She cast one sleepy glance toward the gas space heater by the bathroom door. But already her lids felt weighted down with coins, and she was lucky to make it back to bed before sleep overtook her.

Steve frowned, reading the curt note a second time:

Sorry, but I don't feel well today. I'll have to cancel out for tonight. C.

He glanced next door at his neighbor's rose stucco apartment building. Redbrick steps led to a solid oak door with a diamond pane. Flanking the door were two orange trees in wooden tubs.

Cancel out. No mention of calling, he thought. No "welcome home, how was the trip?" As if she were cooling out toward him?

Lost in reflection, he plucked the mail out of the box, hoisted his Samsonite, and climbed the narrow wooden stairs that ended at his third-floor apartment. Inside, he threw his suitcase on the bed and popped a compact disc into the player. Then he showered, shaved, and changed into clean clothes. Feeling halfway human again, he paused near the phone and debated calling Corinne.

No, he finally decided. If she really didn't feel well, she might be in bed. And if she had lied, as he suspected, then what would calling her accomplish—besides making him feel like he was groveling?

Despite this compelling logic, he lifted the handset and punched her number into it. A rude busy signal rewarded his effort.

He hung up and glanced at his watch. It was almost six. Breaux had said he would be at the Ragin' Cajun tonight. Steve decided to grab dinner somewhere, then look him up.

He waited five minutes and tried Corinne's number again. Still busy. Frowning again, he hung up. Outside, he paused in the deepening shadows to glance at the silent front of her building. His eyes lifted toward Corinne's balcony. Light spilled out the uncurtained French doors, bathing the pots of bright zinnias and jonquils.

He squinted slightly as he tried to figure out what looked different tonight.

Finally, unable to pinpoint what it was, he crossed Decatur and merged with the neon darkness of the night.

C. J. Guidry raised five and Breaux slapped hands with him. "W'assappenin', old sleuth? How you makin' it?"

"Same shit, different day, cap," Breaux replied.

Without asking, Guidry drew a foaming schooner and plunked it down on a bar napkin. Breaux eased onto his usual stool at the end of the bar. Nearby, a sales type in an ill-fitting toupee was wolfing down boiled crayfish and bitching to a waitress about the Saints' lousy passing game.

The detective's random gaze ended at the Mardi Gras countdown calendar hanging on the wall between the dartboards: Ten more days until Fat Tuesday.

He felt a slight stirring of belly flies.

(*Something was wrong with his voice, the way he looked at her. . . .*)

"What the hell you moonin' about?" demanded Guidry. He planted two beefy elbows on the bar in front of him. "Old lady cut you off?"

Breaux gave him a pitying glance. "No woman has *that* much willpower."

Guidry laughed with derision. "Don't blow smoke up my ass, pilgrim!" He lowered his voice and added confidentially, "If some sweet thang begged you to slip her six inches, you'd have to fuck her twice."

Breaux eyed his chum's expansive girth. "Least I

can assume the missionary without incurring a man-slaughter rap."

"The bigger the cushion, the sweeter the pushin', coonass."

C. J. slapped his belly proudly and moved down the bar, dealing out bright foil ashtrays shaped like alligators. The waitress, bored by the toupeed sales-man's bar-stool quarterbacking, wandered over to the Wurlitzer and fed it some change. Otis Red-ding's "Dock of the Bay" throbbed to life. Once again Breaux let his gaze wander to the Fat Tuesday countdown calendar. He was still staring at it when a strong hand gripped his shoulder.

"Buy me a drink," Jernigan greeted him, "and I'll tell you one hell of a story."

Chapter 21

"You're on," replied Breaux. He caught C. J.'s eye and held up two fingers. "But let me tell *you* one first."

He started by bluntly stating his conclusion that someone in the NOPD had developed deliberate myopia concerning the deaths of Robert Jernigan and Dale McGinnis. He summed up the main points from his check of the death records — the unusual fact that the Chief of Police himself had signed both reports; the failure to initiate a routine homicide probe; the unlikelihood that McGinnis, a former Navy SEAL, would die accidentally on a river as placid as the Pearl.

"I guess maybe Dad mentioned he was in the service," mused Steve, watching Breaux closely. "He never said he was a commando. You ruled out the weather factor?"

"I checked. Some heavy rain, but no flooding. The rivers were normal."

Breaux explained the additional problem of the Medical Examiner's note concerning the type of

186

fracture found in the senior Jernigan's skull.

"No one fact by itself amounts to much," Breaux concluded. "But now I tend to agree with you. The whole thing just won't spend."

Breaux knuckled some foam off his salt 'n' pepper mustache. "What I'd like," he said thoughtfully, "is a chance to grill Pearlman."

"Pearlman? Clinton Pearlman, the politico?"

Breaux nodded. "He was the chief then, signed the reports."

Both men were silent for a minute, each alone with his thoughts. Finally Breaux reminded him: "I bought you that drink."

It was Steve's turn to nod. The two men had been tiptoeing around it for over a week now. It was time to drag the word out into the open.

"What would you say," he began slowly, "if I told you—seriously—that I left town to visit a folklorist who specializes in the study of the so-called evil eye?"

Breaux's face remained politely impassive. But something like relief glimmered for a moment in his eyes.

"I'd say two things," he replied. "May I buy you another drink, and please keep talking."

Steve acquiesced to both suggestions. He summed up the reasons for his suspicions about the Emperor, emphasizing the incredible odds against chancing onto the scene of three separate, probably related deaths. He described the technique as Lisa had, wherein enthusiastic praise or approval disguised a more insidious intent. Steve also mentioned the well-documented evidence for the efficacy of "overlooking." He concluded by admitting he was convinced the Emperor was obsessed by, and constantly watching, Corinne. But Steve stopped short of alluding to his latest suspicion, which was still embryonic.

"There's some whopping holes in the theory," he conceded. "For one, why would non-believers be susceptible, assuming they even knew or suspected that the Emperor was a . . . fascinator?"

Saying the word made him feel foolish. Breaux, however, looked anything but skeptical. He, in turn, ran through developments at his end, beginning with the Medical Examiner's report that cause of death was indeterminate for Jeanette Manders and the Holman child.

Breaux met his eye. "The first time we kicked this around? You mentioned feeling something. Something hard to describe, but real?"

Steve nodded once, waiting for more.

"Sheila Holman described it in almost the same words."

Breaux paused and glanced away. Steve followed his eyes and saw he was watching the Mardi Gras countdown calendar again.

Ten days . . .

"This is nuts," the cop muttered, but without conviction. He looked at Steve again.

"I've *almost* got enough to at least approach the precinct captain. Almost. But, Jesus, I'd be staking my retirement bennies on it. How would I explain being able to do all this extra legwork while still babysitting the CBD? I need something specific, not just a string of impressive coincidences. Since

188

the parade accident the day you left, the public-
relations situation is especially hairy. Right now the
nail that sticks up gets hammered down. And
they'll flatten me quick if I raise a threat to Mardi
Gras tourism."

"What parade accident?"

"Relax. I thought about that too. This was just a
particularly nasty but routine incident. Apparently
some asshole spooked a horse into the crowd. A
teenage girl was killed and two others hurt."

Both men nursed their beer for a minute in silence.

Breaux said, "Tell me more about your lady
friend Corinne. I already know she's pretty. What
do you mean, something's happening to her?"

Steve opened his mouth to speak, abruptly pausing as something occurred to him. He glanced toward the pay phone by the cigarette machine, then
stood up and fished a quarter out of his pocket.

"Excuse me a minute," he told Breaux.

He tried Corinne's number. Again he received an
intermittent busy signal. Steve hung up slowly, staring at his distorted reflection in the chrome panel
of the telephone. When Breaux had mentioned Corinne, Steve finally realized what had bothered him
earlier as he glanced up at her balcony: The French
doors were closed. She always left them open, even
when it was cooler than today.

Why did that seem so important? It wasn't, he
admitted while returning to his seat. But nonetheless a premonitory *frisson* tingled along his spine in
icy pinpricks.

"Have another drink," he told Breaux. "I'll be

189

back."

Steve waited impatiently for a break in traffic, then jogged across Canal and into the gloomy shadow of the U.S. Custom House. He rounded the corner and followed Decatur near the waterfront, weaving his way among the dawdling tourists who still hadn't converged on Bourbon Street for the night. The air was thick with a dank humidity that left blurry gold halos around the streetlights.

It was eight blocks to Corinne's building. He was halfway there, almost abreast of the Jackson Brewery, when he spotted the Emperor hurrying toward Canal on the opposite sidewalk.

Impulse, more than anything else, sent Steve angling across the street.

The Emperor didn't spot the younger man until it was almost too late to avoid a collision. He started to duck around him, but Steve deftly sidestepped, cutting him off.

A streetlight glowed directly overhead. For a moment the pasty-faced mime stared into Steve's eyes — long enough for the latter to notice that his left eye was brown, the right blue.

And long enough to feel as if he'd just peeked into the putrid soul of some vile, reptilian basilisk.

The Emperor tried to duck around him again. Steve gripped one of his elbows.

"Who *are* you?" Steve demanded. "What are you up to?"

Again their eyes met. For a fleeting millisecond, staring into those piercing, mismatched eyes, Steve lost the last vestige of his skepticism. At that moment, he was sure it was true. All of it was true. . . .

"Turn the old dude loose, jack, or you're gonna have some kneecap problems."

Steve spun around. A trio of merchant marines stood glaring at him. The spokesman was burly and belligerent-looking, with at least three inches and fifty pounds on Steve.

The old mime wrestled out of his grip and scuttled away.

Jesus, screamed the revived skeptic in Steve. *What the hell are you doing?*

Corinne, urged the believer in him. *He's been watching Corinne. . . .*

"—omebody closer to your own age, asswipe?" he heard the sailor demand.

But Steve executed an abrupt about-face and hurried along on the sidewalk, oblivious to the derisive shouts behind him.

The front entrance was not locked until eleven P.M. After buzzing her number with no success, Steve let himself in.

The ground floor was well lit but silent, the dead silence of a house where no human has lived for years. Bulbs in frosted-glass and brass fixtures lined both walls of the narrow hallway. Somebody's ten-speed was chained to the steam radiator at the end of the hall.

There's a woman involved in all of this, isn't there?

The stairwell was just inside the door. Steve took the steps two at a time, dread heavy in his stomach.

You're rescuing a beautiful young damsel who's in the clutches of some sinister Svengali.

The second floor was also well lit and mausoleum still. Faintly, at the end of the hall, Steve could hear a TV set yammering away. Hearing it somehow comforted him and dispelled the illusion that the house was devoid of humanity.

Slow, wasting diseases . . . nervous or mental disorders for which there is no apparent explanation . . . all manner of ill luck, disease, and death . . .

Steve smelled it as soon as he reached her landing, and the heavy odor shocked him to the core of his soul.

Her door was locked. But now he imagined he could hear the serpentine hiss of the escaping gas inside.

"Corinne!"

He hunkered down and slammed his shoulder into the door, feeling more like he was harrowing hell than breaking into an apartment.

Chapter 22

"Cannibals," said Professor Eric Winters, "eat their victims' hearts, believing that they are also thus ingesting their courage. I see a few of you are wincing? Of course. Others are smiling condescendingly at such primitive quaintness. But actually, cannibals have the right idea—only the wrong organ. And there are more . . . efficient ways of subsuming the attributes of others."

Winters paused, his brilliant eyes sweeping the classroom like cobalt beacons.

A few of the students had noticed something different about Winters this morning. He was less caustic, more enthused. He seemed wired, strung out, like a manic riding the last moments of a high. So far today his lecture had been riveting. Even the normally disgruntled Donald Carr forgave him for wandering so far afield this morning. Carr took in the rumpled suit and scratchy cheeks, and wondered if the tightass had actually gone out and enjoyed some carnival revelry over the weekend.

"Why do I mention cannibals?" Winters bellowed

rhetorically, and the peroxide blonde in the last row giggled nervously. "First, let me remind you of our key research question this semester. Namely, what is the true capacity of the human brain? We already know that most researchers feel the brain is grossly underutilized."

He caught Carr's eye and held it, adding, *"We* . . . also agreed to define 'mental activity' beyond the parameters of a standard IQ test—a new definition which includes so-called psychic abilities. We concluded by hypothesizing a wonder drug of the mind: MBM or Maximum Beta Mode, named after the electrical frequency at which our brains perform at an intellectual—I use that word loosely— peak."

Carr sighed his here-we-go-again sigh and glanced away.

"Back to cannibalism," said Winters, briskly rubbing his hands together and leering with mock dementia. It was the first time they had ever seen him ham it up, and the class loved it. When the laughter subsided, Winters continued.

"Consider this. About ten years ago a graduate student in chemistry—let's call him Larry and his college State U.—came across a professional article which fascinated him. In this article, two respected biochemists summed up an experiment in chemical-learning theory. They had constructed a special aquarium complete with a complicated maze, then stocked it with fifty goldfish that had never encountered the maze. For several hours the goldfish avoided the maze altogether. Then, slowly, one by one, they ventured into it, each requiring several more hours before it had learned the maze sufficiently to swim quickly through."

Winters paused rhetorically, gazing out the classroom window into the slate-gray sky over the lake.

"However," Winters resumed, "it was the next stage of the experiment which truly intrigued Larry. Our researchers removed the goldfish and extracted, from the brain of each, the various chemicals involved in synapse or transmission of neural impulses. These chemicals were then injected directly into the cortices of another fifty goldfish that had never encountered the complicated maze. And—*mirabile dictu!*—the new batch of goldfish promptly proceeded to negotiate the maze without the long hours of acclimation and learning."

Winters smiled. His blue eyes swept the class again.

"Now, the point of all this was not lost on Larry. True, he was not exactly Rhodes Scholar material. But the essential point was clear to him. 'Learning' is accompanied by chemical equivalents in the brain, and those chemicals—and thus, the skills they correspond to—can be introduced *from another brain.*"

The class was now an enthralled audience. Not one pen moved. Carr, who already glimpsed the gruesome outcome of this apparent digression, felt the hair on his forearms tingle.

Winters met his eyes, smiled cryptically, then glanced away.

"Unfortunately, Larry was also as mad as a

March hare. Two things were happening to him simultaneously. First, he was developing a fanatical admiration for a certain professor of calculus whose brilliance was known throughout the academic community. *And* he was failing out of graduate school, in part because his own math skills were mediocre at best. Larry lost sleep, quit eating properly, began to abuse drugs and alcohol. Naturally this only exacerbated his mental disorder — as did his obsession with a topic that had fascinated him since doing a report on it in grade school. . . ."

His voice trailed off. He caught Carr's eye again. Winters smiled. "And what *was* that topic, do you suppose, Mr. Carr?"

Carr, who had missed breakfast that morning, felt his stomach do a quick series of flutters. "Cannibalism, sir?"

"Precisely. Cannibalism."

Winters surveyed the rest of the class. "I see from your shocked faces that most of you have anticipated our grisly denoument. Larry, now thoroughly insane, decides that the key to his academic survival is the brain of his calculus professor — or more precisely, the essential chemicals associated with said professor's celebrated mathematical ability. Larry lacks the precise anatomical knowledge to know exactly where such chemicals would be located — an isolated region in the cerebral hemisphere of the forebrain. But his knowledge of cannibalistic belief renders such distinctions unnecessary. And after all, digestion *is* a process of

. . . absorption. At any rate, one night he waylays the professor, kills him, and crudely extracts his brain. Over the next week, part by unpalatable part, he devours nearly 75% of the brain before he is apprehended by police."

The blonde in the back row looked like she needed a courtesy bag. Several students exchanged incredulous glances.

"Is this *true?*" one of them finally ventured.

"See me after class," Winters promptly responded, "and I'll give you the relevant journal citations. It was quite a *cause celèbre* in the academic world."

Another student asked, "Where is this guy today? Wall Street?"

Laughter rippled through the class. Winters smiled his tight little smile.

"Today he is in a mental institution in Chicago. He's officially classified as a schizophrenic of average IQ. Yet he can multiply two fifteen-figure numbers in his head, or calculate the square root of a sixty-figure number in seconds."

The class sat in shocked silence. Finally, someone laughed. A second person then decided the prof was having them on royally and joined in the laughter. Within seconds the room was a chorus of laughter and jeers as students razzed those next to them for being such suckers.

Only Carr refrained from joining in. His eyes met those of Winters. He saw something in their deep blue depths that made his back break out in sweat. When the noise subsided, he spoke up.

"Doctor Winters—that list I left on your desk? Last time I spoke with you, you said we could also discuss some . . . pragmatic topics related to our career goals?"

Winters smiled with mock deference and nodded briskly. "Of course, Mr. Carr, of course. So tell us—what's eating you?"

The class erupted again. Winters grinned triumphantly, watching pink roses suddenly blossom in Carr's cheeks.

Chapter 23

By early afternoon huge gray clouds had stacked up like boulders on the southern horizon. But the sky over the lake was lambent with thinly veiled sunshine. For the first time in a week, Tree's "Punch-a-train Express" made the crossing toward north shore and the marina near the mouth of the East Pearl River.

The lake was moderately choppy. Tree and Steve glimpsed only a few other boats, rising and dipping between swells, until they finally spotted the barely visible cluster of cabanas marking the distant shore. Ten minutes later, Tree docked next to the clinker-built dinghy.

"That's one kick-in-de-butt frown you wore all the way over," remarked Tree as they lugged the trawling motor down from the boathouse.

Steve nodded. "Female problems."

Tree flashed his quick gap-toothed grin. "Hot flashes?"

They both laughed, almost dropping the motor. The moment seemed to ease the burden of gloomy thoughts Steve had been strapped with since Saturday night when he broke into Corinne's apartment. He'd found her—alive—but rendered semiconscious from gas fumes—and dragged her onto the landing. Later she'd insisted it had been an accident . . . something about how she was considering turning on the gas when she fell asleep, and must have acted on the thought.

Possible, thought Steve as they mounted the small outboard. Still, hadn't the Emperor been racing away from her neighborhood at the same time?

Correlation, he reminded himself almost wearily, *is not causation.*

An hour later the same warring thoughts still plagued him as the two men negotiated the sluggish bayou zigzagging its way through the lush wild grotto of Honey Island Swamp. Once again the split-slab shack surprised them by suddenly springing into view all at once as they rounded the sharp bend just before it.

Tree killed the engine. A heavy silence fell over them, broken only by the shrill conversation of birds and the rhythmic, deep-throated croaking of frogs.

The shack perched on its hummock, a huge gray toad squatting against the dense curtain of green behind it.

"You ax me," said Tree, stepping ashore behind Steve, "I think you otta check it out. Won't be shit to pry that Jax sign off the window."

Steve nodded in agreement. "If it's still deserted, let's do it."

A few seconds later, however he spotted proof that the shack had recently been visited. Hard rains during the past week had left a muddy swale in front of the door. Someone had thrown plywood duckboards down across the muck.

The two men exchanged glances. Tree shrugged.

"Anybody home?" Steve shouted.

His words were immediately absorbed by the dank growth surrounding them.

Steve moved closer to the duckboards and squatted on his heels. Divots of dried mud caked one edge of a plank where someone had obviously scraped his shoes before going inside. Steve found several prints in the soft ground between the duckboards and the nearest corner of the shack, prints made by hobnailed boots. He squatted again and felt the edge of one of the depressions, as crusted and dry as a dead stick. At least a couple days old.

"Brah!"

Tree was examining something near the same corner of the shack where the footprints disappeared into the thick saw grass. Steve joined him, glancing toward the spot where Tree's finger was pointing. Someone had poked a forked stick into the dirt. Stretched in a straight line behind it, its chiseled white skull propped in the Y of the stick, was the skeleton of a water moccasin. The hollow eye sockets gazed out over the bayou with atavistic patience and cunning.

"It's a witch-eye," explained Tree, reading the incomprehension in his friend's puzzled stare. "More petro cult jive."

He stood back up and pointed out across the sluggish brown water.

"Witch-eye spoze to protect a house from attack by water. Whoever put it there shurnuf knows the old stories about this swamp. Everybody claims the Pearl is a ha'nted river from the old days of Jean Lafitte. Bunch of Spanish settlers got surrounded by redskins real near here. They knew the Indians would torture 'm bad, so the whole regiment marched into the water to fife-and-drum music, drowned to the last man. Now people claims you can hear music at certain spots, comin' from underwater."

Tree glanced at Steve. Then he shifted his gaze to the shack and continued. "None of my business, but I still say this is somebody wants people to *think* he's onto *vaudau*. Dunno what you're lookin' for, cap, and I ain't gone ask. But I'll be happy to tear that sign off the window for you."

Steve tried the door, again peeked through the chinks of the hinges, but to no avail.

"No," he finally decided. "Somebody was here, and there's a good chance that same somebody is the legitimate owner. But this is his last chance. Next time I'm going inside, come hell or high water."

"You're the skipper. Me, I'd go in now."

"Why?"

Tree flashed his grin. "Cause I'm nosy, that's why, and I wonder what'n the fuck you're looking for so hard. First I thought it was a woman. But no woman worth the money you're shucking out would live in *that* piece of shit."

Tree nodded toward the shack, then drifted out back toward the burning barrel.

Again Steve moved closer to the weathered gray surface of the door. He reached out, touched the wood with his fingertips.

(*haunting white faces, one of them transforming into Corinne's face twisted into a scream*)

The door refused to budge. But now, as before, Steve felt a vaguely pernicious tinge in the air, like charged ions.

He turned around. Across the bayou, the drooping oaks on the far bank seemed like simian arms reaching for him across the water. The shrill, steady hum of insects, the rusted croaking of frogs amplified until they were needlepoints pricking his eardrums.

Steve didn't realize he was doing his fist-tightening exercises until—at some indefinable point—he felt someone watching him.

His palms broke out in a sweat.

He turned to see Tree staring at him.

"Where yat?" his friend asked uncertainly. He eyed Steve's outstretched arms curiously.

Steve nodded toward the shack. "We'll wait till next time. But you're right to be curious. There's something bizarre inside there," he said with conviction.

After dinner Steve graded a stack of student lab manuals, then tried to call Corinne. There was no answer. Alarm flared up briefly within him, and he considered going next door.

But no. She'd claimed that what happened Saturday evening was an accident. He longed to give her the benefit of the doubt, especially as the two alternative explanations made for a no-win predicament. Either she was suicidal, or his bizarre suspicions about the Emperor were justified.

So instead he turned the night over to Taj Mahal and a glass of German hock. Pulling on a sweater against the damp early evening chill, he moved out to the balcony and stretched out in a canvas chaise longue. He sipped the wine and tried to impose some order on the confused riot of his thoughts.

Overriding everything was his growing hunch that, somehow, some way, the two threads were related. His search to solve the mystery of his father's death could be connected to whatever it was that was visiting unholy terror on the Crescent City. Exactly how, he couldn't even begin to speculate. Nor was he close to being convinced that he was right. After all, he reasoned, what single shred of *proof* did he have that this feeling was not just some chimera, some monstrous offspring of his overwrought nerves? Every fiber of his scientific being cried out for Verifiable Data.

Instead, he was becoming practically obsessed with a weird old man and a spooky shack.

For a moment, unbidden, he again saw Winters's face as it had looked this morning. What was it that troubled him about it? But a new stampede of images and thoughts soon drove the question from

204

his mind.

The hock started to work its magic: He felt his muscles loosening, the pace of his thoughts relaxing. He grew heavier as he sank into the chair. Behind the wide-open French doors, an overhead fan with cane-inlaid blades revolved slowly, its shadow hypnotically caressing the bentwood chairs, Persian rugs, and varnished hardwood floors.

Traffic noise receded to an airy murmur. Overhead, the steel sky darkened toward magenta. The damp air was laced with whiffs of seafood and mimosa. All of it—sound, sight, smell—synthesized in a sensory meltdown as the lonesome, husky notes of a saxophone escaped into the night around him.

His mind finally reached the plane where it was not the slave of external stimuli. *Don't you understand what's happening?* demanded the voice of innermost being. *What's happening is that—*

He started, his wine glass shattering on the floor of the balcony, when the doorbell chimed.

Cursing the interruption, Steve stepped carefully around the shards of glass and back into the apartment. He swung past the stereo to turn the music down a tad, then opened the hallway door.

"Care to join me?" Corinne said, greeting him, proffering two bottles of Guinness Stout. "Or is this a bad time to debauch?"

She was vulnerably pretty in a camisole blouse and cream-colored tiered skirt that offset the deep copper of her eyes. For a moment, before he replied, Steve fought down an impulse to kiss the delicate white hollow of her throat.

He stepped back, swinging the door wide.

"It *was* a bad time," he admitted. "Now it's getting better."

He took the bottles from her and excused himself, stepping into the kitchen to open them and pour the stout into tapering glasses. When he returned she was browsing through his music collection.

"So how're you feeling today?" he asked, handing her a glass.

"I still look like hell, but I feel a lot better."

He studied her face. There was more color to her cheeks, and the haggard pockets under her eyes were less puffy.

"If this is a glimpse of hell, I won't be wanting last rites."

She smiled. "I'm not *that* dearly won."

Their eyes held for a moment. A second later they each glanced self-consciously away. Steve swallowed with difficulty.

"I want to thank you again," said Corinne. "It's corny, but . . . you're my knight in shining armor. I still can't believe that I owe you my life."

Something inquisitive in his eyes prompted her to turn away.

"Steve, I've gone over and over everything in my mind. I *must* have turned that heater on in my sleep. The last thing I remember thinking was that it was getting nippy in my room."

He nodded. "I believe you. In fact, I wouldn't be surprised if it wasn't even your idea to do it."

He saw her shoulders stiffen. She set her glass on an end table, then turned to stare at him. "I don't get it."

"Neither do I," he said. "But let's start comparing some notes."

"About what?"

"Try 'About whom?' "

"All right, teacher. About whom?"

"The Emperor."

He watched one of her eyelids twitch. She paled slightly, crossed to a chair, sat down on the very edge of the cushion.

"I'm listening," she said quietly. Her voice was tight with barely suppressed emotion.

"He's been watching you," said Steve. It was not a question.

She nodded.

"What else do you know about him?" he asked.

Corinne concentrated for a moment. "I know that I don't like him. Everywhere I go, he's there. Sometimes he stares right at me. Usually, though, I'm just *aware* of him, you know? I couldn't prove he's watching me then, it's like he's looking . . . I don't know exactly, around me, or past me."

"What else?"

She dropped her eyes from Steve's. "Promise not to laugh?"

"Unfortunately—yes."

She told him about the elderly black woman who had made that vaguely familiar gesture while passing him in the street. Corinne's session with the encyclopedias had confirmed it to be a sign to ward off the fascinator's eye. By the time she finished explaining about the Italian tourist who called him *jettatore,* Steve's face was livid with emotion.

"You wondered too? So that makes *three* of us who kept our mouths shut?"

At her puzzled glance, he added, "I'll explain later. Listen. I never mentioned why I went to Ann Arbor, did I?"

"It was none of my business," she said lightly.

"Yes it was. I wish I'd told you sooner. I . . ."

He saw some deep-rooted fear suddenly flash in her eyes, and hesitated. She appeared a little better, yes, but she still looked peaked and sleep-starved. At that moment he considered the situation from her point of view. She was understandably close to the brink, and one careless move might push her over. He decided to gloss over it for now. She had a right to know, but he had an obligation to inform her in doses she could handle.

"I went to do some research along those same lines."

"And?"

"And I'll tell you more about it later. For now I just want you to do me a little favor."

Her voice softened. "I owe you more than a little one."

He grinned. "I kind of like having you in my debt."

"Maybe," she said, "collecting it will be even better?"

"Maybe."

His grin vanished, and once again he swallowed a hard lump in his throat. A brief flaring of groin warmth greeted her innuendo. "Much better, I'm sure," he amended.

"That favor?" she reminded him.

"Just this. Did you find the present I left for you?"

"*You* left it?"

He watched her slip one hand deep into a pocket of her skirt and emerge with a necklace twined around the fingers. It was chiefly red coral, with nickel-sized iron charms shaped like tusks evenly spaced around the necklace.

It was only a protection, Lisa had explained to him, not a cure. Protections could supposedly prevent or even temporarily reverse the effects of *malocchio*. But the victim remained susceptible. Only a full-blown cure stopped the influence permanently. Above all, it was essential that the suspected fascinator never see the protection. Knowledge of a protection was a key to thwarting it.

"It's . . . interesting," she told him. "Thank you."

"Yeah, I know it's not too elegant. But how 'bout indulging me and promising to wear it for awhile. Just for luck. And always wear it out of sight."

She glanced at him, curious. Corinne started to ask him something, abruptly decided against it. Instead, she lifted both hands behind her neck and fastened the necklace into place.

"Somehow," she said, "I suspect I'm not going to like what you have to tell me."

He said nothing.

She stood up, her eyes never leaving his face. "Will you please come over here?"

He did. She leaned up into his arms and pressed her soft warmth against him. They kissed, tasting each other hungrily.

"Would I be abusing my knight-in-shining-armor status," he said, his voice husky with wanting her, "if I invited you to stay the night?"

She smiled, slipping a hand into her pocket and coming back out with her toothbrush. "I thought you'd never ask."

But a few minutes later the smile faltered. Corinne looked hard into the gray-green depths of his eyes.

"I'm scared, Steve," she told him, recalling something that made her shudder. "I don't understand what's happening to me, and I'm just so scared. I don't want to die!"

Chapter 24

Dallas Jordan tapped the dottle out of his pipe and reloaded with a pinch of fresh Prince Albert. He listened attentively until his visitor had finished his request. Then he spoke.

"Political commercials? Straying a little out of your bailiwick, aren't you?"

Alan Breaux assumed the innocent face of a cherub. "Nothing human is foreign to me," he said piously.

Jordan made a farting noise with his lips, his intelligent, shrewd eyes watching the cop closely. "Why?" he persisted, curiously. "What's in the pipeline?"

"I promise," Breaux said. "You'll be the first reporter to know, if and when there's anything to know."

"Deal. But I'm warning you. . . ."

Jordan paused to fire up his meerschaum. He glanced toward the City Editor's desk, and lowered his voice. "Hell hath no fury like a teed-off news-hawk. Don't forget me, baby."

After graduating from Dillard University, the young black whiz-kid's political acumen and incisive humor had quickly catapaulted him to the top among observers of the state's political scene. The journalist still found time for the occasional hard-news feature, and had once teamed up with Breaux to expose a million-dollar health-care scam preying on Social Security recipients. Now he scented another potential scoop.

"Count yourself lucky if I do stiff you," Breaux assured him.

"That bad, hanh? Better and better. C'mon."

Jordan led him back out to the main lobby, then down a flight of tiled steps.

"How's the book coming along?" said Breaux.

"It's not a book until it's published. The sticky wicket right now is the title. What else can you call a study of Louisiana politics, besides *Sewer Gumbo?* My agent says that's an 'off-putting' title."

The steps led to a set of double doors marked LIBRARY AND ARCHIVES, EMPLOYEES ONLY. Inside, a middle-aged woman with her gray hair in finger waves sat at a desk reading a paperback. One long wall was lined with reference books, the other with gunmetal filing cabinets. Along the shorter back wall were several microform projectors and a 25" color TV crowned by a wireless remote VCR.

The librarian smiled. "Good day, Mr. Jordan."

"Top of the morning to you, Alice. Look up a video for me, darlin'?"

While she located the tape, Jordan turned to

Breaux. "We file copies of all political spots. Pearlman, huh? There's one mediocre man who really thinks he's hot shit. That's why he was a lousy Chief of Police. Good cops can be dumb, but they can't be ambitious."

"I like you too, desk jockey."

"You?" Jordan grinned. "Whoever said *you* were a good cop, white boy?"

"My wife thinks I've got potential."

"I've met Cindy, remember? Frankly, she deserves better."

Before Breaux could return the insult, Alice returned with a video cassette and handed it to Jordan.

" 'The Eyes of Louisiana,' " Jordan read, leading the way toward the TV at the back. "Oh, yeah. I remember this baby, all right. In just one month of saturation, it helped move Pearlman from dark-horse status to a whopping sixty-two percent of the vote. Even card-carrying Democrats who'd never violated party loyalty before swung over to him."

Jordan laid his pipe aside and popped the cassette into the VCR. They viewed the brief spot several times. Breaux, especially, watched the screen carefully.

The message was just as he'd remembered it. Everyday people streamed across the busy intersection of Magazine and Poydras in downtown New Orleans. An unctuous voice-over quickly cataloged the asininities and fopperies and outright lawlessness of Pearlman's competitors. Meantime, the screen darkened until only the pedestrians' eyes

213

were visible moving with disembodied ghostliness across the screen. They too faded out, until only one set of piercing blue eyes remained.

"The eyes of Louisiana are on the future," urged the sonorous voice while the eyes stared outward, unblinking. "Vote Clinton J. Pearlman, State Representative."

"You agree it's a successful spot?" said Breaux after Jordan finally ejected the cassette.

"Does Dolly Parton sleep on her back? Damn straight it was successful. That was the only ad he ran during the last month of the campaign."

"Why does it work? Because it's hypnotic?"

Jordan shrugged. "Hard to say. Almost all advertising is hypnotic in some way. Actually, from a technical standpoint it's a fairly simple spot. I'd say the success is in the bald directness of the appeal. Ad moguls spend millions on subliminals and 'high concept' approaches until finally Joe Viewer is inured to all of it. This caught them off guard. Some faceless, omnipotent voice is saying, 'Look at me! Just do what I tell you and piss on the gimcrackery.' It's comforting to a lot of people, man. Like being in the Army—no decisions. You get up each morning, you already know what you're gonna be wearing. No problems."

Breaux nodded thoughtfully. "Just skip all the psychologizing and tell me straight from the shoulder. Do you *personally* feel this ad has anything special going for it?"

"Personally?" said Jordan, speaking around the stem of his pipe as he stoked it back to life again.

"Personally, I think it's tripe. So are velveteen paintings, but they sell. No accounting for taste, *hombre*."

"No accounting," Breaux agreed distractedly. He added, "Who would've been in charge of producing this?"

"Probably Pearlman's campaign manager, working with a PR company."

"Who was his manager?"

"Some slick, button-down Yankee named Roger Gazaway. Last I heard he was in South America doing special consulting for Rand Corporation."

Breaux nodded. He stared at the cassette in Jordan's hand. "Any chance of getting a copy of that?"

"Good chance," said Jordan. "But tell me. Have you got Pearlman by the short and curlies on something?"

Breaux hesitated, trying to ignore the voice that nagged him: *You have nothing except insane speculations.*

"If what I have pans out," he replied finally, "consider your next book sold."

The morning was brilliant with spun-gold sunshine when Breaux emerged from the *Times-Picayune* building. Lost in worried reflection, he headed toward the multilevel parking garage on Canal where he'd left his car.

Once again doubt assailed him.

What, demanded that skeptical voice he had

215

never managed to shake, *are you looking for?*

But he couldn't say. He was caught in a maze, unable to see the next stage of his journey and blinded on all sides. But he had to grope forward and trust there would be a way out somewhere down the line.

Two costumed carnival revelers staggered past him, and Breaux stopped to glance around.

Only a week now until carnival season culminated in Fat Tuesday. The crowds were growing. Hotels were jammed, cabbies were smiling, and the souvenir shops were as busy as frontier cathouses on a Saturday night. The world's biggest free party was gearing up.

Watching the costumed drunks caper in the streets, Breaux thought: Christ knows, modern cities are already havens for psychopaths. The madness of Mardi Gras is like throwing down a welcome mat for every rubber-room candidate in the world. How do you monitor madness in a city of sanctioned insanity?

Breaux resumed the trek to his car, unable to quell the image of the Emperor vindictively wadding up a page from that Mardi Gras countdown calendar.

The cash register hadn't stopped ringing all morning. Corinne finished restocking one revolving rack of postcards, then started on the next one.

Nearby, a young couple were smothering laughter as they sorted through the bawdy T-shirts. Corinne saw the girl elbow her companion, showing him one that said, IF MAN WASN'T MEANT TO EAT PUSSY, WHY DID GOD MAKE IT LOOK LIKE A TACO? "I feel like dining a la Mexican tonight." he quipped back, and she slugged him on the arm.

A second later they both glanced over and caught Corinne eavesdropping. She flushed and returned to her task.

Busy jotting down stock-replacement numbers, she was startled when Maddy said conspiratorially, only inches from her ear, "I saw you and Steve having breakfast this morning at Tally Ho."

For a moment Maddy maintained her pretense of casual curiosity, as if it hardly mattered to *her* if Steve and Corinne had slept together last night. But Corinne knew she was itching for the torrid details. A second later a mischievous smile slipped past Maddy's composure. "You had quite an appetite, babe," she added with exaggerated innocence.

Mercifully, a customer approached the counter and Maddy left to ring her out. By the time she returned, Corinne had it together enough to warn her, *"Don't* say it, whatever it is, smartass!"

Maddy's big Nile-green eyes widened in self-righteous amazement. "But, puss, I was only gonna ask if the earth moved."

Corinne surprised her. "Several times," she confessed, flashing a grin, and Maddy beamed like a proud mother hearing baby's first words. Her glance dropped to Corinne's neck.

"What's this? Oh, babe—the coral's pretty, f'sure, but those metal thingamabob's're kinda

217

tacky."

Maddy slipped a finger under the necklace and lifted it out from under Corinne's blouse to examine it closer. "Where'd you get it?" she added.

"Present," said Corinne cryptically.

Early this morning, as they lay entwined in each other's arms, Steve had told her more about the strange necklace and its supposed protective effects. He had also filled her in on his research into *malocchio*. Never mind if it all sounded like something from *Elvira's Movie Macabre*. All she knew was that Steve had left the necklace with her on Saturday night, two days ago, and already she felt and looked better.

The fierce headaches had become only occasional dull throbbings. The nagging listlessness no longer plagued her. The chronic nausea was almost gone and the fatigue pouches under her eyes were now mere shadows. Even the klutziness seemed to have passed. So what if it *was* just some silly placebo trick? In fact her body was probably just rallying, as if it finally realized its responsibilities now that she had been selected to work with one of the country's finest sculptors. But she'd wear the necklace anyway, as she had promised Steve.

"Present, huh?" said Maddy dubiously. She examined it one last time. The bangles lining Maddy's arm clicked and clinked as she tucked the necklace under Corinne's blouse. "Oh, well. Maybe he has weird taste in jewelry, but he sure is cute."

Maddy hastened back to the register, where another queue was already forming.

He was sure *that,* all right, thought Corinne, busying herself with the stock again. He was a lot of things she liked. But he was also holding something back, something terribly important to him. If it was his business and his business alone, then fine. She had no desire to snoop through each and every nook of his personal life. It was just this incessant suspicion lately that whatever preoccupied him somehow touched her life too — touched it even more intimately than just romantically or sexually.

If nothing else, his saving her life had insured that.

Corinne glanced over her shoulder, checking the sidewalk out front. Nobody was watching her. She thought again about what Steve had told her. One finger rose to the necklace and made contact with a cool iron tusk.

Tuccari ferru, she thought, finding a guilty solace in the words.

Chapter 25

"Ma jolie!"

Startled, Corinne glanced across Decatur Street. Georges Lagaće waved at her. The old artist was carrying a sack of fresh vegetables home from the French Market.

She waved back. Corinne was about to continue on when something occurred to her. Instead, she crossed the street.

"Still interested in drawing my portrait?" she greeted him.

His countenance lit up. "What dream voice is this I am hearing?"

"Make you a deal. I'll pose for you—dressed," she added hastily, momentarily dulling the new-found gleam in his eyes. "In return, you tell me what you know about Katerina Zverkov."

The old French Canadian narrowed his eyes shrewdly. Finally he said, "My answer would be no, if I believed I could thus spare you from this unhealthy curiosity. But I see the fire which smolders in those oh-so-bee-yootiful eyes. You will find out without the help of old Georges, *non?* And he? He will lose the treasured portrait of *ma jolie!*"

He rolled his eyes tragically, then winked. "And so, to borrow an Americanism: Name the time, sweetheart."

"The sooner the better."

"In that case . . . shall we seize the moment?"

Corinne nodded. He glanced apologetically at his purchases.

"I live only a block from here. Would it be disrespectful if I invite you to my home for the portrait? *D'ailleurs,* we can talk better there."

Corinne agreed and fell in step with him. Georges rented the ground floor of a two-story lavender stucco on Chartres. He led her around to a covered veranda in back that served as his studio, then excused himself to go inside and put his groceries away.

Corinne glanced around. The "studio" was airy and bright, but looked more like a cheery waiting room than an artist's atelier. Mums in bright Japanese baskets dotted the tables and stands. Georges was into collecting miniature liquor bottles, and hundreds of them lined a tier of shelves along one wall. Another wall was a showcase for vintage advertising posters by Toulouse-Lautrec. But she saw very little of Georges's own work.

He must have gallery inside, she decided.

As if to confirm her supposition, he now returned carrying a framed drawing. Knowing Georges, Corinne had fully expected him to sheer deftly off the subject of Katerina. But now he handed her the drawing.

"She was a princess, *non?* Eyes that were sapphires, skin of wild honey. She graciously allowed me to do this."

The stunning beauty of the woman in the colored-pencil sketch actually took Corinne's breath away.

"You knew her?" she asked.

"*Knew* her? Pouf!"

Georges led Corinne to a cane-bottom love seat, then took his place in a canvas director's chair about five feet away. He opened a sketchbook and, crossing his legs, balanced it on one thigh. Georges worked quickly while he spoke, dividing his attention between Corinne and the likeness rapidly coming to life under his pen.

"We were the best of friends—not lovers, I regret to say. Katya unburdened her heart to me as she did to few others. We spent long hours working side by side, talking, practicing the English so new to both of us."

"Tell me about her," Corinne encouraged him.

Georges expelled a histrionic sigh. "*Ars longa, vita brevis,* eh? The best of her life has survived in her work. You, pretty one, must set your thoughts ever forward toward your own career, not on a tragic past which is not even your own."

He saw she was about to say something and raised his free hand, stopping her. "Yes, yes, I know—you're *curious.*"

Georges frowned, shook his head, and muttered something in French. He worked for a minute, the silence broken only by birds quarreling in the yard behind them.

"What would you like to know?" he said finally, his voice resigned.

"You said she was learning English. She wasn't born here?"

Georges shook his head. "She was born in Russia, although there is surely no record of this. Her father was a powerful official in the regime which came to power in the Bolshevik Revolution of 1917. Unfortunately, her mother was not her father's wife — she was his mistress. You must understand, this was a time of even greater moral hypocrisy than one finds today in Russia. A Bolshevik, a moral paragon for the sacred proletariat, could not admit to the bourgeois decadence of a mistress! The woman was sent abroad to give birth. Katya and her twin brother were born in Rome."

"Twin brother?"

"Shh," said Georges, "do not look quite so directly at me. There, just so."

Reluctantly, he continued speaking as he worked. "Not merely twins. What are called . . ." He hesitated a moment, his brow creasing, until he found the word. "Siamese twins. Joined at the skulls and hips. No one expected Katerina and Alexey to live, but surgery was performed nonetheless. The operation proved to be less complicated than anticipated,

223

and both children survived. Physically they were 'normal.' But . . ."

Georges shrugged and trailed off, concentrating for a moment as he shaded an eyebrow. Finally he resumed his narrative.

"Fate had other plans for them. The mother died at childbirth. Of course the publicity surrounding the operation and her death eventually exposed the true identity of the twins' father. He was promptly executed by Mother Russia as an enemy of the people, leaving the twins orphaned. Fortunately he had previously made arrangements for the care of his estranged children. They grew up in a mountain village in southern Italy, raised by a nurse until they were old enough to make their way in the world."

"How did she end up in New Orleans? Did her brother come with her?"

Georges nodded. "Naturally it was impossible to emigrate legally. But they lived near a seaport and arranged for freighter passage to the United States. Katya spoke little about this to me, but I fear they were forced to rely on her . . . charms to ensure the expenses of their passage. New Orleans was their port of entry. They liked it here, especially Katya. They were young—younger even than you. But the nurse who raised them had a natural son who spoke some English, and he had taught them what he knew. Alexey, with his brilliance, continued studying until he was fluent. Somehow they survived here. In many ways, this was a good city for such as they."

Georges stopped drawing for a moment, lost in some troubling memory.

"What do you mean, 'such as they'?" Corinne asked, prompting him gently.

Georges chose his words carefully. "They were . . . different. You must remember the circumstances of their birth, try to understand what life was for them, growing up alone and forsaken. Two children alone in an uncaring world. They were close . . . perhaps *too* close. Do you understand me?"

Corinne looked puzzled. "You don't mean . . . they were lovers?"

"Exactement! It was not clear to all, perhaps, but I eventually understood. There were unmistakable signs. And I forgave. They were different in other ways also. As you have seen, she was an artist of true greatness. He brother did not possess her creative genius, but he was gifted with the great intelligence."

Georges shrugged one shoulder. "Some say he was gifted — cursed — with something else."

"What do you mean?"

"People talk," he said evasively. "Where brains lag, tongues wag."

She was about to press the point when Georges announced briskly, *"Voici,"* and turned the sketchbook so she could see it.

"I like it!" she admired truthfully, confronting herself. "You do wonderful work. I wish I could

225

hatch so effortlessly."

He tried not to look too pleased. "Merely a journeyman's pathetic attempt to capture true beauty. The eyes are the challenge."

His last words seemed to reverberate around her for a moment. Finally Corinne said, "But what happened to them? Katerina and Alexey, I mean?"

Georges set his sketchbook aside and gazed through the screen toward a clump of broad-leafed banana trees shading the house. For a moment his old eyes were misty as memory transported him.

"What happened to them?" he repeated softly. "I often wonder."

He took a deep breath, looked at her. "It was in 1958. They had been here several years. Alexey had somehow acquired identity papers and was enrolled at Tulane, where he quickly became the undergraduate . . . what is the word? . . . the undergraduate prodigal?"

"Do you mean prodigy?"

"Just so! Katya had no formal learning, but her genius was quickly recognized and respected in the Quarter. Some compared her to Rabouin."

Georges gazed outside again, as if seeking comfort from the sun. His eyes brushed past Corinne's for a split second, and she saw they were blurry with unshed tears.

"Georges, I'm sorry. I didn't understand. No more."

"Ah, but you will hear it! You must learn the price of curiosity in this devilish world, my pretty

226

Corinne. It was Mardi Gras, 1958."

"Don't," she said helplessly.

"Mardi Gras, 1958," he repeated stubbornly. "Among all the artists in the Quarter, Katerina Zverkov is selected to be our royal artist, the youngest and most promising—the one chosen to represent us among the official court of the King Rex Parade."

His eyes held hers with pitiless despair. "Someone as talented as you, *ma jolie*. She rode in the back of a long black convertible. A hearse, you might say. She was bee-yootiful, so bee-yootiful in a blue velvet gown trimmed with sheer white lawn, matching her crown of white gardenias. No one will ever know what happened. Someone throws a bottle, perhaps. All of an instant, a policeman's horse leaps, Katerina is knocked from the car, the horse goes up, comes down, goes up and comes down again, each time landing with iron hooves on our princess. The screams, they were so horrible. . . ."

Georges visibly shuddered, but hurried on before she could stop him.

"God might have been merciful and killed her. Instead He left her grotesquely mutilated—her spine shattered, her skull misshapen. She was paralyzed, there was the brain damage."

Corinne felt gooseflesh when he looked at her, his face pallid.

"I saw it all. I will never forget. But perhaps even more terrible was the face of Alexey. He was

227

riding as her official escort, he was the closest. He saw everything, but was unable to help. Watching him—oh, I have seen the sadness and pain of this world, *ma jolie!* But nothing before or since could be as that face."

Her grip tightened on his shoulders, and he reached up gratefully to cover her hand with his.

"So now you know it. The city was shocked, *mais oui,* and the contributions poured in. I assure you, many a street artist went without his third meal of the day to give our Katya the best care. However, there was little 'recovery' to speak of. I saw Alexey once or twice and attempted to learn about her. But he was beyond reaching. Eventually he acquired money somewhere and moved away with his sister. No one I know has seen or heard from them since."

"I should have kept my mouth shut," said Corinne, furious at herself.

"Yes," agreed Georges. Then he mustered a smile and a wink. "But you did not, did you?"

Now he narrowed his eyes and studied her tired face closely as she stood near him.

"The eyes," he announced with somber disapproval. "They are lovely, but very tired. You must take better care of yourself, my pretty one. Life is not just work."

For a long moment Corinne recalled last night with Steve. It was the first time in a long while she'd missed so much sleep for such a pleasant cause.

Georges, as if reading her face, smiled knowingly and winked again. "Good! Beauty should not be an unplucked fruit left to wither on the branch."

As he escorted her out through the house, Georges touched her elbow and guided her toward a long room off the central hallway.

"My private stock," he confided. "Few see these but I. And now your radiant face will lead my collection beside Katya's."

He flung open a set of double paneled doors. Corinne gaped in surprise. Perhaps a dozen sketched portraits lined the immaculate white walls. All were of young women, all attractive. When she had a longer look, she realized she recognized many of them. Then she understood that they were all artists or performers who had worked in the Quarter.

"My muses," said Georges proudly, leading her further inside. "My beauties."

Corinne was about to comment when a cool galvanic tickle of premonition moved down her spine. The portrait nearest her, smiling as if to welcome her to a unique Gallery of the Dead, was the beautiful, chestnut-haired puppeteer, Jeanette Manders.

The Emperor ignored the increasing buzz of his brain's vastly overworked synapses.

To his hyperacute senses, the midday sunshine bathing Jackson Square was a brittle white alkali glare as stark as his makeup. Normal speaking voices were magnified to jet-engine screams. He smelled not only the usual smells of seafood and Lucky Dogs and lush gardens, but the dank-jungle musk of sex, the sheered-copper tang of blood, the bloated-carcass stench of death.

Only a week now, urged the inexorable voice that always dominated when he crossed over. You must press on. You must define the operational limits of your great power, of your great, pure love. *Thou shalt destroy the righteous with the wicked!*

He glanced at a businessman seated on one of the iron benches in front of the cathedral.

The Emperor felt an invisible mental sphincter tighten.

He looked at the businessman again and thought: *Your left armpit itches.* Idly, still perusing the sports section of his *USA Today,* the man reached up and scratched his left armpit.

Exhilaration washed over the Emperor in benzedrine rushes. He glanced toward a fruit stand at the corner. He ignored the vendor and selected a pyramid of melons out front, concentrating. A moment later the pyramid collapsed and the melons rolled helter-skelter.

His pleasure reduced him to a trembling weakness like the immediate aftermath of orgasm. It was true. *He was no longer limited to the glance.*

He stared out toward the twin streams of traffic on Decatur. Again the mental sphincter tightened. A resounding collison of metal was followed by horns and angry shouting.

But a moment later the Emperor's triumphant grin faltered. His throat went tight with rage as he remembered his initial attempt, on Saturday, to influence without eye contact. Obviously, in light of the fact that he had spotted her afterward, Corinne Matthews had somehow thwarted him. But the beautiful little Whore of Babylon *would* succumb.

And now her man. *That* man. The Emperor had recently understood everything in a powerful epiphany of cosmic insight. The scenario now unfolding had been drawn up by Destiny. It was not by chance alone that the son had inherited his father's mission. This city, this Sodom and Gomorrah of the New World, had become a great battlefield. Soon it would be a grisly abattoir, the ultimate site of the endgame between the Righteous and the Wicked, between the wronged and their wrongdoers. Those who had sown iniquity would soon reap punishment.

For a moment—a fleeting, tender moment of something almost like sanity—he pictured the remote bog where the shattered hope of his life lay enshrined.

Two teens approaching him veered wide to avoid the old weirdo. One of them carried a jambox bouncing off his thigh. A fragment of patter between tunes reached the Emperor.

". . . this year's Mardi Gras floats go well beyond the papier-mâché and iridescent paints of the past. They introduce such high-tech innovations as moving eyes and arms, and some floats are even self-propelled. . . ."

Should be exciting, thought the Emperor, his eyes two pools of burning acid.

The old mime took up his place in Jackson Square. Soon the bottom of his silk hat was carpeted with silver and bills. Tourists were especially impressed today. His gay smile was tragically offset by the oh-so-convincing tears shimmering in his mismatched eyes.

One week, repeated his silent crossover voice. *One week . . .*

Chapter 26

"I beg your pardon for speaking so candidly about one of your colleagues," Donald Carr apologized. "But there's something very . . . odd about Professor Winters."

Jesus, fellow, you're telling me? thought Steve, watching his visitor across the wide, cluttered desk. But he kept his tone carefully neutral.

"What do you mean?"

Discreetly, knowing Carr's voice might carry through the partially open office door, Steve nudged the volume up slightly on the portable radio beside his elbow.

"Specifically," said Carr, "he seems completely unable to put our course in brain physiology on track toward any practical goals. He's brilliant, yes, but absolutely irrelevant. Most of the others agree with me. We just want to be good medical practitioners in the real world, not pioneers in the vanguard of abstract brain research."

Steve, who could only guess at the content of Winters's lectures, watched Carr closely.

"It's true," Steve replied, "that Professor Winters is one of only a few on the faculty with a medical degree instead of a doctorate. But he's done little actual practice in neurosurgery outside of a lab. So naturally his interests are research oriented."

Carr listened attentively, his sense of fair play causing him to concede the point with a nod. He was only twenty-one, but the prematurely receded hairline, thick glasses, and owlish squint added a decade to his appearance. He balanced his backpack on one bluejeaned knee like Santa holding a child.

"I understand that," Carr said patiently. "The man is brilliant, clearly brilliant. I'm sure he's wonderful for the reputation of Delta College. It's just . . ."

Carr's voice trailed off and he briefly searched Jernigan's face for an invitation to continue carping. He found it.

"It's just that he seems obsessed with the theoretical topic of maximizing brain potential, to the exclusion of *any* practical concerns about brain disorders or injuries."

Steve decided he'd learn more by playing the devil's advocate. "Brain capacity is a hot area of research right now," he pointed out reasonably.

Again Carr nodded. "Definitely. And rightly so. I even agree with him about the paranormal angle. But I—"

"Paranormal angle?" Steve cut in.

"Not actually 'paranormal.' Not according to

234

Professor Winters. Even so-called psychic powers could be routinely reduplicated, he claims, once we pinpoint the exact neurochemical transmitters in the brain."

Steve felt his armpits dampen with sweat. This was a side of Winters he had heard nothing about.

"Of course," Carr added deferentially, "that line of thought has caught on generally since your father's work gave it new credence. I've read some of his articles."

Steve nodded absently. Carr said, "At first, when I complained and Professor Winters invited me to submit a list of less speculative lecture topics, I thought he was coming around a little. Now I realize he was just throwing a bone to the dogs. Frankly, he doesn't give a damn what we need or want."

"You know," said Steve, "if I *am* going to help you, it'll be necessary for me to review those lectures first. I recall that you took excellent notes in my class last semester. May I borrow the notes from your class with Winters?"

Carr nodded. "No problem. I'll need my notebook for other classes this morning, but I can Xerox them and leave them in your department mailbox this afternoon."

Carr was obviously still bothered by something else. His hands fidgeted nervously with the flap of his backpack.

"If it was only the lecture business, I'd probably just tough it out along with the others," he explained. "But there . . . there *might* be another problem—one that would help explain my first complaint."

Carr looked up at him, using one finger to push his heavy glasses further up on the bridge of his nose. He said, "I think Professor Winters might be a drug addict."

Spurred on by Jernigan's dumbfounded expression, the student added, "I know it's a serious accusation. But I think he's addicted to whatever substance he carries in that little silver pillbox."

Steve frowned. "You mean his blood-pressure medicine?"

Carr looked doubtful. "So he mentioned to us one day. Have you ever heard of anyone taking blood-pressure pills twice in one hour? Twice a day, maybe, but it's usually once a day or even one every other day. During our last class, though, he definitely took two."

"Maybe he just forgot?"

"Maybe," Carr agreed halfheartedly. "But he's not exactly the absentminded-professor type. And that's not the first time lately I've noticed him taking a second pill in one morning. Besides, his moods have been noticeably . . . erratic in the past week or so. Last class, he actually clowned around and cracked jokes—*funny* jokes."

Steve stared as if he'd just found out the Pope smoked pot. "Eric Winters clowning around?" he said incredulously, momentarily forgetting his pose of neutrality.

Carr nodded. "He looked pretty strung out too. Dilated pupils, trembling, losing his train of thought . . ."

"Tell you what," Steve said finally. "My authority around here is limited, to put it mildly. But you drop those lecture notes off, and I promise to look into it."

His first opportunity came earlier than he expected. After Carr left, Steve locked his office and was rounding the corner into the main corridor when he spotted Winters. He was jackknifed over the drinking fountain, calfskin briefcase resting against his leg.

He held the silver pillbox in his left hand.

Winters raised his head from the spouting water, swallowing to wash a pill down. He was finishing another drink when Steve moved in on him quietly and snatched the pills from his hand.

"What the—?" Winters sputtered, whirling around.

He recognized Jernigan, and the hard blue eyes filmed with angry blood.

"*Give* me those," he snarled, grabbing for the pillbox.

Steve stepped deftly out of range, watching the other man's face closely. For a moment, as their eyes met, the film of anger was transformed to a glaze of desperate fear.

"*Give* me those, damn you!" Winters repeated, lunging again.

Another professor and several students had

paused to see what the commotion was all about. Steve glanced at them, then at the filigreed silver object lying on his palm. Finally his eyes returned to Winters's stoney-eyed glare.

"Sure," he said finally. "No need to get upset. Here."

He tossed the pills carelessly toward his colleague, then spun on his heel and left. Not until Steve was unlocking his Mazda in the parking lot, still mulling over the incident with the pills, did he realize something else. Now he knew what it was about Winters's face that had been nagging him like a half-remembered dream image. It was the ash-blond eyebrows. They knitted together, forming one solid line over his eyes.

"Lieutenant!"

Breaux paused, wincing when hot coffee sloshed over the lip of its styrofoam cup and over his fingers. He looked across the lobby at the woman calling to him through the top of a Dutch door. A fake cedar plastic sign over the door announced FORENSIC LAB REQUESTS: RING BELL FOR SERVICE.

"I ran a spectro on that film you dropped off yesterday."

Breaux glanced around the precinct building, glad it was still early. No one else had heard her.

Taking a big swallow of coffee to minimize further self-injury, he crossed to the Dutch door.

238

"Already?"

The woman sergeant smiled. "You said chop-chop, so chop-chop it was."

Her smile grew a little more conspiratorial. "Did I overlook the supervisor's authorization on the work order?"

Breaux sipped his coffee, hiding a grin. "I don't know. Did you?"

Cheryl Towers looked at him askance. "What new can of beans are you trying to open now?"

"Nothing. I'm just indulging my senility."

Cheryl was in her late twenties, but it was common knowledge around the cop shop that the lab technician preferred much older men. This was tragic news to the males under forty or so, in light of her blonde hair, Malibu tan, and D-cup breasts. Breaux occasionally exploited her Daddy Complex, taking care not to overdo it. He had no serious qualms about adultery. But he suspected that, despite her proclivity for older men, in bed Cheryl would prove an erotic combatant who took no prisoners.

She confirmed his suspicions now as her eyes traveled the length of his body in frank appraisal.

"Senility, huh? The rest of you sure looks healthy enough."

"Must be the Vitamin E."

"I've read about that stuff. Does it work?"

"Not miracles," he replied reluctantly, enjoying one last, lingering glance at the voluptuous swell of her blue cotton blouse. "So what turned up? Anything?"

Cheryl shook her head. "Nothing on the image reconstruction. The face wasn't just underexposed, it was burned completely off the film with a laser trace. It's a common technique used in special effects."

Breaux tried not to look disappointed, but she caught the momentary distraction in his eyes.

"If it's any consolation," she told him, "I can tell you that, whoever he was, the guy was wearing one contact lens."

His eyebrows rose.

"Spectrometer confirms it," she explained. "The wave-length readouts never lie. His left eye is brown, but he's wearing a specially tinted contact to correct it to blue like the right eye."

"Interesting," said Breaux. "Thanks, lady."

"Anytime," she replied, making the word resonate with layers of possibility.

By the end of most school days, Donald Carr always felt as if he were coming apart like a sloppily knit afghan. So he especially enjoyed the therapeutic mile-and-a-half walk home along the lake front. This daily mental tranquilizer doubled as aerobic exercise, thus saving forty more minutes he could apply toward his monomaniacal goal of maintaining his medical scholarship.

He leaped the row of half-rotted logs dividing North Campus from the lakefront, then paused to adjust his backpack and poke his glasses back up on his nose. When he resumed his trek he gradually angled away from the asphalt walkway the other students were following, opting for his usual shortcut. Because of the last fierce-glowing burst of dying sun, he failed to notice the car swinging out of the faculty parking lot. It turned right onto Lakeshore Place and, following the road about twenty yards behind him, headed in the same direction he was.

He was especially distracted this evening. Earlier he had photocopied his notes from Winters's class and left them in Steve Jernigan's department mailbox. Carr was convinced his case against Winters was at least just, if not advisable. Still, he couldn't help a faint belly-stirring of guilt, mostly spawned by his innate pragmatism and respect for authority. Especially scientific authority.

(*There are more . . . efficient ways of subsuming the attributes of others.*)

Carr's face lapsed into its familiar owlish squint when he gazed out over vast Lake Pontchartrain and watched the waning sun flame the water a scarlet-edged gold. He took long, swinging strides, his backpack shifting lopsidedly each time he leaped a rock or a supine trunk.

(*So tell us, Mr. Carr . . . what's eating you?*)

He was only vaguely aware when the car eased to a stop just ahead and to his right up along the shell berm of Lakeshore Place. Carr had reached a swampy stretch where gravel had been trucked in

241

behind the sea wall, forcing him to watch his step more carefully. Occasionally he miscalculated and winced as a pointy fragment of shell pricked at the soles of his Pro Flyers.

Up on the berm, a car door closed with a thick muffled *chunk*. A white, disembodied oval of face gazed in Carr's direction through the grainy haze of gathering darkness behind the flaming lake.

Even as it happened, Carr was both helpless spectator and willing participant.

Responding to some invisible prompt in the atmosphere, the usual flow of his thoughts—a busy amalgam of calculus problems, chemical equations, and anatomical nomenclature—began to skew like iron filings scattered by a magnet.

The part of him Carr seldom allowed onto the stage of conscious awareness—his too-long-neglected libido—now emerged with a vengeance. It was as if his very being was centered around nothing but erotic gratification. Even the motion of walking, causing his jeans to gently pressure his penis, ignited a fierce loin heat ten times stronger than any adolescent lust. His erection was so hard he was forced to limp, his breathing accelerated to an animal panting, his testicles ached for release.

The white face floated nearer on the blue-black sea of twilight, monitoring Carr with silent absorption. The preternatural vibrating of the air pitched itself an octave tighter.

Now he was a walking hardon, one bad mojo case of unsated lover's nuts, a mean sac of back-

242

logged sperm roiling for release. Walk more carefully, Carr commanded himself, sure he would burst upon impact if he tripped.

A precise drill-field voice only he could hear barked, *Eyes, left, cocksman!* He obeyed. A four-wheel-drive Blazer was parked near the water. And the pretty Hispanic woman who had parked it there was aiming her 35-mm. Pentax out over the lake, recording the glorious Southern sunset.

You need pussy, cocksman, whispered the silent voice. *Oh, man, do you need release. HARCH!*

He covered the first ten yards quietly. Then a stick snapped loudly under his foot and the woman spun around.

At first, squinting to see him better in the dying light, she smiled a generically polite smile. The greeting became more tentative, then faded altogether when she got a clear look at the abomination approaching her.

His left fist pumped great guns on his exposed, blue-veined erection. His right clutched a long, pointed rock like a deadly poniard, raising it to split her head open.

Free-lance photographer Anna Padilla—a two-time rape victim who had learned her sexual politics in the *barrios* of L.A.—didn't scream or run or beg for mercy. She dropped the Pentax and dipped her right hand into the pin-grain gadget bag on her shoulder, emerging with a Browning .380 Auto.

"Stop right there!" she commanded, part of her secretly hoping he didn't.

She got her wish. But besides the rage and hurt burning deep within her, the early teachings of church and family were strong.

"I'm warning you—stop! If I kill you now you'll go to hell, mister! Stop . . . STOP! I won't wound you, motherfucker! I'll *kill!*"

Carr ejaculated with a powerful grunt and leapt at her growling like a savage animal. A moment later he felt his skull explode in a noiseless white flash, and several chunky clots of something like wet cement smacked into the rocks just microseconds before he did.

Chapter 27

Doctor Eric Winters woke up feeling like an Amtrak had rolled over him sometime during the night.

Pain had sunk deep roots into his neck and shoulders, its fiery stems and branches lashing all the way up to his hair follicles. His thick pancake makeup should have been carefully removed before he returned to the house. Instead it had rubbed spots into the pillowcase, coating it moistly like glazed sugar.

He winced at the additional explosions of pain that assaulted him as he sat up. Near-panic quickened his pulse when he saw he still wore the summerweight black suit. He had *never* risked wearing it home before. Somehow, he must have managed to claw the lace jabot off. It lay crumpled on the thick pile carpet just inside the bedroom door.

As usual when he had overindulged in Maximum Beta Mode, he had no memory of the preceding twenty-four hours. But he felt the overwhelming conviction that he had achieved a major breakthrough toward realizing his ultimate objective.

Then his eyes slowly focused on the purple Mardi Gras beads dangling from the doorknob.

Winters broke into a cold sweat.

No!

He struggled out from between the sweat-rumpled sheets and crossed on unsteady sea legs to the digital clock radio on top of the dresser. It was 8:40 A.M. He thumbed the radio on and flipped the selector dial to the area's twenty-four-hour news station.

". . . on the West Bank and Gaza Strip, Palestinian youths armed with stones and Molotov cocktails . . ."

The newscaster's voice assaulted him like twin slaps to the ears. Winters cursed and reached for the volume knob. While the newscaster reiterated the familiar, unchanged litany of international woes, Winters stripped and crossed to a bathroom adjoining the bedroom.

Leaving the door open, leaning one ear toward the radio, he rubbed cream into his face and rinsed off his badly smeared mime's visage. Next he dampened a stiff-bristled brush and ran it through his hair and knitted brows to remove the spray-on tint that turned them from their real ash-blond to a silver white. Finally, he opened a plastic lens case beside the spigot and removed a tinted contact. Throwing his head back, he inserted the lens that made his brown left eye blue like the one on the right.

Twenty years younger, he returned to the bed-

246

room just as the newscaster turned to the metro news.

"Here in the Crescent City, an attempted rape marred last night's positive Mardi Gras spirit and resulted in the shooting death of the assailant, a twenty-one-year-old New Orleanian. Donald Eugene Carr, a full-time student at Delta College, was pronounced dead at the scene last evening, killed by a single gunshot wound to the forehead. Released after questioning was Anna Maria Padilla, twenty-six, a free-lance photographer from Los Angeles. Padilla is currently compiling a photo essay on the Deep South for *American Leisure,* a travel magazine."

Winters turned the radio off, his face numb with shock. For a moment his frown was as stern as a centurion's.

Again his eyes drifted to the purple Mardi Gras beads adorning the bedroom door.

All right, so it was possible.

But whatever had happened, no irreparable damage had been done to his plans for Fat Tuesday.

Again his eyes were drawn toward the door, toward the hallway and a second door opposite his bedroom.

No. He was sure he had done nothing to lead them *there*.

For a moment it bothered him, the idea of these curious memory lapses during which Jekyll became Hyde and did things he — Winters — had to read about like everyone else. But he argued that it was similar to a great artist trying to recall his mind-set

247

during the creation of his greatest work. It was as impossible as separating the dancer from the dance.

Quickly, not wanting to call attention to himself by being late for his ten o'clock class, he dressed in a clean suit and tie, black nylon socks, and honeycomb open-weaves. Then he returned to the dresser. There, among some loose change and his keys, was the filigreed silver pillbox.

(*God is mentally ill*)

Winters squinted, trying to grasp at a cluster of thoughts just beneath the surface of his subconscious.

(*the invisible worm that flies in the night!*)

But it was no use. He placed a pill on his tongue, carefully noting the time so he wouldn't overdo it again today. Then he pocketed his medication and left to face the city he had only just begun to punish.

Corinne set her cup down and said, "Steve?"

He glanced across the table at her. "Hmmm?"

"Have you ever heard of a local artist named Katerina Zverkov? She was involved in a horrible accident during Mardi Gras of '58."

"Sure haven't. Why?"

Corinne hesitated to watch two pigeons wage a tug-of-war over a scrap of doughnut. It was only noon, but carnival visitors had already overrun the covered patio of Cafe du Monde. Waiters hustled everywhere like stock-exchange gofers, and the hearty good-morning odor of coffee and roast chicory laced the musk and creosote smell of the nearby river.

"Just curious," she finally replied. She was still thinking about the tragic tale Georges had told her yesterday, though she wasn't in the mood to repeat it now. Instead, Corinne only nodded toward the nearest lithograph. "She did those."

Jernigan glanced at the pictures, then took a second, longer look. "I'm no connoisseur, but I'd say she must've been pretty good."

"Very," agreed Corinne, trying not to notice they were using the past tense.

"Speaking of artistic talent, did you call this guy what's-his-name, the sculptor?"

Corinne laughed, her strong white teeth flashing. " 'What's-his-name!' " she teased. "Belgard Davis just *happens* to be the greatest outdoor sculptor in the Deep South, and one of the top five in the nation, *that's* all."

"Scoozay-*moi*," said Jernigan with a chivalric bow. He tried to look properly abashed.

"Yes, I called him," she answered happily. "We're getting together in a couple weeks to discuss preliminary sketches."

Steve saw her eyes glint like crystal for a moment. He reached across the table and covered her hand with his. "It's good to see you smiling again."

"It's good to *feel* like smiling again."

Corinne picked his hand up and brought it briefly to her lips. "For the first time in a long while I'm *happy* again. I can't believe I'm saying it, but it's true. I'm happy about my career, I'm happy about my health improving, I'm happy about *you*. I feel guilty. People aren't supposed to feel this happy. If it wasn't for this . . ."

She trailed off, the dark cloud of a frown momentarily scuttling her sunny mood. He understood what "this" was and squeezed her hand.

Corinne's free hand slipped under the collar of her blouse and pulled the red coral necklace out into view for a moment. Then she tucked it out of sight again.

"It's crazy," she said, somberly. "It has to be! But I keep telling myself, how can we *both* be going crazy together?"

"We can't be," he assured her. "Our explanation is shaky, granted. But something is happening, and we're going to find out what."

She searched the gray-green depths of his gaze, wondering for a moment whatever had become of her emotional suit of armor.

"No, we're not going crazy together," she agreed. "But there is something we should be doing together."

He raised a surprised eyebrow.

"That too," she said, "but it's not what I meant."

"Shucks."

Her lips pursed in an ironic smile. "Big talk."

"Yeah? Try me."

"All this exuberance even after so little sleep last night?"

Lightly, he brushed her fingertips with his. "Change your mind about staying with me again tonight and find out."

"Tempting as the offer is, no. I told you, I refuse to use you as my security blanket. And anyway, don't distract me from the issue. You still haven't asked me."

"Forgive me, I'm lust-simple. Asked you about what?"

"What kind of beau are you? Have you forgotten this Tuesday is Mardi Gras?"

Steve glanced around at the costumed tourists, the sea of masked pedestrians flashing by on the sidewalk, many already drunk or high. "You're pulling my leg!" he exclaimed with mock surprise.

"I'll pull your *nose* if you don't invite me to at least one parade!"

He grinned. Her remark had triggered an unexpected internal alarm, but he was damned if he was going to put a damper on her happiness.

"It's a date, foxy lass. Name your procession."

Despite his quick, upbeat response, Corinne glimpsed the momentary uncertainty in his eyes. *She rode in the back of a long black convertible. A hearse, you might say . . .*

Fear. Fear of the dark, fear of the Unknown Thing under the bed. Fear of love, fear of success, fear of life itself. Did it end only at the grave, or could she oust its crippling influence and have the kind of life she really wanted? Corinne wasn't sure, but she knew that she could not slay a monster without first confronting it.

"King Rex rolls on Tuesday," she said finally. "Take me to the King Rex parade."

They have no right, the Emperor told himself fiercely.

Unobserved in the morning shadow of the fountain, he watched Corinne raise the man's hand to her lips.

A fierce, tight smile devoid of any mirth distorted his chalk-white face.

Hate seethed within him — a gnawing, burning rage like acute gastritis. These two were together everywhere now. He knew the enjoyment they were having of each other, the transcendent bliss that resulted when those young healthy animals coupled. *And they had no right!* Whores and sons of whores! They would die with the rest in this city of murdering Sodomites. . . .

The Emperor's face abruptly flushed warm as he watched Corinne pluck her necklace out into plain view for a moment.

Tuccari ferru . . .

So they finally knew. For how long?

His lips quivered with barely suppressed rage when he thought about the time he had wasted trying to influence her. But he consoled himself with the reminder that she had just rendered her protection impotent by revealing it to him.

Besides . . . He fingered the silver pillbox in his jacket pocket. Traditional protections presupposed traditional powers. He was now amplifying his with exponential strength, thanks to the accumulated dosage of MBM. If he chose, he could swallow

252

another right now, and . . .

But no.

No.

Not today, cautioned the "self" who took over during crossovers. He must maintain enough competence during the next few days to synthesize the final batch of MBM with his medication.

(*And his dark, secret love does thy life destroy.* . . .)

Katya . . .

Oh, my lovely, lovely Katya . . .

A quivering tear oozed from one eye and fell on the gardenia in his lapel. Wetting it, he thought, but not staining it a horrible carmine as her blood had done.

Again his rage flared—a fast explosion of anger like gasoline catching fire. The Emperor knew he was on the verge of snapping, destroying his plans for Fat Tuesday. Abruptly, he spun on his heel and made blindly for Decatur.

But the inner rage only flamed deeper as it demanded an immediate outlet.

His deep-set, intense eyes scanned the cluster of costumed carnival-goers waiting for the light in front of Jax Brewery.

Hedonists, were they?

Revelers?

Savage barbarians enjoying a Dionysian debauch?

Then by all means, *let the festivities begin.*

He flexed a psychic muscle. This time, thanks to the hundredfold booster effect of the MBM derivative, it was effortless — as easy as an eyeblink, so unlike the sustained concentration of the days when he'd relied solely on his own ability and the crude lessons from Alain, the son of the woman who'd raised him and Katya. So easy, in fact, that he barely managed to stop himself in time from killing *all* of them.

A slight flex, an invisible push, and the masked woman in the ostrich-feather skirt tumbled off the curb, just as an RTA bus flew past.

Heads inside the bus and out turned fast at the solid *thunk* sound when she was sucked up into the wheel well. Spectators on the sidewalk watched, their faces freeze-framed in horror, as she was jammed between rubber and metal and dragged like so much old linoleum for another quarter of a block until the bus could finally stop, smearing a bloody trail of lurid green feathers.

Chapter 28

"I figured something wasn't jake with Pearlman," explained Breaux, "when I noticed those sloppy reports about your dad and his partner. It was after you told me about your little research trip up north that I decided to have the video analyzed."

"It's definitely a contact?" asked Steve.

"Definitely. *One* contact—and don't it make his brown eye blue?"

"I'll forgive that one," Steve said, watching the detective signal C. J. Guidry for two more drafts. A spillover carnival crowd had the Ragin' Cajun living up to its first name. But he ignored the pulsing Wurlitzer and the clamoring patrons, concentrating on what Breaux had just told him.

He and the cop had already concurred on one crucial point. The Emperor could well be the unknown star of that political message, just as his oddly mismatched eyes were somehow behind the recent tragedies in the Quarter. There were now too many connections—definite and probable—to attribute to coincidence, despite the fact that the Big

Picture was still fuzzy around the edges. But now Steve was almost sure that another piece had just fallen into place: The Emperor and Eric Winters were the same person.

The contact, of course, solved the obvious problem of the difference in their eye coloration. The age disparity — the Emperor's silver hair versus Winters's ash-blond — could be accounted for by skillfully applied makeup. There were still some gaping holes, some glaring questions about logical motivation for such apparent insanity. But the bizarre input was beginning to form its own insane logic, to weave a coherent pattern out of meaningless ink blots. Especially since Carr had dropped off those notes Steve requested. His flesh had crawled as he scanned them. Those lectures read like mere updates of his father's work!

Guidry thumped a pair of schooners down, startling him.

"Bring us a couple shots too," said Breaux.

Guidry faked severe shock. "Nawlins, lock up your chirruns! The West Bank Piker is calling for whiskey! His old gal musta give 'm sumpin to celebrate!"

He poured both customers a double of Jack Daniels, then tipped a little more into a water glass and set it near them.

"Case I get busy," he explained.

After the bartender hustled off, Breaux stared at Jernigan's hands for a few moments, then remarked, "Anybody special you're looking to throttle?"

Startled out of his reflection, Steve unclenched his left fist and rested both hands flat on the bar. "Nervous habit."

Breaux glimpsed at him sidewise for a moment. He watched the younger man's jaw muscle bunch tight as he fought some terrible indecision.

"Yeah, my old lady," said Breaux. "God love her."

He looked Jernigan in the eye and added, "She says I'd be a better cop if I thought more creatively."

Jernigan understood this invitation to open up. Why not, he reasoned. Could anything seem farfetched after what they'd already concluded? But if somehow he was right, then Steve also knew that Winters could have been involved in killing his father. It wasn't just a matter of abstract justice, this was the blood of his own. Breaux was a decent enough guy, but he was also a cop—a cop who was talking more and more about the possibility of approaching his superiors before Mardi Gras.

Fine, let him do his job and protect the city, if need be. Steve had no intention of hindering him. Hell, he'd do what he could to help. But Steve wanted the option of confronting Winters before the police did. Or even worse, before the police blew it and tipped their quarry off.

Breaux saw that his gambit had failed. He sighed

257

stoically and dropped the subject.

"The way things're going, I've decided to take a few of my personal leave days. Captain bitched until I volunteered to work crowd control on Fat Tuesday. Now I'm free to put a tail on the Emperor."

Steve nodded. Again he thought about those lecture notes Carr had dropped off. The utter insanity of the idea paled when he considered the things that had already happened. But if he *was* right . . . He recalled Lisa's notes on *malocchio*.

If all else failed, and if somehow this evolving nightmare was true, there was a possible weapon of last resort. Unfortunately it was said to be as risky as it was effective. Thinking of risks reminded him again that Corinne's building was unprotected tonight—and that the Emperor was out there somewhere, prowling around.

"I'm heading back to my place," he told Breaux. "Offer you a cold beer and some civilized music?"

Breaux shook his head. "Thanks, but I'm heading home too. The wife is threatening to turn in a missing person's on me."

This time when their eyes met, both men glanced automatically toward the Mardi Gras countdown calendar.

"Should be a good one this year," said Steve.

"They always are," Breaux assured him. "Down here we know how to throw a party."

* * *

258

Give it up, little girl, whispered the voice of a ghost in the semidarkness. *You can't do it!*

Corinne lay tense in the big brass bed, unconsciously fingering the iron charms of her new necklace. Tonight she had resolved to forgo the usual ritual of her bogeyman check. Nor had she left two lights burning, as usual. Only a pale splash of light spilled past the crack of the bathroom door.

But she was too frightened to rally herself to her cause. It just wasn't working. The pillow felt like a hand on the back of her head, the blankets were arms pinning her to the mattress. She knew that looming presence at the end of the bed was only a shoji screen, but the knowledge didn't stop it from seeming to melt and shift, to change shape in the darkness.

What's under the bed, little girl? whispered the ghosts in the shadows. *You didn't check!*

"Go to hell!" she said out loud.

The words fell like stones into a bottomless well, leaving only a menacing stillness punctuated by the rapid explosions of her heart.

What's under the bed, little girl?

Fear prickled her scalp. Corinne glanced toward the opposite wall of her studio apartment. A stray shaft of moonlight illuminated the gold-framed photo of her parents. They both seemed to stare at her with malevolent eyes.

We've left for the night, Corinne. What's under

259

the bed?

Sighing in exasperated surrender, Corinne kicked the covers back. For a moment, when she swung her legs down to the floor, cold lips kissed her spine as she waited for someone to grab an ankle.

She stepped quickly away from the bed. Tugging her sleep shirt straight, she crossed to swing the bathroom door wide open. Light poured into the apartment. On her way back to bed she stopped at her work table to flick on the tensor lamp. More light shooed away the last lingering shadows.

But it was no use. She couldn't skip her ritual. The Sisters of Mercy would not approve, she thought grimly. Her bogeyman check was more deeply engrained than nightly prayers.

Corinne crossed the room and plucked the bright yellow tennis ball off the dresser. She returned to the bed, dropped to her knees, and sent the ball on its way with a quick sidearm toss. Reflexively, she rose to retrieve it from the other side, waiting for the familiar cork-popping sound as it hit the wall.

The ball failed to roll out.

Blood pulsed in her ears, her armpits broke out in a cold sweat. *No,* Corinne thought desperately, oh no no *no!*

She was frozen in her kneeling position, too terrified to move.

(Twenty-five years old and still afraid of the dark, still afraid of bogeymen lurking under the bed.)

260

Hesitantly, her hand trembling, she reached toward the edge of the chenille spread.

(You are an artist, not a detective! Develop the talent God has given you, and the Devil take the rest!)

Catching her bottom lip between her teeth, biting so hard she tasted the salty tang of blood, Corinne clutched the spread.

(You must learn the price of curiosity, my pretty Corinne. . . .)

Crying out, she flipped the spread back.

Light rushed in under the bed. Corinne stared, terror dilating her pupils into big black buttons. The tennis ball had stopped halfway under, snagged by one of her white fur slippers.

But instead of relief, a powerful sob suddenly wracked her chest. Her face crumpled in fear and shame and sheer, inexpressible frustration. She doubled up on the floor, hugging herself, rocking back and forth, giving vent to her tears.

"Merciful God, *help* me!" she implored over and over. The prayer was still on her lips when, not bothering to crawl back into bed, she finally fell into a deep, dreamless sleep.

Chapter 29

"Damn, he's good!"

"*Good?* He's unbelievable! He hasn't moved for a half hour!"

"Wish my old lady could keep her mouth shut that long!"

"Such expressive eyes . . ."

"Mama, is that man a statue?"

"No, hon. He's called a mime."

"My God, the discipline . . ."

"Almost spooky . . ."

The Friday morning French Quarter throng formed a ragged semicircle before the long steps of St. Louis Cathedral, watching the old mime create a human still life more eerily impressive than any daring acrobatic stunt.

Breaux edged closer through the crowd. He could see the Emperor clearly now. The white, immobile face could have been carved out of pure marble, but the oddly mismatched eyes seemed wired for current. They fairly glowered with some keen inner energy.

(I can't believe, said Cindy, that I actually voted Republican!)

A tourist, draped in a psychedelic tunic to honor Mardis Gras, stepped forward and dropped a handful of change into the old man's hat.

"You *believe* that character?" said the man beside Breaux admiringly. "He's something, isn't he?"

"Something," agreed Breaux, watching the fervent eyes.

But what?

Again his stomach churned acid as Breaux reminded himself that Fat Tuesday was only three days away now. He desperately needed some concrete evidence if he was going to approach his superiors in time.

The detective excused himself as he brushed past spectators and edged even closer. The Emperor paid no attention to his movement, gazing out over Jackson Square with the detached equanimity of a man who has astroprojected himself elsewhere.

Curious, Breaux followed the line of his gaze. There was nothing but scattered pockets of carnival-goers, an early morning juggler doing his thing on a unicycle, and a girl drawing a portrait of an elderly couple. Sunshine momentarily pushed saffron fingers through a thin strata of cloud cover, forcing Breaux to avert his glance before he recognized the artist as the pretty girl he had seen with Jernigan.

Breaux slid his wallet out and peeled a dollar out of the bill compartment. He moved within two feet of the Emperor and flipped the money into his hat.

Casually, keeping his voice low, Breaux said, "The eyes of Louisiana are upon you."

The crowd murmured its surprise when the mime suddenly started as if he'd been goosed.

Breaking the sphinxlike role, he swiveled his head sharply to stare at Breaux.

Their eyes met in a visual shoving match. And now, despite their two-tone coloration, Breaux recognized those intense eyes as the persuasive gaze featured in Clinton Pearlman's political commercial. He recognized something else: a malevolent, psychotic, murderous purpose that filled Breaux with a cold dread. It was like staring into the very maw of Hell itself.

Dream about this forever, kids!

The next moment the Emperor bolted through the crowd, with Breaux dogging his heels.

Steve nosed his Mazda into the curb and parked out front. He watched the house for a few more moments before he killed the engine and got out of the car.

It was a squat California bungalow, the type popular in many of the city's middle-class suburbs. Heavy wrought-iron bars covered all the vulnerable windows. Neat yew hedges lined the front of the house. Pink-blooming azalea bushes dotted the front and side yards. There was no garage and no car parked on the gleaming white crushed shells of the cul-de-sac.

As Steve approached the front door, he thought about the shack in Honey Island Swamp. But glancing up at the slowly massing dark clouds, he decided that if threatening weather had kept him and Tree away today, it had probably dissuaded anyone else as well.

Unless someone was *staying* at the shack . . .

Despite a lack of objective evidence, he was now convinced that shack was tied to his search. There were the dreams, the powerful sense of menace the place triggered in him. It was just too implausible a "coincidence" that his father, Dale McGinnis, *and* the shack were all linked to Honey Island Swamp.

Deep in thought, he had reached the front stoop. Steve hesitated for another minute or two, studying the silent house.

So far the day had proven mostly frustrating. He had been unable to waylay Winters on campus because Delta, like all schools in New Orleans, had closed in recognition of the final weekend of Mardi Gras. Then he had had no luck finding Eric Winters's address in the city directory. Luckily, Steve had finally dug up a Delta College faculty-staff directory and found this address in the outlying suburb of Kenner.

He stared at the front door. It was iron-reinforced oak. He tried the bell, waited thirty seconds, then tried again. Nothing. The place was as still and quiet and lifeless as a small-town cemetery.

Was Winters staying here? There was no name on the mailbox. On a chance, he reached down and flipped the jute doormat over. There was no spare key.

Again he thought about the shack.

No . . .

But why not?

For a few moments Steve recalled the lecture notes Carr had left for him. Fear tickled his stomach when he thought about the official notification of Carr's death the Dean of Students had sent him yesterday. The newspaper version had been much more lurid. It just wouldn't square with Steve's image of the hapless student.

In his notes Carr had placed a huge asterisk beside the gruesome incident featuring the cannibalistic grad student who consumed his professor's brain.

Food for thought, he had punned in a morbid marginal note.

Along with that shack, Steve reminded himself, this place might somehow also hold a key to Carr's baffling fate. He was still reeling from his recent conviction that Winters—and his probable alter ego, the Emperor—was up to something catastrophically evil. Like Breaux, he was desperate for some kind of concrete proof. Carr's death only boosted his desperation—another hint that some deadly net was tightening fast.

Steve wandered around back to check for any possible means of entry. But the place looked as secure as a bunker. The back door too was solid oak reinforced with iron bands. He could see nothing through the shuttered windows flanking it.

He was testing one of the locked shutters when a realization hit him: Winters wasn't at home.

Nor at school.

Even if Steve's wild hunch about Winters and that shack was right, he probably hadn't braved this weather to reach the swamp today.

So where *was* he?

The answer insinuated itself in his mind like a lewd suggestion.

Corinne!

He raced around front toward his car, trying to ignore the voice that cried like a heartbeat—*too late, too late, too late!*

Friday certainly didn't begin like a tragic day.

Corinne was up at the first blush of sunrise, her appetite ravenous. After a quick wake-up shower, she fixed herself a Spanish omelette and enjoyed it with two steaming mugs of black coffee. Thus fortified, she ventured out to conquer the new day.

It was only eight o'clock when she arrived at Jackson Square and rolled back the steel curtain of her sidewalk studio. Mist hovered over the cobblestones in shifting little patches, and ominous dark thunderheads were massing over Lake Pontchartrain. But Corinne refused to let the weather put a damper on her mood.

For a moment, as she hung out her display drawings, she slipped several fingers under the neckline of her pullover and made contact with the necklace Steve had given her.

Already the events of the past couple weeks seemed unreal. She felt like a half-awake dreamer trapped between the world of truth and the world of fantasy, but dwelling in neither. She admitted she was viewing the Emperor through a distorted haze of paranoia induced by her declining health. If it *was* only paranoia, Steve was sharing it with her.

Soon her first customers arrived and Corinne gladly surrendered this troubling line of thought. Thanks to this year's record Mardi Gras crowd, she stayed busy for the next two hours.

She wasn't sure exactly when the Emperor started watching her.

One moment she was concentrating on her portrait of an elderly couple from Ohio, a charming pair who confessed they had selected her only because she reminded them of their daughter. The next, she was aware that a crowd had gathered near St. Louis Cathedral. At first she assumed they were watching the wisecracking juggler on the unicycle. But a brief, sickeningly familiar spasm in her stomach prompted her to look closer.

A moonstone-white face was gazing in her direction above the sea of tourists.

The spasms became more intense, developing into a tight cramp that made her wince.

A familiar ache settled in behind her eyes. But this time it was far more intense. Despite her powerful caffeine buzz, exhaustion washed over her in intermittent waves.

Somehow she managed to complete the portrait. After the couple paid her and departed with their new drawing safely tucked between sheets of protective cardboard, Corinne hurriedly closed her studio. Nausea filled her with an oily queasiness, and now the headache was so bad the clip-clop of passing mules struck her like blows.

Had to hurry . . . She was on the verge of chucking up her breakfast, right out here in front of everyone.

The necklace, she thought as she pulled the sliding curtain down and slipped the padlock through the hasp. Obviously it wasn't working now. Had it ever?

She was too distracted to notice the Emperor bolt around the corner of the cathedral onto St. Peter Street. Steve had told her about Alan Breaux, but she had never met him, so she wouldn't have recognized the middle-aged man who peeled himself away from the crowd to follow the fleeting performer.

Her hands fumbled, all thumbs now, failing to snap the lock shut. The harder she tried, the more she botched it. Until the padlock suddenly slipped from the hasp and clattered onto the cobblestones.

Damnit . . .

Gastric acid spurted up her throat, bitter and burning. Near tears now, she fought the urge to vomit. When she stooped to retrieve the lock, a fierce flaring of internal pain made her gasp.

It had never been this bad before. What was happening to her?

Appendicitis, whispered an insidious voice. *Kidney stones . . . or maybe even the Big C, hmmm? Student Health could easily have screwed up those lab tests. . . .*

Preoccupied with the physical symptoms, Corinne wasn't aware of a corresponding disease blighting her thought.

Something was troubling her. Steve had moved to the Quarter about the same time her health had started to deteriorate. He claimed the move

270

was merely a whim, that he was bored with his apartment on the lakefront. But was the overlapping of their lives merely coincidence?

You paranoid little fool, argued another voice. *Steve gave you the necklace. That's when you started getting better.*

So true, countered the first voice. *And now you're worse than ever, aren't you?*

Deep within, an invisible demon turned the screws tighter, and a fiery explosion of pain made her cry out.

Oh, God, help me, she pleaded, panic causing her pulse to fire boosters.

God, whispered that voice from the mouth of Hell, *is dog spelled backwards. Hang it up, cunt. . . . You're worm-fodder now. . . .*

Maddy . . . she had to get to Maddy. Maddy would help her.

Leaving the lock where it lay, Corinne turned and headed across the square toward Toulouse Street. By now the costumed revelers were out in force. It was all she could do to weave her way among them without collisions.

Masked faces leered at her. People jostled her roughly. Buildings and trees became an organic, living force bent on terrorizing her with their looming presence. Even the mules pulling the fringed surreys seemed to glower at her malevolently. And throughout it all, the pain increased until it seemed as if every nerve ending in her

271

body had been stripped raw and held up to a flame.

I'm going to die, she thought. *Oh, merciful God, please no!*

Toulouse Street was a madhouse. The French Quarter gay community had organized their own parody parade and now filled the street, their bodies brightly painted and skimpily costumed. Gritting her teeth against the incredible pain, Corinne fought her way toward Maddy's shop, making slow progress.

Only a half block, she told herself fiercely. Maddy will help. . . .

But now she was caught in that old childhood nightmare where monsters were chasing her and she could only take slow-motion steps. Each step was like trying to walk underwater. The shouts, the pounding drums, the laughter. All of it formed a hideous, painful roar that brought tears to her eyes.

Corinne was within twenty feet of Maddy's shop when a group of female impersonators in tights and bouffant skirts suddenly formed a circle around her. They began to spin around and around as if she were a maypole. The weird masks blurred until all she saw were the eyes — staring, prying, opening her up like an oyster to gouge out the vital pith of her soul.

Corinne was drowning in a sea of pain, clutching at consciousness as if it were a life preserver.

272

Sound melted into sight. The twirling gays were a fast blur of color. Her pain was increased by a power of ten. She cried out.

Corinne was well beyond the point of being able to notice the chalk-white face now staring at her from the group of spectators lining the opposite side of the street.

It was not just an oblique gaze this time, but a steady, fixed stare.

For a long and blissful moment the pain eased, and she felt a warm inner glow of happiness and peace. She smelled homemade bread baking, recalled the peaceful lake where she used to swim as a little girl. Instead of the raucous parade noises, she heard a pure, beautiful singing like the crystal-clear voices of angels.

It was the last thing she was aware of before a voice from Hell whispered, *Welcome home, bitch!* and she collapsed in a pathetic huddle amongst the whirling dancers.

Chapter 30

Breaux kept the Emperor in sight as he tailed him along St. Peter Street, but immediately lost him when the old man cut over to join the parade pandemonium on Toulouse.

"Cool it, fuckhead!"

"Hey, man, watch where you're going!"

Breaux muttered terse apologies, elbowing spectators aside, stepping on toes as he fought his way along the sidewalk. Twenty feet ahead, in the motley confusion of costumed celebrants, he thought he glimpsed a white face.

He was vaguely aware, as he clawed his way forward, of the twirling group of gays dancing on the opposite side of the street. Breaux frowned when he realized the white face *was* the Emperor's — and he was staring hard toward the whirling dancers.

Breaux followed the old man's gaze across the street. At first he didn't understand. Then, with a cold shock of realization, he recognized the person at the hub of that hectic circle as the same girl he had seen with Steve Jernigan.

"I'll be go to hell," he said slowly, cold sweat breaking out on his temples.

The Emperor stared harder. Now the girl faltered.

"Hey!" Breaux shouted. *"Grab him!"*

He held his wallet high, displaying his photostat ID. "Grab that man!" he shouted again.

It was useless. His words went as unnoticed in the din as tears in a rainstorm. His pulse throbbed in his ears as Breaux tried to fight his way closer to the Emperor.

Suddenly the girl collapsed like a rag doll.

"Shit!"

Breaux grunted. He gripped the top of a metal barricade and vaulted it smoothly. But a marching band flashing by impeded his progress. The dancers had stopped and one of them was kneeling to check on the girl. Breaux heaved a sigh of relief when he saw another one frantically signaling to a nearby team of parade medics.

Breaux didn't know if she was still alive, but he did know there was nothing he could do for her. Instead, he decided to continue following the Emperor.

The crowd was especially dense, and Breaux made agonizingly slow progress. Again he glimpsed white and realized the Emperor was looking back over his shoulder, watching for him.

(*And what if he stares at you?*)

275

His stomach turned into a solid lump of ice, but he pressed forward. At least, he thought, the crowd was also impeding the old mime. He didn't speculate about what he was going to do when he finally caught up with him. Despite what he had just seen, the reality wouldn't sink in that he was trying to catch a devil by the tail.

But what he saw next turned him into a True Believer.

He had been steadily gaining as the Emperor was virtually stopped by a human chokepoint of spectators. A moment later those same spectators were being scattered like bowling pins by some invisible force, spewing them left and right, opening a passage in front of the fleeing mime.

Motionless with horror, Breaux watched a woman fly fifteen feet in the air and return to the pavement head first, her neck snapping at a grotesque angle. An obscenely fat man rose clumsily heavenward like the Goodyear blimp, his day-glo dashiki flapping in the wind. Then he plummeted back down into the middle of the marching band, crushing a trombone player. A young girl and her pet golden lab went airborne, a cruel parody of Dorothy and Toto being sucked up by the twister. Breaux averted his terrified gaze when they landed under the wheels of a tractor-driven float.

Then came the explosion, tearing loose great chunks of concrete and belching a gouting spume of smoke and fire.

Screams filled the air. The music abruptly stopped as the parade came to a halt. Still too stunned to move, Breaux watched the Emperor slip away through the passageway he had cleared like Moses parting the Red Sea. The last thing the policeman was aware of was the Emperor ducking into the parking lot of the nearby Big E-Z Motel complex.

Then a panicked wall of fleeing spectators slammed into him, and Breaux went down in a writhing confusion of limbs.

When he regained consciousness some time later, the place looked like the aftermath of a battle. The dead and dying lay scattered everywhere, the injured groaning pitifully. One man, fully conscious, sat against a lightpost, hugging his exposed guts and begging for a priest. Witnesses of the inexplicable carnage cried hysterically. Several ambulances were at the scene and Breaux could hear sirens screaming as more arrived, hampered by the blast rubble.

He struggled to a sitting position and gingerly felt the huge goose egg over his left ear. Then he remembered, and his eyes turned toward the motel complex. Groaning, he struggled to his feet and made his way unsteadily toward the office.

He paid little attention to the dapper, late-fortyish businessman type who emerged from one of the rooms, a briefcase in hand. For a moment the man watched him with cool, detached, ice-blue eyes. Then he disappeared around the corner of the building.

Alan Breaux was perched on the stoop when Jernigan returned to his apartment building early in the afternoon.

"Hey, old sleuth! How . . ."

A glimpse at the ugly knot over the detective's ear brought Jernigan up short.

"What the hell happened to you?"

Then he read something in his friend's eyes that made him pale slightly. He glanced next door toward Corinne's balcony.

"I take it you haven't been listening to the radio?" Breaux said.

Steve shook his head in numb confusion. "Corinne," he whispered, not making it a question.

Breaux nodded. He stood up unsteadily. He looked as if he had aged at least five years since Steve had seen him last.

"She's at Presbyterian Hospital," the policeman explained. "C'mon. I'll explain on the way."

"Hospital," Steve repeated stupidly. "How . . . how bad?"

Breaux met his eyes, then glanced away. "Let's go," he repeated. "I'll fill you in on the way."

"How *bad?*" Steve demanded.

Breaux took a deep breath to steel himself. "Bad," he said. "Very. She's in intensive care.

They don't expect her to make it."

Steve stood immobile for a full minute. His face registered nothing. When he spoke, his voice sounded tiny and faraway.

"Give me a few minutes. I've got a call to make first."

"We don't *have* a few minutes," Breaux snapped.

Some color returned to Steve's face. "Tell me," he said, a raw edge creeping into his voice, "what the hell did the hospital do for Sabrina? We both know damn good and well that no hospital is going to help her now. Wait for me. I'll be down in a few minutes."

He took the steps two at a time, praying to God that he could reach Lisa in Ann Arbor before it was too late.

Corinne's voice drifted back to him from that first night they had spent together: *I'm scared, Steve. I don't understand what's happening to me, and I'm just so scared. I don't want to die!*

Ten years younger than Breaux, Police Chief Hal Cameron was perceived by most of his fellow cops as middling—middling tall, middling competent, middling honest. Trained in business as well as criminal science, he was an efficient administrator who kissed a minimum of ass and was not on the payroll of any sleazeoid element. But like most of the able numbers-crunchers, he thought a "hunch" was something you corrected surgically.

All this had looped through Breaux's mind after he dropped Jernigan off at the hospital and returned to the main precinct in the City Building downtown. He spent twenty minutes pacing in the waiting area outside Cameron's office, across the corridor from Internal Affairs Division. Then the paneled door finally burst open and a knot of clamoring journalists suddenly streamed out, racing for the banks of pay phones in the lobby.

A minute later Cameron appeared in the doorway, loosening his navy rep tie. "Breaux," he said simply, too enervated from the press conference to inject any feeling into it.

He pushed his door open wider, and Breaux read it as an invitation to enter. He selected a pea-green vinyl chair squatting before a huge wall-poster bar graph of the current NOPD budget.

"Fucking scoops," Cameron said wearily. "Bunch a goddamn piranhas." He sank into the swivel chair behind the desk. "I take it you know by now what happened in the Quarter?"

Breaux nodded. "I had a ringside seat."

He turned his face enough for Cameron to see the prominent swelling over his ear.

The chief whistled. "Get it looked at?"

"Sure," Breaux lied.

A moment later Cameron frowned. "Why didn't you mention this to me before now? Could've used you around here."

The first response that popped into his head was almost true, anyway, so Breaux went with it for simplicity's sake. "A friend of mine was hurt. I had to help her."

"Sorry to hear it. She okay?"

"Too soon to tell."

Cameron shook his head. "Just what we need with only three days till Mardi Gras."

"That's why I'm here," Breaux interjected. But Cameron, still pumped up from his press conference, missed the comment. He shook his head again in disgust and pointed at the budget illustration behind Breaux.

"Why should *I* take the heat for a Department of Utilities screwup? Price of crude dips any lower, we're talking some deep cuts in the city budget next year. I've got good officers leaving every day because Atlanta and Miami and Nashville and where-the-hell-ever can pay decent wages and offer some competitive bennies. Mayor's task force is screaming at me, put more officers on the beat. Where the hell'm I spozed to *get* them when the City Council cuts each recruit class by five percent?"

Breaux nodded, saying nothing. It was Cameron's favorite spiel, and Breaux already knew it by heart.

Cameron had more lamentations to sing, but suddenly seemed to realize what Breaux had said earlier. He looked at the older man. "What's on your mind, Lieutenant?"

"What went down today, among other things. I don't think it was a Department of Utilities screw-up."

Carefully, trying to be as precise as he could, Breaux explained what he had witnessed today. He was especially careful when describing how the victims had been hurled into the air *before* any actual explosion.

But the difficult part concerned his suspicions of the Emperor. Only now, faced with the task of describing them, did he realize how frustratingly subjective his "case" was. Try as he might, Breaux simply could not bring himself to the point of actually naming the mime, or even baldly stating his conviction that the old man possessed unnatural, powerfully destructive powers. After all, there wasn't one scintilla of tangible proof. He had to satisfy himself with a pallid, sketchy overview: his suspicion that recent deaths in the French Quarter were linked to the "accident" today—and that even more carnage was in store for Fat Tuesday. The lack of hard evidence, the huge gaps, made his concluding plea for special security on Mardi Gras seem ridiculously futile.

When Breaux finished, Cameron watched him for a long moment, wondering just how hard that blow to his head might have been. But the chief kept his voice carefully neutral.

"Look, Al. Frankly, I'm hearing a lot of fantastic generalities here. You want to name some names, provide some dates, prove some crimes and probable causes, maybe that's a different ball game. But we're talking *three days* till Carnival."

Breaux nodded. The impossibility of what he was trying to do now confronted him starkly. Cameron read the confusion in his face.

"Hell, you're a good cop," the chief said in a tired, consoling tone. "But let's face it, guy. If I even *suggest* interfering with the usual Mardi Gras itinerary, I'm gonna make the grinch who stole Christmas look like a folk hero. Not to mention the fact that I'll end up in Cowpie, Nebraska, palming doorknobs until I retire."

Breaux nodded, his face a study in misery. Cameron watched him a moment longer, then added, "Tell you what. Since this obviously means so much to you, I'll see what I can do about maybe setting up a couple hundred more volunteer crowd marshals with police armbands. All right?"

Breaux said nothing. If what he and Jernigan suspected was in fact true, such a gesture would merely be shoveling sand against the tide. But evidently it would have to do. The only alternative was to press harder and risk a psychiatric leave from the force.

He rose to leave. "Thank you, sir," he said without conviction.

283

"Cheer up, Al. Christ, people screw in the streets on Mardi Gras, *you* know that. What the hell we gonna do?"

Breaux nodded again. But Cameron's words followed him all the way home and hounded him long into the night, keeping sleep at bay: *What the hell we gonna do?*

Chapter 31

"Where y'at, cap?"

Startled out of his gloomy thoughts, Steve nearly dropped his coffee cup.

"Tree! You made it."

His friend's usual snake-swift grin was replaced by a puzzled frown as he measured the troubled gray-green depths of Steve's eyes. But he said nothing, only turning to nod at the elderly black woman standing beside him.

"This here's the lady I told you 'bout when you called last night, brah. Della Claiborne, meet my friend Steve Jernigan."

Steve rose from his seat at the cafeteria table and took her gnarled, hard-knit hand in his for a moment. The old voodoo *mambo* was tall, nearly as tall as Steve, and wore her grizzled salt 'n' pepper hair cut close to the scalp. Her huge, coffee-colored eyes slid away from him, resting on the hospital employees and the early visitors filing through the breakfast line.

"Uhh . . . look," Tree said awkwardly. "I got

Miz Claiborne outta bed pretty early this morning. I don't 'magine she had time to grab much to eat."

It took Steve a few seconds to understand that Tree wanted to say something to him in private. He hastily reached for his wallet and slipped out a five-dollar bill, handing it to the woman. She smiled briefly, flashing a mouthful of nicotine-stained teeth, then ambled off with slow dignity to join the breakfast queue.

"Listen, brah," Tree said as soon as she was out of earshot and the two men had sat back down. "My gran'mama said to tell you — Della's poor as a church mouse, but *don't* offer her no money for her services. That's spoze to be bad luck and it'll only piss her off. What you do is, you tell her you want to mail a contribution to the church she belongs to."

Steve nodded. Tree hunched forward on his elbows, his shiny black dreadlocks framing his puzzled face. He shot a curious glance at the paper bag beside Steve's cup.

"I ain't gonna ax you what the hell you're doing. None a my business. Just tell me this much. Is that old shack part of it?"

Steve hesitated, recalling last night's phone call to Lisa. She had reminded him that, according to folklore, once a victim succumbed to *malocchio,* mere protections were useless. Only an outright cure might help the victim — a cure brought about by only the most powerful white magic. Deeply puzzled and angered by his reticence, Lisa had nonetheless relayed strict instructions for a supposedly powerful healing ritual. She had also emphasized that only a recognized priest or priestess of white magic could undertake any curative attempt.

Steve nodded finally. "I think it also," he volunteered, "has something to do with what happened yesterday during the parade on Toulouse."

Tree studied him closely.

"What happened yesterday," he repeated. "You sayin' it wasn't no gas main blowing up?"

Four persons had been killed and a dozen others injured in yesterday's carnage. Despite the seriousness of the "freak accident"—perhaps even because of it—city officials were adamant that Mardi Gras festivities would go on as planned. And that included the grand King Rex parade on Fat Tuesday.

But Breaux had insisted to Steve that the actual explosion had come long *after* those victims were hurled into the air. Meaning, thought Steve grimly, that Eric Winters—a.k.a. the Emperor—had somehow graduated to new levels of demonic terror. *An unnatural ability,* Robert Jernigan had written in his journal, *augmented by an unnatural hatred.*

"Let's just say a gas main isn't all it was," Steve replied.

Both men watched the old *mambo* stop at the cash register to pay for her meal.

Tree said, "How long you gone need her?"

Steve shrugged one shoulder and glanced apprehensively at the clock over the cafeteria entrance. It was not quite eight A.M. Upstairs in Intensive Care, Corinne lay dying. And he still hadn't figured out a way to circumvent the medical staff long enough to conduct the ceremony Lisa had prescribed.

"Tell you in a minute," he replied. Seeing Alan Breaux giving him the high sign from the cafeteria entrance, Steve excused himself and hurried across the dining area to meet him.

"You call him?" Steve asked.

Breaux nodded. "His wife wants my ass on a silver platter for waking them up, but he's on his way."

Part of the massive weight lifted up off Steve's chest.

"All right! I just hope to hell he has some muscle around here."

Breaux looked doubtful. "Even if he can, *will* he? Don't forget he's a doctor."

"Yeah. And I'm a scientist and you're a cop. Do *you* believe it now?"

Breaux still looked like a man trying to figure out what century he had awakened in. "I don't know. Even after yesterday. I mean, I saw it, but I still don't believe it. Did your friend come through for you?" The policeman glanced toward the table where Tree was sitting.

Steve nodded toward the old *mambo,* who was

returning with her tray.

Breaux tried to grin. "She eats Wheaties."

Steve was too preoccupied to appreciate the wry humor of his remark. "Nothing else on the motel?"

The cop shook his head. "Zip. Right now the place is filled to capacity for Mardi Gras. It'd take a week to run a make on all those names. The manager insists that no one has registered under the name Winters. I think you're right, though. If the guy has been leading two separate existences, he'd need a safe place to change. And that guy I saw leaving the place yesterday definitely fits the description you gave me of this Winters character."

Steve had already filled his friend in on the Winters-Emperor nexus. "I doubt if he'll go back there now," Jernigan said. "And by now he knows we're after him. So the question is, where will he be hiding between now and Tuesday?"

Breaux met the younger man's eyes. "His house or, if your hunch is right, that shack?"

Steve nodded. Before Breaux could say anything else, they both saw a neatly bearded, extremely unhappy-looking man hurrying toward them.

"Cross your fingers," said Breaux. "Here comes Grodner."

After Breaux introduced the two men, the trio retreated to Grodner's office in the administrative-staff wing. The physician sat in passive silence, staring into a cup of Folger's Instant, as they outlined what they planned to do. Time constraints, among other reasons, forced them to gloss over the background details. They concentrated instead on the ceremony they wanted the *mambo* to perform.

"We can't get in there without your help," Breaux concluded. "Only immediate family and clergy. Plus we have to be guaranteed some privacy for a half hour or so."

Grodner shook his head. "I don't believe this," he said slowly. "You got me out of bed to—"

"Look at me, Doctor," Breaux cut in sharply. "*Look* at me! I'm a cop! For thirty years I've been dealing with street scum, listening to bullshit, even bouncing a few ratshits off the curb. Do I look like your average fruitcake who goes in for Ouija boards and tarot cards?"

Grodner watched him for a minute, idly flipping through the Rolodex on his desk. He was clearly surprised by the peremptoriness of the normally mild cop's tone. "I'd say a Madame Blavatsky you definitely are not," he admitted finally.

"Hell no! And just look at the situation here. This is the *third* healthy young girl to drop for no apparent reason. All pretty, all talented, all living and working in the French Quarter. Now I ask you, how does *that* rate on your Scale of Medical Weirdness?"

"Pretty damn high."

Grodner sat quietly for a moment, his face lost in troubled reflection. Finally he picked up the phone and punched in an extension.

"Sharon? Bob Grodner here. Say, have you got any update on the Matthews girl in Unit 17?"

He waited a moment, then nodded. "I see. Still no working diagnosis? Nothing? I see. Yes, thanks, Sharon. No, that won't be necessary."

He hung up. His eyebrows almost met as he frowned.

"Doctor," said Steve, "what do you lose by humoring us? At worst it will just be a waste of time."

Grodner sighed. He rose from the desk and began pacing. After a minute or two, he looked at Breaux.

"Last time you told me you suspected there was 'something odd' about Sabrina's collapse. Assuming I agree to help you, are you prepared to get more specific?"

Steve and Breaux exchanged glances. "If we explain it to you," Steve suggested, "you still won't believe us. But tell you what. Give us a hand, and maybe we can *show* you what we mean."

Grodner studied his medical diploma on the wall, as if apologizing to it for what he was about to do.

"All right," he said, surrendering finally. "It's nuts, but I'll see what I can do. No promises, though. This is the craziest damn thing I've ever heard of."

Steve hated to admit it, even to himself, but Corinne looked beautiful as she hovered on the very threshold of death.

The unconscious girl was surrounded by a high-tech confusion of tubes and IV bottles and electrode leads. Her wan face was almost as white as the skimpy hospital johnny she wore. Grodner paused at the foot of the bed to read her chart. He shook his head, obviously not very encouraged by whatever he saw there.

Just before Grodner's intervention had finally snipped through the red tape, clearing the way for this visit, Steve had sequestered himself with Della Claiborne. Her huge, dun-colored eyes had remained politely distant as he explained Lisa's meticulous instructions.

Clearly, from her point of view, he was covering old ground. Now, without a word, she took the bag from Steve and moved beside the bed. She carefully traced the outline of Corinne's body with a handful of evenly spaced animal claws and teeth that Steve had found in a small French Quarter shop specializing in voodoo paraphernalia. When this was finished she drew out a silver necklace, from which hung a single charm in the image of a bluebird. This she draped around the head of the bed, the bluebird dangling near the unconscious girl's face.

The three men were startled when, upon finishing this task, the old *mambo* made the sign of the cross and uttered the first words they had heard her speak all morning. Her voice echoed deep and resonant in the silent hospital room.

"Eye and Evil Eye! And break his eye.
Let envy die, and the Evil Eye explode!"

Grodner met Breaux's gaze, then looked away, shaking his head. The physician stood before a gleaming cardiac-monitoring unit. He was most concerned with the digital readout on the screen of the electrocardiograph, a measure of critical electrical-pulse changes in Corinne's heart.

The *mambo* crossed to a corner closet and opened the door. She rummaged through the few items of clothing hanging within, finally removing the blouse Corinne had been wearing when she was rushed to the hospital.

Without a word she dropped it into a metal trash receptacle. Then she removed a Zippo lighter from the pocket of her skirt and set the blouse on fire.

"Wait a minute!" Grodner objected. He fell silent when the other two shot him warning looks.

Still muttering, Grodner cranked the room's only window open, letting the smoke dissipate before it triggered the alarm. After the *mambo* had thus symbolically destroyed the curse of *malocchio,* she dug back into the bag and removed a

293

medium-deep ceramic dish. She filled it half-full with water from a plastic bottle and made the sign of the cross over it. Then she set the dish at the foot of the bed.

"May the Loa mount you and heal your suffering," the white witch muttered. "May the Devil's curse return back and injure the one who gave this curse of the evil eye."

From a smaller bottle she placed a drop of olive oil on the end of her middle finger and dropped it into the water in the dish. Slowly, one by one, she let five more drops fall into the water. She stared intently, frowning when the oil spread out in a large circle.

She shook her head, mumbled something in Creole dialect, and glanced at Steve.

"The curse is powerful," she pronounced. "The most powerful ever I see. I cannot hope to harm the Overlooker by returning his curse, only to *perhaps* help this girl."

Steve nodded. He swallowed with difficulty. "Please try," he said.

The *mambo* hesitated. "It might kill her, you understand?" the witch warned. "She dies anyway, but if the curse fails, death comes faster. It comes *now.*"

Steve nodded again. He avoided the glances of the other two men. "I understand. Please try."

She removed a thin silver knife from the bag. Carefully, she cut the oil on the surface of the water in the shape of a cross. This done, she crossed to the window and emptied the dish. Three more times she repeated the entire process with the oil and water, and emptied it. The fourth time she skipped the oil and added a pinch of salt to the water instead, repeating:

> "Water and salt,
> I hope that whatever
> The witches devise will *fail!*"

She tossed it out the window and turned to stare at Corinne's inert form.

Steve too stared at Corinne.

Breaux watched Grodner.

Grodner stared at the cardiac monitor, his face draining white above his beard.

"We're losing her! *Shit,* we're losing her!" he shouted.

He leaped for the emergency call button beside the bed. Reacting instinctively, Breaux grabbed him in a bear hug and restrained him.

From the bed came an ominous rattling, like pebbles caught in a sluice gate. Corinne's lungs were giving up the ghost.

"You idiots!" screamed Grodner, his face twisted in panic. "You fucking idiots, she's dying! You're *killing* her!"

What the old *mambo* did next was not in the ritual Lisa had carefully prescribed.

Snatching up the thin silver knife, she leaped toward the bed.

"Stop her!" Breaux commanded.

But before Steve could move, she had plunged the knife into her own thin, brown arm. As her blood splattered the sheet, she screamed, "My blood for your power, damned Fascinator! *Done,* in the name of the Loa!"

Steve froze. His flesh crawled against his shirt, as Corinne abruptly sat up, scattering tubes and IV's every which way. The hideous voice that roared from her lips blasted them like a simoom from the furnace of Hell.

"Does mine eye offend thee, cocksuckers for the Messiah? Then *pluck* it out!"

A protracted bark of harsh laughter issued from her throat as she fixed gleaming-coal eyes on each member of the room. Then she uttered a piercing scream of agony and pain and collapsed back into the pillow.

Chapter 32

It was still well before noon when Breaux parked his Toyota on the crushed-shell cul-de-sac in front of Eric Winters's house.

Dark, heavy clouds were racing in from the gulf, threatening to obliterate the sun. In the muted light, the squat California bungalow seemed to hunker down behind the yew hedges out front, ready to leap on any trespassers. The iron-reinforced door, the barred and shuttered windows, gave it the impression of a fortress.

"No car around," said Breaux, trying not to sound relieved.

Steve was the first to open his door. "Place looks like it did last time I was here. I'll try the bell again just for drill. Why don't you go around back? No one'll see us there."

Breaux nodded. He opened the glove compartment and rummaged among the contents for a moment, removing several copper shims. "Hate to get cute on you, but what do you do if he answers the door?"

Steve met his eye for a second or two before looking at the house again. His face was rough with the blue-black shadow of beard stubble. He tried to ignore the cool sweat breaking out under his arms as he considered the question.

For a moment his right had wandered to something round and hard protruding from the pocket of his sport jacket. Its touch was vaguely reassuring.

"He won't be home," Steve answered finally. He didn't bother to add what both men already feared: *If he is, it may be the last doorbell we ever ring.*

Shells crunched softly under their feet as they stepped out of the car. Breaux slipped out of sight behind a clump of azalea bushes at the nearest corner of the silent house. Steve hesitated only a moment before ascending the trio of front steps and leaning against the doorbell.

A minute later he whispered muttered thanks that no one had answered. Trying to ignore the voice that warned him that Winters could be hiding inside, he went around back to join Breaux.

The cop had already worked a shim between the jamb and the lock mechanism of the heavy oak door.

"Been a while since I've done this," he said. "These newer locks're a bitch to—"

With a quick metallic *snick,* the tumblers moved and the bolt snapped back.

The two men exchanged a long look. Then, without a word, Breaux eased the door open.

Sunshine flooded a big kitchen, pushing shadows back into the corners and setting miniature galaxies of dust motes aglitter. The room was silent except for the low hum of a coppertone refrigerator. Several dead plants lined the windowsill over the sink, their leaves brown and crumpled from a lack of water and light. The house smelled dusty and vaguely medicinal.

A short hallway flanked by a closed door on either side connected the kitchen to the front of the house. The pair took a quick glance around the living room to make sure it was empty. Then, their steps muffled by the thick pile carpet, they returned to the hallway and tried the door on their right.

It was unlocked, and opened with a slow creaking groan.

"I'll be damned," Breaux whispered softly.

Both men stared at the crumpled lace jabot lying on the floor just inside the room. Something rattled against the door when Breaux pushed it open wider. He reached around and plucked the purple Mardi Gras beads off the inside door handle.

They exchanged another glance but said nothing.

A few moments later Steve emerged from the adjoining bathroom, a hairbrush in one hand. Its stiff bristles were tinted silver white.

A quick but thorough search of the bedroom turned up nothing else of obvious importance.

"I'd say our theory was right," Steve conjectured. He stared at the jabot lying on the floor like a discarded banana peel. "He rented the motel room so he'd have a safe spot to change. That way the neighbors couldn't make a connection between him and the Emperor."

Breaux nodded. Without a word, both men turned at the same time to stare at the closed door on the opposite side of the hallway.

It seemed to stare back, inviting them—*daring* them—to enter.

" 'Ah, but a man's reach should exceed his grasp, or what's a heaven for?' " Breaux quipped, fortifying himself.

He reached the door first and tried the knob. It was locked. Not bothering with the shim, both men heaved their shoulders into it. Wood splintered and the door banged open. Breaux slapped at a light switch just inside the entrance.

After several flickering false starts, a set of fluorescent lights hummed to life overhead. It was a basement—or what passed for a basement in New Orleans, where the nearby water table made deep digging difficult. A half-dozen unpainted wooden steps descended into a cool, well-lighted area with central air-conditioning and a concrete floor.

His pulse throbbing in his ears, Steve eased past his companion and descended. He paused at the bottom of the steps and did a double take.

"This time we win the cigar," he called over his shoulder to Breaux, making no attempt to suppress the excitement in his voice.

The cop joined him. A moment later his jaw dropped in astonishment.

The area had been converted to a small but sophisticated lab. There were four long, zinc-topped counters crowded with electron microscopes, specimen jars, beakers, and butane burners. Breaux had no idea what purpose the long bank of monitors and gauges and computer-linked VDT's lining the far wall served. But it wasn't the high-tech dazzle that had arrested his attention. Instead, his eyes were rooted to a huge specimen jar reigning alone in a glass-fronted cabinet in the middle of the room.

Floating in the murky solution was the huge, off-white cauliflower of a human brain. Or rather, what was left of one. Several sections were missing, as if some capricious snacker had taken a bite now and then in passing.

"Alan Breaux," said Steve, his awed tone belying the morbid humor of his remark, "meet Mario Townsend."

Breaux shifted his shocked gaze to the younger man. "Townsend? The psychic? You mean . . . ?"

Steve nodded, moving closer. After five years of fruitless searching, hundreds of sleepless nights, thousands of hours of idle speculation, he had just struck pay dirt.

"How can you be sure it's him?"

301

Steve opened the cabinet and poked the jar with the tip of his index finger.

"Technically, I can't. Not right here and now. But see those missing sections—there, and there, and right here? Large chunks of the cerebral cortex are missing, as well as the entire pituitary gland and hypothalamus. According to my father's research, those were the areas most advanced in Townsend's brain. It was to facilitate study of those specific regions that Townsend left his brain to my father and his associate. And look there."

Steve pointed to a small stainless-steel gadget on a shelf below the specimen jar.

"That's a pill press. Seen one before?"

Breaux shook his head.

"Pharmaceutical companies and the narco mobs use them to press out all those little tabs that contain the measured doses of whatever. Winters was somehow extracting the chemical transmitters from Townsend's brain, re-synthesizing them with his blood-pressure medicine. A perfect system. Finding a safe inert base for new chemicals is time-consuming. He could ride piggyback on the legitimate medicine, using its base as the carrier for his chemical extraction."

As he spoke, Steve was rifling through a stack of record books in the bottom half of the cabinet. One was labeled DAYBOOK: MAXIMUM BETA MODE in neatly printed letters. He flipped open the cover. Taped to page one was a faded yellow clipping from the June 5, 1977 *New York*

NOTED PSYCHIC WILLS BRAIN
· TO UNIVERSITY RESEARCH TEAM

They scanned the lead. Then both men looked up and locked glances again.

"Anymore doubts?" Steve asked.

Breaux shook his head. He no longer felt motivated to play the devil's advocate.

"All right," he surrendered. *"We* know. But even with all this, we've got no conclusive proof of legal wrongdoing. Just hope something concrete turns up at that shack this afternoon so I can take this to the heavies. If we're right, we've only got two days to find that crazy bastard. We're talking a million-and-a-half people on the streets for Mardi Gras. We don't stand a snowball's chance in Hell of locating him without help."

Again Steve eased his fingers into his jacket pocket and nudged the hard object within.

"Even *with* help," he mused, "we may not stand a chance."

He lapsed into silence while he flipped through Winters's daybook and thought about Corinne. True, after uttering those terrifying words and collapsing earlier today, her recovery had been nothing short of miraculous. Only moments later she had opened her eyes — normal, copper-colored eyes dazed with confusion but devoid of that demonic gleam.

303

But according to the last notations in this record, on Fat Tuesday Winters planned on increasing his dose of MBM by a factor of ten.

Two days . . .

They didn't understand why, but in two days — a mere forty-eight hours and counting — a human monster would embark on a holy jihad that would turn the world's biggest free party into a supernatural bloodbath.

Steve felt his scalp go cool with sweat.

"Let's get the hell out of here," he suggested, and Breaux didn't seem inclined to challenge the idea.

Chapter 33

Even nature herself had decided to abet the cause of Eric Winters.

Steve and Breaux were forced to postpone their Saturday afternoon visit to Honey Island Swamp, preempted by the huge black thunderheads which had suddenly blown in off the Gulf of Mexico. The storm began ten minutes after they left Winters's house and ushered in a torrential, wind-driven rain that lashed New Orleans mercilessly until late Sunday afternoon. Ten inches of rain in just twenty-four hours stripped leaves from trees and flooded streets, forcing National Guard and civilian volunteers to sandbag several key levees in the outlying parishes.

Then, as abruptly as it had begun, the storm stopped. Depleted clouds scattered like ashes in the wind. By four P.M. Sunday, Mardi Gras revelers were pouring into the streets, rejoicing in the return of Sol. The world's biggest free party was back on track with a hedonistic vengeance, making up for lost time.

"Here, babe," fussed Maddy, handing Corinne a blanket. "Better tuck this around you. It's still a little nippy out here."

Corinne, basking in the sun, felt as lazy as a lizard on a hot rock. Reluctantly, she shifted in the lounge chair to look up at her friend.

"Maddy, would you stop mother-henning me to death? I'm not an invalid, I feel fine!"

"Don't push your luck, puss. The doctors told you to rest."

"I *am* resting! They didn't tell me to smother myself."

Only one other patient shared this corner of the hospital sun terrace with them, a woman in her seventies who had long ago nodded to sleep over a copy of *Reader's Digest*. Five stories below, Mardi Gras was building to a fever pitch. The crowd ebbed and flowed in a colorful human tide. From this height Corinne and Maddy could even see Jackson Square. Its mass of revelers was punctuated by a record number of jugglers, mimes, unicyclists, palm-readers, fortune-tellers, and break dancers. A BBC filming crew was recording the action from a wooden platform in the middle of the square.

"Good God, have you ever seen the carnival crowd this big?"

Corinne surveyed it all, a smile momentarily lifting the corners of her mouth. Somewhere a brass band struck up "Dixie," and the smile

306

slowly faded to a pensive frown as she recalled Friday's fateful parade.

She remembered so little about it. That had been only two days ago, but already the images and impressions were as vague as a childhood memory. Corinne dimly recalled the nightmare of fighting her way through the crowd, and the horrible pain just before she blacked out. After that, nothing—until she came to in the hospital with all of them ringed anxiously around her bed. A bearded stranger was bandaging an old black woman's arm, and the sheets were spattered with blood. And yet, she had felt fine. Later, Steve carefully filled her in about everything, supplying whatever missing pieces he and Breaux had gathered.

Now the events of the past few weeks seemed like something she had merely hallucinated.

Dimly, she became aware of Maddy's voice penetrating her reverie.

"Attention, K-mart Shoppers!"

Corinne glanced up at her guiltily. Maddy stood over her chair offering a steaming wide-mouth thermos. Her fingers were brilliant with rings, her arms covered nearly to the elbows by her omnipresent bangles.

"Heah y'go, babe. Hospital food won't cut it. You need some of Aunt Maddy's special-recipe seafood gumbo."

"I'm not hungry right now."

"You eat, girl! You may feel fine, but you're so skinny you could walk through a harp! Put some meat on those bones."

Corinne gave in with a sigh and accepted the thermos. She set it down beside her chair and absently handed her friend a Kleenex. Without a word, Maddy automatically dabbed at the lipstick smearing her teeth.

The brass-bound lobby doors swung silently open and a readheaded nurse burst onto the terrace, her bright smile rivaling the late-afternoon sunshine. She crossed to her elderly patient, leaned over the chair for a moment, then returned by way of Corinne and Maddy.

"The doctors want you to nap, young lady," she ordered. "You haven't slept since late morning."

She glanced reprovingly at Maddy, including her in the admonition. "I'm trying," Corinne said. "I'm just not sleepy right now."

The nurse relented with another smile. "Mardi Gras fever. Tylenol won't help it. Twenty more minutes," she added for Maddy's benefit. Then she returned to the lobby.

Below, the din of the celebrants seemed to increase with each passing minute. Vehicle traffic had crawled to a standstill. A group of drunk Joe College types, cutting through the hospital parking lot to reach the Quarter, glanced up and saw Maddy standing near the tubular-steel railings.

"Show your tits!" one of them screamed.

"Show your dick!" she taunted back.

A moment later Maddy stepped away from the railing, her face aflame. "My God, the asshole *did* it!"

But Corinne missed the bawdy little interlude, her face blank with concentration.

(*They were close . . . perhaps too close. Do you understand me?*)

"Babe?"

(*Some say he was gifted—cursed—with something besides intelligence.*)

"Babe!"

(*It was Mardi Gras 1958 . . . Mardi Gras . . . Mardi Gras!*)

"Corinne!"

Slowly, Maddy's face came into focus, as if Corinne were surfacing from deep water.

Maddy's eyes were the first thing she noticed. Eyes that studied her closely, intently. For a moment, they didn't seem like eyes at all. To Corinne, they were weapons—a pair of psychic bullets piercing into the warm vital life of her. Again she thought of the *ahmaw,* the vampire soul. Corinne turned her face quickly away.

"Quit *looking* at me!" Corinne snapped.

The hurt was plain in Maddy's surprised face. "Well, shit! Why don't you just tell me to hit the bricks and get it over with! I'll talk to the sensitive artist later when she comes down off her *fuck*-ing high horse!"

She flounced toward the lobby doors. Then Maddy hesitated, turning to look at Corinne again. Her voice was softer.

"God, in His infinite wisdom, decided we should be good friends. Until you tell me otherwise, I'll assume He knew what He was doing. If you need *any*thing, puss, you give me a call, hear? Visiting hours or no, I'll get in! And look. I'm sorry about that sensitive-artist crack. You're my best friend, and I love you."

A moment later Maddy was gone. Corinne called out behind her. But Georges's words again drifted back from the hinterland of memory.

I saw it all. I will never forget. But perhaps even more terrible was the face of Alexey . . . watching him—oh, I have seen the sadness and pain of this world, ma jolie! But nothing before or since could be as that face!

Steve switched on the quartz running lights, and twin pencil beams of light probed almost futilely into the black velvet folds of the premature twilight.

Occasionally, traced in the weak margins of the lights, shadowy forms scrambled up the low banks of the bayou. Eyes watched them from out of the night, momentarily glinting like gemstones when the light caught them.

After his brief appearance at the hospital on

Saturday morning, Tree had been called south to Boothville to report for an emergency salvage operation. But he'd agreed to leave Steve a key to the north-shore boathouse where the small trawling motor for the dinghy was kept. By the time the storm cleared on Sunday, and Steve and Breaux reached the mouth of the East Pearl River, waning daylight had left the entrance to Honey Island Swamp a murky haze.

When they had navigated the last switchback before the shack, Steve cut the engine. He strained to make out the face of his companion in the crepuscular light.

"Shit-oh-dear," Breaux said softly. "I guess we're here."

They could just make out the shadowy mass of the shack. It perched menacingly atop its low hummock, guarding the bayou like Cerberus watching the River Styx. There was no apparent sign of habitation. Besides the musty stink of dead plant life, the air felt charged with some venomous perturbation—a pernicious, sulfurous stench that tickled their gag reflexes.

Steve threw the steel rim overboard, then leaped ashore first, dragging the nose of the dinghy a few feet out of the water. Breaux handed him a short handspike and one of two flashlights. Then he followed Steve onto the bank.

"Why don't we keep the lights off for now," Steve said in a voice barely above a whisper.

311

"Hundred to one the place is deserted. If some-body was inside, there'd be a light on, and some of it would have to spill through the cracks some-where. Still, let's play it safe until I pry that door open. C'mon. I'll knock first."

"Sounds neighborly," Breaux agreed.

The spongy ground felt like a thick carpet be-neath their soles. Insects and frogs sounded their eerie cadence against the silent backdrop of the swamp. A few feet from the shack Steve drew up short, catching his breath on a hissing intake.

"What is it?" Breaux whispered.

There was silence for about ten seconds. Steve passed the handspike back to Breaux. When he finally answered, his voice was wooden with barely contained fear.

"The door," he said, his voice croaking. "I think it's already open."

Fighting off a wave of panic, Steve reached one hand slowly forward and made contact with the scaly, weather-beaten door.

As he reached out toward he knew not what, Steve wanted to touch the reassuring solidity of the object lying snug against the flashlight in his jacket pocket. But somehow he resisted the temp-tation.

He saw haunting white faces, one of them transforming into Corinne's face twisted in a scream.

Steve touched the wood and pushed. An invisible cat mewed in the darkness as the rusted hinges gave way under protest.

And like the clue to it all, the gray weathered door of that shack swinging open . . . he could see nothing in the shadowy-cave depths beyond the door.

Moving in slow-motion dream time, his pulse thudding hard against his eardrums, Steve removed the flashlight.

Nothing but darkness. Until, heart scampering, he stepped further into the shack and the door thumped shut behind him triggering the brittle, cackling laughter of the foul hell hag who lurked within, waiting just for him.

Dreading the simple movement more than anything he'd ever done in his life, Steve aimed the flashlight toward the interior of the shack and flicked it on.

As he watched Jernigan reach forward in the darkness to test that half-open door, Alan Breaux raised one hand to the shoulder holster under his jacket and unsnapped the Colt .38 Police Special.

He wrestled mightily with his fears, losing the battle but at least sustained by the struggle.

Breaux wasn't quite sure at what point he had come to the realization that this case—unofficial or not—was his last real stand as a cop, the final victory he wanted to take into old age. It was his consolation prize for losing the race against mortality. He was defending the city of his birth, his home. This was the ultimate test of those words printed on the door of every blue-and-white cruiser in New Orleans: TO PROTECT AND SERVE.

The door creaked open, its hinges crying, *"Rrr-uuu-nnnnnn!"*

Beside him, Steve directed the flashlight beam into the darkness.

"My *God,*" breathed the detective. He was dimly ashamed of the hot urine suddenly spurting down his thigh.

Corinne would have recognized the face from the sketch Georges had shown her. But the intruders wouldn't know until later that it was Katerina Zverkov who lay on a crude but clean shakedown against the back wall. Exactly how long she had been dead was impossible to say. She wore the same blue-velvet gown trimmed with sheer white lawn that Georges had described to Corinne. She was also wearing her Mardi Gras crown of gardenias. Both the flowers and the encrusted, rust-colored blood coating them had obviously been chemically preserved for eternity years before. So had Katerina's grotesquely deformed body, still humped and gnarled like a human pretzel from the accident which had destroyed her.

The two mystified men recognized the lace ja-

314

bot twined through her fingers.

Though it was impossible to tell when she had died, the intruders could clearly see the probable cause.

Her lover had also chemically preserved the stillborn infant at Katerina's breast. The oddly mismatched, brown and blue eyes of the child's father glittered like pastel marbles in the flashlight's steady beam.

They had come into the world literally as one. The surgeon's knife that cleft them in twain had not been able to sever their single spirit.

Desperate with inexpressible grief and rage after her cruel maiming, he had written a heartfelt plea to the widow of his dead father, then living in comfortable exile in Europe. Moved by pity for the illegitimate offspring of her husband, she had been generous with money.

Constantly at her bedside in the private hospital in Florida—except for brief trips back to Louisiana to make certain practical arrangements—he nurtured his dream of revenge in the long hours of silence as he watched her languish. He could not know then if the seed germinating inside her had been snuffed out along with the flame of her vitality. But that seed was their secret. She had sworn him to that. If he was to protect that secret—and spare her the gross indignity of pity-

315

ing, prying eyes—he knew her next home would have to be as inconspicuous as possible. Special arrangements through a discreet New Orleans attorney and an absentee realtor had secured the land and shack in Honey Island Swamp.

The hospital could do little for her beyond providing sedation for the excruciating pain. "Physical therapy" was a cruel joke. Her spine had been shattered beyond surgical help, leaving her paralyzed from the neck down. Her once lithe, supple body now looked like a Cubist nude with its anatomy viciously misproportioned. Day by day he helplessly watched her pale-sapphire eyes lose their color like fading autumn flowers. He saw her honey-hued skin turn as anemic and white and flaccid as a bedridden octogenarian.

Upon Katya's release he had spent another small fortune arranging to transport her by private ambulance and helicopter to the shack. By then she was far beyond caring about her physical surroundings. But she insisted she would rather die than be seen by any more strangers. All the while the child still grew inside her twisted body.

During those final months their only visitor was Alain, the son of the nurse who had raised him and Katya. Alexey felt the old jealousy flare up at each visit—the jealousy he had long ago learned to live with because Katerina clearly did not return Alain's obvious love—at least, not that kind of love. It was as if Alain were her true

316

brother and Alexey her grieving beau.

But only Alexey was there with her the night her final ordeal began. Only Alexey.

And he would never forget the obscenely bright red blood.

"Alex! Oh, Alexey, it hurts, it hurts, it hurts so much!"

"Be strong, my darling Katya, you must be strong, my darling!"

"Alexey! Ohh, Alexey, help me, please, dear God, HELP me, HELP ME, please, dear God!"

"I'm here, Katya, I'm with you, my sweet love, don't leave me! PLEASE!"

"The blood, oh, dear merciful God, how can there be so much blood, Alexey? Oh, my darling, stop it, STOP IT, there's so much BLOOD!"

The living nightmare had lasted well into the next morning. Somehow he had delivered the still-born child himself, trying everything he could to stem Katya's massive hemorrhaging. But her shattered spine and pelvis had resulted in internal disfigurements as well, and the trauma of birth proved too much for her ravaged womanhood. He held her fragile, bent body. Tears streamed down his cheeks. Great sobs wracked him like blows. Then it came: that horrible, awful moment when the last spark of life faded from her eyes.

For a long, agonizing moment his insides were twisted in an invisible fist. "I am you, and you are me," he whispered in a voice ghastly with

317

clarity. "There is no I, but only we."

He laid her down gently in the blood-soaked bedding and staggered outside toward the bayou. He dropped to his knees. And the words sprang from his lips before he knew he was speaking. "Oh, my Katya," he moaned. "My pretty, pretty Katya!"

Only then did the rage overtake him. A white-hot glow wrenched the agonized cry from his throat: "NO!"

It would be many years before he was again capable of doing what happened next.

He stared at a huge live oak on the far bank of the bayou. Alexey concentrated his rage. The tree suddenly snapped off at the ground with a sound like a giant whip cracking. It came crashing down onto the trees around it.

A possum wallowing in the mud began to scuttle clumsily for shelter as the tree descended. A flock of goldfinches lifted like a black-and-gold dust cloud from the surrounding trees. Alexey trained his raging, mismatched eyes on the birds. A moment later they swooped down on the unsuspecting possum. Chattering madly, they pecked at its eyes. Alexey watched in grim fascination as the birds savaged the helpless, screeching animal, fighting amongst themselves for a chance to rip out the next piece of flesh.

But still the fury boiled inside him like spiritual lava. Alexey concentrated on the lazy brown sur-

318

face of the bayou.

Within seconds the first hissing snakes of steam were writhing and dancing above the surface. Moments later the water began a slow boil, quickly turning frenetic. A wall of steam enveloped the shack, blotting out the morning sun.

As quickly as it had flared, his rage was spent.

Wisps of steam still licked at Alexey like vaporous tongues of fog as he stumbled back inside to be with her once more. For the next twenty-four hours he remained in a cocoon of numbing shock. He did not move . . . or eat . . . or think. The next day, when he stirred to life, he kissed his sister-bride farewell, and vowed to her that all hell would stir for this double murder.

With chemical potions he preserved Katya and the child eternally in their rustic wooden shrine beside the bayou. The rest was patience and planning. Years passed and he applied his great genius toward his new scientific career. It was easy to forget Alexey Zverkov and become Eric Winters. Alexey had died when Katerina died. He lopped off his beard, tinted his hair. A theater textbook taught him everything else he needed to know about the art of transformation through makeup. In a stroke of genius, he had come up with the additional persona of the Emperor. Thus could he infiltrate the French Quarter without fear of compromising "Winters"—or of being recognized by some of the older residents of years past.

As time passed, he watched for his opportunity. It came in the form of a 1977 New York Times article. Like a scene from a surrealistic phantasmagoria, he had broken into the laboratory in Ann Arbor and stolen Mario Townsend's brain. But it wasn't until he learned that Robert Jernigan and Dale McGinnis were closing in on him that he discovered the true extent of his own natural talent. Long before he discovered how to extract the necessary neuro-chemical transmitters from that purloined brain, he had managed on his own to "persuade" Police Chief Pearlman to support his cause.

The cover-up of the two killings had worked like a charm. But Alexey knew that Pearlman's assistance might again prove invaluable, sometime in the future. The brilliant "Eyes of Louisiana" commercial had finally proven his mass hypnotic appeal formidable, even without Townsend's brain. Alexey knew that he possessed "the eye," a legacy of his Russian forebears. He had even received a few lessons in its use from fellow jettatore *Alain. But with the exception of that one grief-stricken morning, he had been unskilled in using it properly—a retarded giant unable to harness his own strength. Those election results showed a hideous strength honed with age. And with the booster effect of Townsend's unique brain, Alexey knew he could increase that strength by a factor of a thousand.*

The Yahweh who was once good was now a god of psychosis and evil. All that remained was to purify the earth — to turn Sodom and Gomorrah back into a Garden of Eden.

"Yes, my sweet, sweet Katya," he vowed many times to the still, grotesquely beautiful form while stroking her cold, white limbs, "all hell shall stir for this!"

Chapter 34

"Sorry, Father, but you can't park here. This is a parade staging area. You'll be towed."

The Brinks security cop smiled amiably and pointed toward the river. "There's a free lot over on Decatur," he added. "It's still early enough, you might find a spot."

The Roman Catholic priest didn't bother to return his smile. He was behind the wheel of a yellow Ryder van which he had parked in front of a chain-link fence surrounding a vast Quonset warehouse on North Front Street. A sign wired to the fence said PARADE KREWES ONLY.

The priest removed his dark wraparound sunglasses and stared at the guard. "Open the gate," he said quietly, "and don't let anyone else in until I leave."

The guard's face dissolved into a mask of confusion. He started to object.

Then he made contact with the priest's oddly mismatched eyes.

His ability to resist was sucked out of him like a yolk through an egg shell.

"Of course," he replied, his voice a 78-rpm record playing at 45.

Early morning sunlight glinted off the guard's badge as he stepped away from the van. Moving sluggishly, he unhooked a key from his utility belt. He inserted it into the thick Yale padlock and snicked it open, then swung the gate wide. Crushed shells crunched under the van's tires as the priest drove into the fenced-in enclosure. One of the huge Quonset's sliding doors was already open. He guided the Ryder van inside and killed the engine.

The interior of the vast building was a multicolored sea of monsters and Spielbergian nightmares.

The Mardi Gras floats were lined up like B-52's in a hangar. Papier-mâché dragons, sponge dinosaurs, iridescent jungle beasts with gold-leaf hides and huge sequined scales abounded.

In a far back corner, a krewe of early arrivers were running their high-tech giant octopus float through its final pre-parade check. They glanced up curiously when the van entered. The foreman, a balding, middle-aged man in blue work chinos, walked across the warehouse to greet the new arrival.

"Help you, Father?" he said as Alexey Zverkov swung down from the van.

"Is that the float you're rolling in today?"

The foreman nodded, his brows rising in puzzlement.

"And is that the krewe that will be manning it?"

Again the foreman nodded. "What can I—"

"Shut up and listen to me. Is your float self-propelled?"

For a moment anger flickered across the foreman's face. Then the eyes that stared at him managed to reach deep down inside of him, shaking his soul like a limp rag doll. "Yes," he replied in the same slow-r.p.m. voice the guard had used.

A smile tightened Alexey's lips. "Good," he murmured. "Call the rest of your krewe together."

A minute later the others were gathered around him in a semicircle, their eyes glazed over like sugar-coated *dragées*.

"Where are your throws?" Alexey demanded.

Like a marionette being jerked about, the foreman turned and pointed toward a row of wooden pallets lining the nearest wall. They were overflowing with boxes of plastic beads, cups, frisbees, and aluminum doubloons.

Alexey nodded. "All right," he said. "Leave most of them behind when you form up for the parade. Instead, there are a dozen ten-gallon buckets in the back of my van. Load them onto your float, and make sure you also load the screwdrivers you'll need to pry the tops off. You'll empty those buckets, at my command, when you reach the main parade-reviewing stands at Jackson Square. Is that clear?"

Slowly, the men nodded, zombielike.

"Do it," Alexey snapped. "And be quick. Once the buckets are loaded on your float, take enough throws to cover them up."

As if in a trance, the men set about following his orders, moving like mental patients on Thorazine. While the foreman opened the rear doors of the van, Alexey examined the huge papier-mâché and sponge octopus more closely. Its movable eyes were the size of huge TV screens. The neoprene tentacles were about fifteen feet long and as thick as telephone poles.

For a moment Alexey's brow furrowed, and he tensed the invisible sphincter of his awesome new telekinetic will. Suddenly one of the tentacles slithered into motion like a giant anaconda in the throes of an epileptic seizure. It cracked through the air like a whip.

One of the living zombies unloading the van paused to glance at it stupidly. Then he continued hoisting a bucket down.

A triumphant smile creased Alexey's face. All of this was just for sport. There was a special soupçon of terror reserved for the VIP's and dignitaries at the end of the parade route. When the contents of those buckets rained down onto the horrified crowd, stage one of the true bacchanalian revel would be underway.

One of his unwitting lackeys shambled by, lugging a bucket toward the float. A large warning label was prominently plastered on the side of the container:

CAUTION: CONTAINS HIGHLY CORROSIVE INDUSTRIAL STRENGTH SULFURIC ACID. HANDLE WITH EXTREME CARE

"Carnival," Alexey whispered to himself. "Goodbye to flesh!"

"Jesus," said Breaux, wincing as he caught sight of his bedraggled reflection in the glass door.

If we really *are* as old as we feel, he thought grimly, then I sure as hell look my age this morning. He shouldered his way through the entrance to precinct headquarters on Canal Street, trying not to associate himself with that bleary-eyed, flaccid-faced ghost in the door.

It wasn't quite eight A.M. He had squandered most of the previous day trying to get in touch with Hal Cameron, his Precinct Chief. But Cameron had been called away suddenly to Baton Rouge, the state capital. Breaux could only pray he'd be in this morning.

The taxidermically preserved bodies in Honey Island Swamp had, of course, been duly reported, then collected by the Medical Examiner's Office. And Breaux had even managed—without having to furnish the usual probable-cause warrant—to authorize an APB on Eric Winters. But spotting one probably disguised man in that human sea of a million-and-a-half costumed Mardi Gras celebrants would be like trying to sift salt from sugar.

Breaux also realized that trying to convince anyone of what was going on would be next to impossible. The best he could hope for at this juncture would be to persuade Cameron that they *must* mount an intensified search before the King Rex parade rolled at noon. It seemed likely that Winters would unleash his ultimate horror as King Rex made its grand entrance into Jackson Square.

His ultimate horror. Once again, in his mind's eye, Breaux saw that woman flying fifteen feet into the air. He felt invisible insects racing down his spine. He reached the stairwell at the end of the main hall and started for Cameron's office on the third floor. Breaux didn't even want to speculate on the form such a horror might take.

Just as he reached Chief Cameron's door, it suddenly opened. Cameron himself stepped into the hall.

"Hal!"

Relief surged through Breaux. For a moment he

327

paid little attention to the nattily dressed man with the Chief.

Seconds later, recognition made Breaux's blood run cold.

Clinton J. Pearlman.

The final pieces of the puzzle fell into place in a horrifying gestalt that caused his breath to catch in his throat. Cameron's unscheduled trip to Baton Rouge . . . Breaux suddenly understood there was more than simply concern about tourism that was behind the soft-pedaling of the recent deaths. If Winters could "enlist" one man to his sick cause, why not two? Or more?

Pearlman searched Breaux's face, to remember. "Breaux," the former police chief turned politico said finally.

"Congressman," the cop replied, struggling to keep his features impassive.

"What is it?" demanded Cameron. Both men were watching Breaux as if the cop was a bug under a microscope.

Breaux swallowed with difficulty. "It'll wait," he said.

Breaux had almost made it to the stairwell when Cameron called out behind him. "Breaux!"

He turned slowly.

"Aren't you working crowd control today?"

Breaux nodded.

The two men in the doorway exchanged quick glaces, then turned to stare at the detective.

"Good luck," said Cameron.

By noon the reviewing stands near Jackson Square were filled to capacity.

Police barricades and mounted cops barely managed to restrain the additional spillover crowd that lined the opposite side of the King Rex parade route. The day had turned out glorious, bathing the thousands of carnival spectators in a wash of flaxen sunlight that spilled out of a seamless blue sky.

Breaux was patrolling a sector in front of the barricades, dissuading over-enthusiastic spectators from dashing out onto the parade route. He had managed to slip Steve a purple and gold armband identifying him as an NOPD Crowd Marshal. Both men were on the qui vive, their eyes alert, constantly scanning.

Breaux tried to fight down an increasing sense of dread as he listened to the *oompha-oompha* of the marching bands on nearby Canal Street that signaled the approach of King Rex from mid-city. Down front, a uniformed cop caught his eye and flashed all ten fingers twice. In about twenty minutes the parade would reach Jackson Square.

Desperately the detective sought to control the images that were assaulting his mind. But one scene kept recurring with nightmare persistence: the gruesome duo preserved forever in the shack on Honey Island Swamp—the symbol of Alexey Zverkov's inexpressible rage and blighted happiness.

Despite the balmy seventy-degree weather, a sudden chill tightened his scalp.

He resumed his close scrutiny of the costumed spectators, trying to convince himself that his worries could be unfounded. After all, they had no proof that Alexey Zverkov had not already spent his rage, or that he would be foolish enough to show up today knowing how the net was closing in around him.

Was the crowd mood growing uglier, more frenzied—or was it simply Breaux's overwrought imagination?

He watched two men across the square whose shoving match quickly escalated into a fistfight. A pair of uniformed cops broke it up, dealing out a few more jabs with their side-handled batons than necessary. Nearby, several rowdy fraternity brothers shouted the familiar "Show your tits!" refrain at a gaggle of coeds. Now one of the men abruptly reached toward one of the girls and tore her skimpy halter top half off. Another fight ensued when her male escort leaped on the offender, his fists flailing the air.

Breaux jockeyed for a better view. He accidentally stepped on a foot projecting under the barricade.

"Pardon me, Father," he said, glancing distractedly behind himself for a moment.

"Quite all right," the priest assured him.

Chapter 35

Only about ten feet away, Steve noticed Breaux speaking to the priest behind him. But something else he spotted in the viewing stands across the way stiffened the hair on his nape.

"Pardon me!" he shouted, forcing his way through the spectators. "Excuse me! Please let me by! *Move,* Goddamnit!"

Reaching the nearest barricade, he vaulted it neatly, racing across the open space of the parade route past a startled cop into the stands.

He spotted it again: a white gardenia adorning the lapel of a blond-haired man near the top.

"Hey! Watch it, asswipe!"

"What the fuck you doing, man?"

Grimly, Steve fought his way closer through the stands, no longer bothering with apologies, earning a few jostles and jabs for his efforts.

Just before he reached the masked spectator, his hand slipped into the pocket of his windbreaker and closed around the object lying in readiness.

Now!

With one fast swipe of his left hand, he ripped the spectator's Howdy Doody mask off.

His right hand froze in his jacket pocket.

The man blinking at him in surprise was in his late twenties, with two very normal green eyes and fair eyebrows that weren't even close to knitting together.

"Jesus," said Steve. "Jesus Christ, I'm sorry. I thought. . . ."

"I don't care *what* you thought, jerk! Look at my fricking mask! You ruined it!"

His mind numb with adrenaline letdown, Steve dug his wallet out and slapped a ten-dollar bill into the offended man's palm.

He paid no attention to the crowd jeering at him as he picked his way back down out of the stands.

Instead, he tried to stave off a desperate panic as Breaux flashed him the high sign. Only ten more minutes until the arrival of the King Rex parade.

By now Alexey Zverkov was flying far too high to notice, at first, *who* the man was who had just stepped on his toe.

He only had eyes for the first float — a replica of a giant sea turtle — as it now eased round the corner of stately St. Louis Cathedral and rolled into Jackson Square.

The power seethed and writhed within him now

333

like hyperpotent sexual energy, eager to be spent. The accelerated schedule of MBM doses had resulted in a dangerous backlog of eldritch potential—a buzzing, thrumming rush that threatened to vibrate his skull apart if he did not soon relieve the awesome psychic power growing within.

The crowd all around him was clearly becoming more agitated, more frenzied, as the atmosphere began to vibrate around him. Men who, minutes before, had exhibited only the mildly flushed faces of early-stage inebriation now stared with glassy eyes, their shouted words slurring into an incomprehensible roar.

Soon, any time now, the final farewell to flesh would begin.

Down closer to the front, a mother started slapping her importunate six-year-old daughter with frightening zeal. No one interceded.

One of the mounted cops suddenly kicked out at a spectator, his heavy jackboot catching the man's lips flush and splitting them open before sending him sprawling to the ground.

Several observers cheered the cop on. One of them dumped his Hurricane Punch on the downed spectator.

Alexey ignored the horrible vignettes being acted out all around him. He stared toward a long black Cadillac convertible now approaching at a crawl. His eyes fixed on the beautiful young princess of the King Rex parade, stunning in a dress of sheer tissue chambray.

It was impossible, above the increasing din of

the frenzied Mardi Gras mob, to hear the words he intoned softly:

"I am you, and you are me. There is no I, but only we."

With fumbling hands, Alexey reached into the pocket of his dark shirt and removed the filigreed silver pillbox. He knew this final overdose would probably kill him, but not before ensuring that — during the half hour or so of life remaining to him — he would become the true Demon Lord of this Dionysian congregation.

Oh, sweet Jesus Christ, Steve thought, *here it comes.*

He could feel it in the air now: a physical, palpable churning.

Steve fought to reach the barricades and join Breaux on the other side. A cheer swelled from the crowd when the floats began lumbering into Jackson Square, forming grotesque silhouettes against the blue sky.

Someone tripped him and he sprawled headlong onto the cobblestones. Breaking the fall with both hands, he lifted his chin at the very last and let his chest take the final impact. He scrambled back up to his hands and knees. Suddenly a sharp-toed kick caught him in the kidney, doubling him up reflexively. But he managed to jolt back into motion before the next kick connected with his face.

Shouting maniacally, he punched and clawed

335

and kicked a pathway to the nearest barricade and vaulted it.

Steve landed in a cat stance only twenty feet in front of the first float. Breaux was signaling to him frantically, waving him across while simultaneously ordering the mounted cops to restrain the crowd that was now trying to scramble down onto the parade route after Steve.

Wild-eyed, Steve lost Breaux in the pandemonium. There, *there* he was. The detective was watching him, his tense face urging Steve to *move it!* But then the dark-haired priest next to Breaux plunged a trembling hand into his shirt pocket. Even before the silver glinted in the sun, a horrifying realization hit Steve head on.

At first Breaux had watched with almost grim detachment as the crowd attacked Jernigan. *Why don't you care more?* he thought, accusing himself.

That inner voice rallied him, *reminded* him, and now he surged forward.

"Steve!" he shouted uselessly. "Get out of the way!"

The first float had already rolled past. Plastic beads glinted in the sun as the riders peppered the crowd with throws. But unlike the sea turtle which had preceded it, the huge octopus next in line was making no moves to avoid crushing Steve beneath its massive wheels.

"Move!" Breaux screamed. "Move, you goddamn idiot, *MOOVE!*"

He was staring at the octopus float when one giant eye rolled halfway around and winked at him.

A tentacle as thick as a hawser abruptly snaked up and *whapped* a woman cop off her chestnut mare. The float lurched clumsily for a moment as it rolled over her, mashing her entrails and leaving her to convulse in slow, agonizing death.

Somebody screamed, "Pass a good time, *cher!*" The crowd cheered.

When he saw two krewe members prying the lid off some type of bucket, Breaux stopped worrying about Steve.

Confetti or paper maybe? The old shredded-paper-as-water trick?

But he was clawing his police .38 free from his holster even before he saw the word CAUTION boldly emblazoned on the label. Breaux didn't stop to evaluate his hunch, nor was he trained to select a non-lethal target. His first shot hit one of the men high in the chest, knocking him off the float. His next steel-jacketed slug went wide, striking the second man in the elbow. But it was too late to prevent him from clumsily heaving the bucket over the side into the first ranks of the crowd.

Breaux saw the rest of it developing from the corner of one eye, powerless to affect the outcome.

Steve leapt out of the way when he heard the first shot crack above the din. For a long moment the sloppily thrown bucket hung suspended over his head. Then suddenly, it upended, spilling its liquid contents into the air. A split-second later Steve slammed into a teenage girl. Wrapping himself around her like a cloth, he knocked her forward as the shimmering amoebas of acid splashed into a dozen upturned faces all around them.

The liquid missed the teen. Breaux watched helplessly as Steve's body tensed like an archer's bow when a broad splash caught the back of his corduroy jacket, searing through to flesh and beyond.

For a moment Breaux lost sight of the pair as they sank in a toppled-windmill confusion of arms and legs. Then the mind-jarring, agonized screams began and the cop lost sight of *every*thing. Except for one fat woman standing nearby. It wasn't a polyvinyl mask that melted like wax in a flamethrower. It was her face.

Steve felt the hard ground rushing up to meet him, knocking the breath from him as the crowd's weight bore him inexorably downward.

Then his spine felt like it was molten iron. He was dimly aware of his own scream joining with the chorus of shrieks surrounding him. A light exploded in his skull. Then everything grew dark and quiet.

When he came to, he noticed through his pain

the horribly scalded flesh that was all around him. Crying out again as hellfire erupted along his backbone, he separated himself from the screaming girl whose life he had saved and fought his way to his feet.

A charnel-house stench thickened the air. Steve staggered toward the priest, his hand groping in his jacket pocket. A tremor of pain shot through him and his hand jerked involuntarily. The object he had clutched in his fingers shattered on the pavement.

Steve crashed forward onto his face, spasming grotesquely. Before he could get up again, the priest caught sight of him.

Steve needed no words to read the emotion behind the eyes as Alexey Zverkov stared at him, recognition burning behind the ravaged intellect. But Zverkov hesitated just long enough. Steve scooped up a large shard of the broken pocket mirror lying near him—the mirror he had dropped a second earlier. He struggled to his knees.

Alexey glared at his enemy, his eyes registering unspeakable hatred. Steve felt long, seductive, penile fingers entering him—exploring him—persuading him it was foolish to resist blissful lassitude. With almost superhuman effort, Steve broke free and jerked the fragment of mirror up toward the fascinator's face.

A second later Alexey glimpsed his own malevolent stare.

The *jettatore*'s body tensed. The air around him snapped and sparked like a downed powerline.

Zverkov let loose a long, agonized scream as his face bubbled and began to rip apart. His mismatched eyes bulged until, one at a time, they popped loose, driven out by streaming gouts of blood. The skull was the last to go, exploding into dust and fragments like a clay pigeon. The final, triumphant thought Steve took with him to eternity was that he had sent the Emperor and his power back to Hell.

Epilogue

She felt languid and lightheaded. Impossible, half-formed images scurried through her mind like frenzied rodents.

She's waking up, said a familiar voice at the end of a long tunnel.

Corinne?

Corinne!

A hand squeezed hers, urging her to flee the sleepy warm safety of the land of Nod. Corinne's tissue-thin eyelids trembled. Then, obediently, they fluttered open.

The fog rolled back and the first thing she saw was a bearded face watching her intently.

"Welcome back," Doctor Grodner said.

Alan Breaux stood at the foot of her bed. The cop smiled wearily, flashing her a victory sign when she met his gaze. Maddy hovered near the left side of the bed, worry lines starched into her face. Slightly behind her — peering curiously over Maddy's shoulder — was the old artist, Georges Lagacé.

"Hey, babe!" Maddy exclaimed. "How you makin' it?"

Something akin to panic flittered across Corinne's pretty, sleep-puffed face. She tried to rise up on one elbow, but Grodner patiently pushed her back down.

"Easy does it, lady. You've been out for a couple days."

His words were slow to sink in. She was about to demand how that could be, when realization slapped her with all its cruel force. The physician had made *sure* she was "out"—out of harm's way on Fat Tuesday.

Corinne sat up abruptly, catching Grodner by surprise.

"Steve?" she asked. Her eyes swept the hospital room, then moved back and forth between Grodner and Breaux. Before either could speak, she could read the grim confirmation in their eyes.

A warm numbness seeped into her. Corinne fell back against the pillow.

Grodner spoke first. "It happened at the parade. There was nothing anyone could do. He died almost instantly."

"Died?" Corinne repeated bitterly. *"Died?* You mean he was murdered, don't you? What about—"

"Alexey Zverkov is dead," Breaux cut in gently. His voice was faintly charged with warning. "There are a hell of a lot of questions about what happened, questions that won't be easy to answer. Matter of fact, at least one cop has been labeled a fruitcake and asked to retire early for trying to answer them."

She glanced at Maddy and Georges, suddenly understanding. Breaux was reminding her that the three of them—she, Breaux, and Steve—had been caught up in a private kind of hell, a supernatural terror beyond the realm of courtrooms and jail cells and logical evidence. Breaux was the first victim of a foolish attempt to explain it to others. Now he was warning her and Grodner not to follow suit.

"*We* survived," Breaux added. "Whether or not Mardi Gras will is up to the City Council. Frankly, I'm guessing it's gonna be like the Tulane basketball program: out for a long lunch before it returns."

Maddy's bevy of bangles clicked as she bent closer to smooth Corinne's hair. "Don't think about any of it now, babe," she purred. "You just get better. My God, just about every artist on the square has stopped by the shop to ask about you."

But Maddy's artificially bright chatter failed to penetrate the growing numbness Corinne was feeling.

"He saved my life *twice*," she said to the room in general. "That . . . that inhuman monster killed him! We can't just pretend we don't know

343

about what really hap—"

"She's tired," Grodner cut in, exchanging a brief but meaningful glance with Breaux. "Time to let her rest."

"Tired!" Corinne cried out, her eyes snapping sparks at Grodner. "I've been out for a few days, remember? Are you going to deny that ceremony you witnessed right here in this hospital? Are you—"

Grodner slipped the hypodermic into her arm before she could resist.

"I'll check with you later," he said soothingly. He signaled the others with his eyes.

"Toodle-oo, puss." Maddy squeezed her hand again. "Hurry up and get better. I'll bring you up some munchies next visit."

Breaux met Corinne's eyes and said simply, "I'll be in touch."

She nodded. The sedative was already taking effect, dulling the sharp edge of memory and making her eyelids feel heavy.

"Doctor?" Georges said timidly as the others filed toward the door. "A brief word with Miss Matthews before I leave? I've been waiting for hours."

"Very brief," Grodner said, acquiescing reluctantly.

When the door swung shut behind them, Georges stepped closer to the bed and awkwardly took one of her hands in his, bowing slightly to

344

kiss it.

"And so, *ma jolie,* the mystery of Alexey and Katerina Zverkov is finally solved. The newspapers are filled with the story of their tragic love."

Corinne nodded, battling to keep her eyes open. "They don't know the full story," she muttered sleepily. "Not the half of it."

"No," he agreed, "they don't. And they never will."

For a moment something in his tone startled her back to the verge of alertness.

"What . . . what do you mean?"

His fleshy lips eased into a smile.

"That day when I drew your portrait, pretty one? I was not altogether forthcoming with you when I told that story. In truth, I lied. Katya and Alexey grew up in France, not Italy."

Corinne's eyes clouded with confusion. She struggled against her growing sleepiness. "I don't . . . don't understand . . ."

"You will in a moment," he assured her. "Do you recall the nurse I mentioned? The nurse who raised them?"

She nodded.

"I told you she had a son of her own. His name was Alain. And he loved Katya every bit as much as her brother did."

Corinne's flesh crawled against her skimpy hospital johnny as she stared at the "French Canadian." Finally she began to understand.

"Alexey Zverkov possessed a raw power," the old artist continued. "But it was Alain who gave him his first lessons in honing that power. And though Katya loved only her twin, Alain accompanied the two of them on that fateful journey to the New World."

Watching the old man's slack, benign face, she noticed that his bleary brown eyes were more minatory and reptilian than she had remembered.

"You?" Corinne whispered.

Her face broke out in a cool sweat when he nodded.

"Of course Alexey didn't realize he was being used all these years, but what could I do? Katya's death could not go unavenged. Yet my life is in the Quarter. My art is all I know. I could not risk discovery. So I planted and nurtured the initial obsession in Alexey, knowing his prodigious intellect would work out the fine details. He is my little brother. He has *always* done what I tell him."

Sleep tugged her inevitably closer to unconsciousness as the sedative took over. Corinne recalled his gallery of dead women, his wistful words: *My private stock . . . and now your radiant face will lead my collection beside Katya's.*

It took him only a moment to remove the single contact lens. Corinne lay petrified with fear as he lowered his two-toned gaze back to her. One eye brown, the other blue. His naked stare drilled

346

its way into her mind, seeking the sacred bastion of her soul.

"So pretty," he whispered, his voice an intimate, deadly caress from the grave. "My little beauty. My muse. I *must* have you for my collection."

THE ULTIMATE IN SPINE-TINGLING TERROR
FROM ZEBRA BOOKS!

TOY CEMETERY   (2228, $3.95)
by William W. Johnstone
A young man is the inheritor of a magnificent doll collection. But
an ancient, unspeakable evil lurks behind the vacant eyes and
painted-on smiles of his deadly toys!

SMOKE   (2255, $3.95)
by Ruby Jean Jensen
Seven-year-old Ellen was sure it was Aladdin's lamp that she had
found at the local garage sale. And no power on earth would be
able to stop the hideous terror unleashed when she rubbed the
magic lamp to make the genie appear!

WITCH CHILD   (2230, $3.95)
by Elizabeth Lloyd
The gruesome spectacle of Goody Glover's witch trial and hanging
haunted the dreams of young Rachel Gray. But the dawn brought
Rachel no relief when the terrified girl discovered that her innocent
soul had been taken over by the malevolent sorceress' vengeful
spirit!

HORROR MANSION   (2210, $3.95)
by J.N. Williamson
It was a deadly roller coaster ride through a carnival of terror when
a group of unsuspecting souls crossed the threshold into the old
Minnifield place. For all those who entered its grisly chamber of
horrors would never again be allowed to leave — not even in death!

NIGHT WHISPER   (2092, $3.95)
by Patricia Wallace
Twenty-six years have passed since Paige Brown lost her parents in
the bizarre Tranquility Murders. Now Paige has returned to her
home town to discover that the bloody nightmare is far from over
. . . it has only just begun!

SLEEP TIGHT   (2121, $3.95)
by Matthew J. Costello
A rash of mysterious disappearances terrorized the citizens of Har-
ley, New York. But the worst was yet to come. For the Tall Man
had entered young Noah's dreams — to steal the little boy's soul and
feed on his innocence!

*Available wherever paperbacks are sold, or order direct from the Publisher.
Send cover price plus 50¢ per copy for mailing and handling to Zebra Books,
Dept. 2732, 475 Park Avenue South, New York, N.Y. 10016. Residents of
New York, New Jersey and Pennsylvania must include sales tax. DO NOT
SEND CASH.*

A CAVALCADE OF TERROR
FROM RUBY JEAN JENSEN!

SMOKE   (2255, $3.95)
Seven-year-old Ellen was sure it was Aladdin's lamp that she
had found at the local garage sale. And no power on earth
would be able to stop the hideous terror unleashed when she
rubbed the magic lamp to make the genie appear!

CHAIN LETTER   (2162, $3.95)
Abby and Brian knew that the chain letter they had found
was evil. They would send the letter to all their special
friends. And they would know who had broken the chain —
by who had died!

ANNABELLE   (2011, $3.95)
The dolls had lived so long by themselves up in the attic. But
now Annabelle had returned to them, and everything would
be just like it was before. Only this time they'd never let anyone hurt Annabelle. And anyone who tried would be very,
very sorry!

HOME SWEET HOME   (1571, $3.50)
Two weeks in the mountains should have been the perfect
vacation for a little boy. But Timmy didn't think so. Not
when he saw the terror in the other children's eyes. Not when
he heard them screaming in the night. Not when Timmy realized there was no escaping the deadly welcome of HOME
SWEET HOME!

MAMA   (1247, $3.50)
Once upon a time there lived a sweet little dolly — but her
one beaded glass eye gleamed with mischief and evil. If Dorrie could have read her dolly's thoughts, she would have run
for her life. For Dorrie's dear little dolly only had murder on
her mind!

*Available wherever paperbacks are sold, or order direct from the
Publisher. Send cover price plus 50¢ per copy for mailing and handling to Zebra Books, Dept. 2732, 475 Park Avenue South, New
York, N.Y. 10016. Residents of New York, New Jersey and Pennsylvania must include sales tax. DO NOT SEND CASH.*